Totally Bound Publishing books by Raven McAllan

Single Books
Hong Kong Heat
Taken Identity
Fairground Attraction
The Duke's Temptation
The Viscount Meets his Match

Diomhair
Secrets Shared
Secrets Uncovered
Secrets Remembered
Secrets Dispatched
Secrets Learned
Secrets Dispelled

Daring Ladies
The Earl and The Courtesan

I0524367

THE VISCOUNT MEETS HIS MATCH

RAVEN MCALLAN

The Viscount Meets his Match
ISBN # 978-1-83943-827-1
©Copyright Raven McAllan 2019
Cover Art by Erin Dameron-Hill ©Copyright May 2019
Interior text design by Claire Siemaszkiewicz
Totally Bound Publishing

THE VISCOUNT MEETS HIS MATCH

Dedication

To David and Josie.

Hope you enjoy your namesakes' story.

Prologue

England, 1817

How good that five minutes in his father's presence no longer had the power to make him feel a criminal. Or ready to commit a criminal act of some sort, probably patricide. His father's antagonism toward his son seemed to strengthen over the years, and David's contempt for the man had increased in proportion to it.

For that matter, David pondered, why did his father, as usual, automatically assume he was up to no good? Luckily their meetings were few and far between. He'd only answered the demand he attend his family's ancestral home because his solicitor had suggested it might be a good idea to discover what was afoot.

There were, Simmons, his solicitor, had told him, rumors that a large number of acres could potentially be for sale not far from David's present home in Yorkshire. As most of that land was Midham land — land belonging to the dukedom — it was cause for concern. Add to that the missive delivered by a liveried footman demanding David attend Midham, or else there would be severe consequences, and David had reluctantly decided he had best see what his parent was up to.

Perhaps it had been petty to stay in his country home the night before and arrive exactly on time at his ancestral home. He knew fine well his papa would have expected him to arrive at Midham the previous day, or to put up in the nearest inn, where no doubt news would be passed back to the duke of his son's whereabouts.

Instead David had spent the last few days at Caldborough, and driven the couple of hours needed to arrive at Midham in time to leave his equipage in the stables and hand his cane and hat to Sleights, the major-domo, as the longcase clock struck eleven. A time chosen, he assumed, because most 'men about town' — even in the countryside — would still be abed. It showed his father had no concept of how David led his life. It was rare he stayed in bed after nine. He preferred to be up and about his business before his peers were around to see what he was involved in. Plus, of course, out of the city there was time to have a good gallop and still be around to attend to any duties or excursions planned for the day.

"Bloody listen to me," his father shouted. "Act your age."

Does he even know my age, I wonder?

David bowed. The sooner his parent said his piece, the sooner he would know what this was all about and could leave. "As you wish. You perceive me all ears."

Had there been a meeting — or a summons — since he was out of short coats, or even before, when his father didn't accuse him of some misdemeanor or other? He didn't think so. One reason he kept out of the man's way whenever possible.

"Bloody rakehell." His father snarled the words. "I won't stand for it, you hear me? You're still not too old for a whipping."

On cue, the thin scars across his back began to ache. David strove to keep his expression indifferent and ignore the reminder of how his father preferred to deal with anything his son did that he didn't agree with. Which was, David mused as he attempted to keep a blank face, most things.

From the first time, when David as a five-year-old wouldn't eat the slimy milk pudding his nanny had thought would be good for him, his father had never spared the rod. Whenever he thought David acted in a way that was against what the duke wanted, punishment would be swift, and merciless. School reports, silly childish acts such as scrumping for apples, to playing cards with the stable lads. All were dealt with in the same way.

Sometimes he had wondered if his father enjoyed giving out punishment, if the elder man obtained some satisfaction from inflicting pain on someone unable to defend themselves. It certainly seemed so.

Until the last time, when —

"Are you listening, damn it? Enough is enough. I won't be made a laughingstock by you."

David, Lord Suddards, Viscount Lyttlethorp, the heir to the Duke of Midham — the man who sat in an overlarge, overstuffed chair and glared at his son — ignored the ache, flicked an imaginary speck of lint from his immaculate jacket and inspected his fingernails. Something which would no doubt infuriate his father and be one more thing to add to the older man's list of grievances.

David was under no illusions about how his sire regarded him, or that the man would eventually inform him what had brought him to such ire. It was a mystery why he behaved in such a manner, and one David could no longer be bothered to solve. He suspected that even if he came clean about his activities, his papa would choose to disbelieve him. It would seem easier to him than to accept he was in the wrong about his so-called errant child, among other things.

The man was an unsympathetic husband, terrible parent, out and out bully—perhaps akin to an unmitigated sadist—and uncaring landlord. His estates, estates David would presumably one day inherit, were in a poor way. The tenants and workers were housed in little more than hovels and, after years of poor maintenance, his lands yielded very little. Some workers were hard-pressed to put food on the table, or stop their windows and roofs leaking. Windows and roofs the estate was supposed to keep in working order. None of which seemed to bother the duke, but did bother his son. David had, when possible, helped out without his parent knowing, but he was conscious it was too little and probably too late. By the time the dukedom was his it would be nigh on worthless. No wonder he had nothing but contempt for his father.

Over the years David had learned not to expect any quarter from the man. Even his mother, whom he doted on, had never truly been able to stick up for her son against her martinet of a husband. David had once asked her if his papa had always been the way he was and been told yes. When he'd questioned his mama about why she had married his papa, she'd told him her parents had wished it, and it was the done thing to obey them. You had to do what your parents demanded. David wasn't so sure.

"I'll rein you in, if it's the last thing I do," the duke snarled at his only son. "Once a rake isn't going to be always a rake in your case."

How very true. Little did his father know. Even so, David still remained silent. What he got up to was no one's business but his own, and those it involved.

"Look at you, sitting there and not giving me the attention I'm due." He struck his hand on the arm of the chair with such force, David wouldn't have been surprised to see the material split and the stuffing pop out.

"It's a pity I can't take my crop to you and beat some sense into your thick skull." The duke glowered. "Not that I'm sure it would do any good, but I'd have a damned good go."

You could try but it would be the last thing you would ever do. As he had no inclination to flee to the continent as a man wanted for patricide, David held his tongue.

"Your sisters now, they never give me or your mama a moment's worry. You? Never a moment's peace. What's this about, eh? Riding bareback down St. James, for heaven's sake? What on earth were you thinking of? St. James of all places! I had to tell 'em you were nauseated. Ill, feverish. No idea what you were doing. And then off to La Calverly's. Gaming there. Uncouth to say the least. How much did you dip, may I ask? Don't think I'll bail you out, my lad, because I will not."

David said nothing. At the age of thirty-five he was no lad, had no intention of asking his father to do anything of the kind and was not about to reveal his personal affairs to his parent. Not any type of affair.

"Bad ton. Not to be thought about," the duke said irascibly. "And now? Now this scandal." He invested the word *scandal* with disgust and scorn as his voice rose. "How dare you? This family will not be ridiculed because of you. Enough is enough. Time to toe the line or else."

David stood impassively—he hadn't been invited to sit—and waited to discover what else his father had decided to lay at his feet. As far as he was aware, there was nothing he'd done to be ashamed of in years.

"Who you take after I have no idea," the elder man said. "Must be from your mother's side. No Suddards is so rackety. I save my money, my lad, and so should you. I know we have to sow our wild oats, everyone does. Ha, even I did, but no one of good ton would ever dream of sowing them in fertile ground before the crop owner."

What on earth was he talking about? David raised one eyebrow, and decided it was time to speak. "Do go on and enlighten me. I fear my mind must be befuddled, I have no clue as to what you are referring to." He hadn't sown anything anywhere for a good six months. He'd been too busy doing his best to save his father's tenants from starvation. These days, his rakish title was far from the truth.

"Balderdash. Lady Whitcombe, of course. Don't try to pull the wool over my eyes. What were you thinking, eh? To give her a slip on the shoulder is not what is expected before she's done her duty to her husband, and well you know it."

"What?" Davis was startled into surprise. Fanny Whitcombe had never interested him and he'd told her so in no uncertain terms, when, after he and his last mistress had parted amicably, Fanny had intimated she was ready to take that lady's place. Was that why she had chosen him as scapegoat?

"I assure you I have never been anywhere near the lady, and if—" He didn't get a chance to finish his statement before his parent cut him off with a slash of his hand in the air. David mentally shrugged. It seemed, as ever, he'd been tried and condemned before he could put his side of the story forward.

"No more!" His father roared the words. "I have it from Whitcombe himself. His wife is increasing and it is not his. Increasing before she's done her duty. The disgrace. He's sent her to the country, of course, but I had a devil of a job to persuade him not to call you out. Said I'd deal with you."

David kept his mouth shut. When his papa was ranting, it was best to let him continue until he ranted himself out. David glanced at the mantel clock. On recent showing he had around another ten minutes to go. He bit his lip as his father spat into the fireless grate and spoke.

"What do you say for yourself, eh?"

David shrugged. "It is interesting to perceive how you believe my upbringing would let me do such a thing." That it was a slight to his father, he doubted the man would understand.

"Well, enough is enough, my boy." To his surprise his papa stood, glared, harrumphed and pulled on the bell rope. "You'll see." The duke once more sat down in the chair he always used and didn't invite David to follow suit. David sighed quietly and looked idly out of the window. The early, summer morning sunshine sent shadows dancing over the lawns that rolled away down to the lake where three swans glided regally over the still water. A beautiful setting, but one he felt divorced from. Midham might be his ancestral home, but it wasn't welcoming to him. His papa had made sure of that. David visited as little as possible and tried, not always with success, to meet his mama elsewhere.

As he waited to discover what was to come, David thought of how he had really spent that last night a week ago. Yes, he'd ridden a horse bareback down St. James. The horse, not him. He'd found the saddle- and bridle-less gelding trotting along Piccadilly and deemed it best to get it into the safely of his own stables until the owner could be found. As the animal had been skittish he'd taken the most direct route there. He hadn't recognized the gelding and still had no idea to whom the animal belonged If it had been involved in a scandal of some kind, the scandal had been successfully hushed up. No accidents had been reported. It was a mystery, and one he suspected would remain so. He'd give it a month and send the horse to his country home.

As for Lady Calverly's salon — it was expected of him, and some things he had to be seen to do. The fact he had lost money was all to the good. It was, if his papa had known it, a drop in the ocean, and he always eventually came out even or ahead. He was a canny and skilled player and knew when to stop. But Lady Whitcombe was one step too far, and he had no idea how to prove his innocence. It was as well he had no intention of explaining his actions to his father or indeed anyone. He saw his chances of retiring to Caldborough, his more modest country home, after he departed from the ducal seat, disappearing before his eyes. He'd need to return to London and discover what the hell was going on.

His father stared impatiently toward the door. When it eventually opened and his mother entered, David jumped. What now? Rarely did his parents get together to face him. In truth, rarely did they get together at all unless society dictated it. A nasty itch slithered across his spine and his cravat threatened to strangle him. David forced himself not to run his fingers between the material and his skin as he accepted the next few minutes were likely to be uncomfortable and he wouldn't like it.

He looked at his father's closed face and his mother's sympathetic one and decided it wasn't worth defending himself.

"So, to that end, you will marry within three months or I will sell off everything un-entailed and make sure you get none of the money to waste. There's a list of likely candidates on the desk here." The duke picked up a sheet of paper and thrust it at David. "Choose one and put your house in order. I tell you now, if you do not do as I say, you'll regret it. Most of my land is not entailed so don't you go thinking you'll be wealthy once I kick the bucket. I'll not have it." The duke thumped his chair arm emphatically. "And don't go crawling to your mama. She is with me in this."

The duchess nodded. "It has to be said and done. You need to grow up and settle down, my son."

David raised one eyebrow. "In that case, there is no more to be discussed." He bowed to them both punctiliously and turned toward the door. "Oh, and this is what you can do with your list." He tore it into tiny pieces and dropped them over his father. How he controlled his rising ire, he had no idea. Nevertheless, he held his increasing temper in check, knowing he needed to get out of the room before he really disgraced himself and told his parents what he thought of their lack of trust. It would do no good, they wouldn't listen — or believe any protestations of innocence. They had decided to be judge and jury and find him guilty. "I bid you farewell."

"Oh no you don't," the duke said. "I need to hear your response."

Did he? Were the scraps of paper that decorated his shoulders and lap not enough? Then in that case he would spell it out. David swung around and looked from his worried mother to his red-faced father. "Go to the devil," he said clearly. "You do not know me. You never have."

On that he walked out of their lives.

Chapter One

London, 1818 – one year later

The lady had a vicious tongue. David was glad he wasn't on the end of the lashing she was in the process of handing out to one hapless peer. Not that the man in question didn't deserve it. He did. It was a given that if a lady replied in the negative to anything a gentleman requested, the said gentleman had to accept she meant no, even if he chose to assume that reply was misplaced. Not so, it seemed, the man in question. He stretched out to grab the lady's arm and she swung around out of the shadows. Even as David took a step forward to aid her, she made a fist—a proper fingers-and-thumbs-tucked-in fist—and hit Lord Algernon Reginald on the side of his nose. For one so slight in stature, she threw a mean punch. The blow was hard enough to make the man sway on his feet. The lady — whoever she was—planted a facer as well as any man David knew. He would remember never to get on her bad side.

"Do not dare to touch me, you oaf." Her tone was scathing and her voice rang with contempt as Lord Reginald's head snapped back with a jerk that made David wince. "Or the next blow will hurt you even more."

He thought he recognized that voice. As she moved fully into the light, he realized he had identified her correctly. Lady Josephine Bowie. Also know by the sobriquet Lady Contumelious—Lady Disdain. Blonde-haired with curls that framed a heart-shaped face, unusual green eyes, a slight but still curvaceous figure, and it seemed, contrary to what he'd previously imagined, a termagant. What on earth was going on?

"May I assist you?" he asked as he stepped into her line of vision and bowed. "You seem to be rather irritated."

"What?" She swung around and frowned. "Oh, it is you," she said flatly when she saw who spoke. "No thank you, my lord. This gentleman"—she invested the word with scorn—"is about to leave." She swung her skirts away from Lord Reginald very deliberately and gave David a quick view of a trim ankle. "He makes the place untidy."

David laughed. "I have often thought so," he replied with a wink she ignored. She appeared immune to his charms. It was a novelty, and one that immediately put his interest on high alert. No young lady of the ton had treated him so cavalierly before and it wasn't a comfortable experience. It was, however, something he thought worth pursuing at a later date.

How his father would laugh. Actually, he decided, no he wouldn't. He would see it as yet one more failing on David's side before dismissing Josephine as the sort of person no heir to a dukedom would contemplate. Blonde-haired chits without obvious assets—or good childbearing hips—were considered insipid, plus her attitude would be seen as an insult to David's status. Unmarried ladies of the ton did not treat lords in such a dismissive manner. They were expected to revere them.

"Ah, so that's the way the wind blows, is it?" Lord Reginald said thickly and sneered as he put his handkerchief over his nose, which now bled copiously. "Why didn't you say you wanted a rake...*ooft*."

David had plowed his fist into the man's stomach. Reginald made a noise akin to a pot on the boil, folded and slid to the floor in a heap of uncoordinated arms and legs. It wasn't easy, but David resisted the urge to kick him and looked at his scraped knuckles ruefully. He'd caught them on Reginald's waistcoat buttons. David sent up a prayer of thanks no one else had seen what happened. Lord help him if his father ever got wind of it all, or discovered the state his son's knuckles were in. All his sire's ideas about David's behavior would be reinforced threefold, something he could well do without. David dusted his hands together, winced as one scrape rubbed against another and held out his arm very punctiliously to Lady Bowie. She glanced at his knuckles.

"You need salve on those." This time her solicitousness didn't seem to be feigned. "You don't want them to get infected." Whether she meant because of the scrapes or because of whom he'd hit, she didn't make clear.

"Later." David dismissed her concern. She intrigued him. This solicitous side of her was something new to him, and he suspected to most, if not all, of the ton. He wanted her attention on him as a man, not his skinned knuckles, not even if her sympathy would be directed at him. Something bothered him about that unwarranted thought. What had brought it on? "Are you all right?"

She raised her eyebrows. "Of course, my lord. He was an irritation I needed to get rid of, no more." She paused and licked her lips.

Did she know what that sensuous gesture — unconscious or not — did to a man? David supposed not.

"I, ah, thank you for your timely intervention, my lord."

Does she mean that or is she pandering to what she thinks is convention? It was hard to tell from her tone of voice. "Perhaps you will let me escort you back to the ballroom?" David asked, loath to let their interaction end. "To take you to your mama, perhaps?"

She looked him up and down with an expression on her face that made him wonder if he had dressed correctly or forgotten to fasten something that should be closed. The impression that he had been weighed up and found lacking, as yet just another annoying male member of the ton, was not a comfortable or, he decided, a warranted one.

"No, thank you, my mama wouldn't want that. She is busy enjoying herself." The way she phrased her sentence intrigued David. As if she herself was not enjoying the ball, which was one of the highlights of the season, or as if her parent did not want her around. Surely not?

Intriguing.

"I came out here for peace and quiet," she continued frostily. "It seems I am forever surrounded by idiots. The last thing I want is to be accosted by them."

David would have taken her words at face value if he hadn't noted the flicker of relief in her eyes when he'd struck Reginald. "That is good then," David said cheerfully, as if he hadn't heard the implied insult. "As I am no idiot, and intend not to accost you, but accompany you instead. Shall we?"

He could almost see the cogs whirring. Dare she trust him? Would he prove to be the same or worse than Lord Reginald? It was understandable. After all, ever since his come out, he had not been known as a steady reliable sort, more a rake and an incorrigible rogue. Strangely—luckily?—not as one who made a man a cuckold. His papa and Lord Whitcombe had never let their belief about Lady Whitcome's child's parentage be known. He had heard nothing more except she had retired, unwell, to the country to wait out her confinement. He assumed the child had been born—it was not, after all, an elephant—but as he'd made a deliberate choice not to discover what sex it was or when it arrived, he was still happily in the dark. As the one thing he was certain of was it could not be his, he needed to know nothing else.

"I assure you, in cases like this," David said, "I am the perfect gentleman."

"I believe you." 'I think', her tone intimated. "Nevertheless, many do not, and I do not want to sully my reputation," Josephine replied slowly, as if she chose her words with care. She sighed. "I am sorry if that appears harsh, but it would do me no good to be seen talking to you, rogue that you are. Life is complicated enough as it is without my parents castigating me for encouraging a rake—or for not encouraging the heir to a dukedom. I have no idea which tack they would take." She grimaced. "I suspect, sometimes it depends how the wind blows."

Her voice seemed to indicate there was no love lost between her and her parents. A little like him and his, perhaps? It was a sad fact his mama had continued to do as his father decreed and had no contact with him. David missed her but had come to terms with it. However, Josephine's parents? Surely not. After all, what could a young, even though not *very* young lady have done to encourage that sort of attitude? Once more, his interest was piqued. "Then we will part before we enter," David said amiably, even though he wanted to shout, 'My persona is not me,' at the top of his voice. He had cultivated it, assiduously, in the past, and even more so over the past year. It had served its purpose well but sadly now it haunted him. Therefore, it was nobody's fault except his own.

Life had a way of making every little thing awkward.

In the distance, David heard the orchestra once more strike up a waltz. "If we move toward the ballroom now, your re-entrance should not be noted. I promise not to follow you. Though I do wish to plead my case. Not everything you hear is true."

"Then you didn't climb those lampposts and put ladies' hats on them all? Or swim naked at Brighton under a full moon?" she asked quizzically, then blushed as if she had just realized she had committed the sort of faux pas no well-brought-up female should ever do. Commenting on a gentleman's less-civilized activities. However, the flush went as fast as it appeared and, to David, seemed unreal. Yet something else to ponder on.

Life was becoming interesting. His body sizzled with the thrill of the chase. Perhaps not sexual—yet—but a definite hint of interesting things to come.

"Guilty as charged but with extenuating circumstances." David decided if he was to be castigated, it might as well be for something real, not imagined. The hats on lampposts had been harmless, the nakedness not quite true. He'd kept his unmentionables on. Nevertheless, the gossips had picked up on the fact his bare chest had been easily visible in the moonlight, and thus a scandal had been created. If it kept his papa's thoughts and interests away from his real everyday activities, it had been worth it.

"Or race down Rotten Row, with others of your ilk?" Josephine finished in a rush.

"Ah, well, I was much younger then," he said apologetically.

For a long moment Josephine considered him, then nodded. "Six months or so younger. Very well. I…" She hesitated as she took his arm and they strolled toward the ballroom doors. "I truly am sorry if I sound rude, my lord, but the complication of my being seen with you is something I can well do without."

Her wording intrigued him. Rake or not, as she had intimated, her parents would no doubt jump at the chance of their daughter being observed conversing with him. David was under no illusions of his desirability as a potential husband. Even with his at-times-less-than-savory reputation, he was considered, as the heir to a dukedom, a catch of the first degree. Minor indiscretions would be overlooked, others put down to an ebullient youth — even now, in his thirties — and women — mistresses — just not mentioned. Every woman, or so he had been told by a good friend, saw him as redeemable — but only by them.

No one had realized he and his papa, who was one of the country's foremost peers, and in the ton's eyes at all times, were estranged. Due to the age gap, they patronized separate clubs and had different pursuits, thus their lack of communication wouldn't be seen as unusual. He had to hope it would continue that way. Because, as the heir to what most people still saw as a vast fortune, it would be automatically assumed any parent would turn a blind eye to some of the escapades of an heir such as he, if it meant their daughter eventually became a duchess.

Was that what worried Josephine? That she might be pushed into marriage? If so, why? She had never shown even one iota of interest in him, or he in her. Even if her mama schemed and plotted, he hoped he was up to snuff enough to be able to avoid being caught.

David was honest — no well-brought-up young lady appealed to him. They never had, and he was wise to every trick any encroaching mama or deb might try to pull to ensure he had to make an offer.

Until now? He quashed that thought to be re-examined later. His tastes had always run to those females who were up to snuff and needed a man to dally with and satisfy them. That usually meant bored matrons — and only those with the requisite number of children of the correct sex, whose husbands accepted dalliance would be the next step. Plus, he didn't approach opera dancers or the demimonde, whatever the grand dames of the ton chose to think. In fact, he ruminated as he glanced at the silent woman next to him, just lately he hadn't had time to dally with anyone. Parts of him could well have seized up through lack of lubrication.

However, he had to acknowledge her lack of interest intrigued him.

Josephine halted just outside the ballroom and the tug on his arm made David stop mid-step. He looked at her inquiringly, and she grimaced before she must have remembered herself and curtsied. A gesture that was correct to the nth degree, he could imagine how much it had cost her.

"This is far enough, thank you. I, ah, appreciate your help," she added stiffly. "Although I could have dealt with him myself, I do thank you for your intervention." She didn't add, 'unnecessary as it was,' but David could imagine her wishing she could.

"Of course you do," he replied genially. "Why would you not? "

She flushed and he wished he had held his tongue, if not his actions. Because with regards to his intervention, he wasn't so sure what his intentions were. Lord Reginald had a reputation for acting first and thinking later — and not always in a good way. The problem was how to divulge the information so she understood, took action and did not ignore him — or indeed overreact.

"Is it all men or only me you have an aversion to?" he asked as she began to walk away. He pitched his voice just loud enough for her to hear. She might ignore his question but there would be no chance of her not hearing it. "For if it is me, what have I ever done to you to deserve your contempt?"

"What?" She turned and took the three steps necessary to get within arm's reach once more. Her blue eyes sparked in a way he had never noticed before and his body responded accordingly and tightened with interest. Again, she tempted him in a manner he would not have thought possible. How he'd like to shake her out of her present mood, but not in a manner that would be at all acceptable.

Not yet, anyway.

Again a notion to contemplate. Was he really debating dallying with this woman? His head said no, the rest of his body, the opposite. Why had he never really examined her luscious curves before? They appeared perfect in every way.

"Dare you not answer me?"

She frowned as if puzzled by his remark. David repeated himself. "How have I earned your contempt?"

"Sadly, as far as I can see, from my knowledge of your sex it encompasses all men, my lord. Although, with your reputation, I would put you near the top of my list."

Well, that told him. David bowed and with a swift look around decided, if she thought she knew him, he might as well live up to the sort of person she thought she was. He grasped both her arms, drew her close and pressed a hard, swift kiss to her lips.

The jolt of immediate arousal was as unexpected as it was exciting.

She was so surprised, she didn't have the nous to struggle. As his scent surrounded her, Josephine lost any wits she had held on to and just savored the sensations that swirled within her. Sensations that were new and she wasn't certain were comfortable, but that her mind insisted she explore. When before, for instance, had her breasts ached in such a way? Her nipples hardened to the point of pain and...her mind closed down.

She leaned into him to discover more, even though she wasn't sure what else there could be. Sadly, before she had time to decide how those tingles and shivers affected her, he drew back, cursed and studied her in a considering manner. The sharp pang of disappointment that coursed through her was as sudden as it was surprising and she swayed and reached for the wall for support.

"Well, that was not as I expected," David said in a guttural tone that she had never heard before. So different from his normal languid and urbane voice, it reverberated through her like a melodic wave of emotion. "You, my dear, have hidden depths."

Her hands fisted and David chuckled. "No, do not hit me. I spoke nothing but the truth."

Drat the man. He was, of course, correct, but even so… "Only a cad would choose to point such a thing out," she said in the frostiest tone she could manage. *Damn him.*

He held his hands up and his eyes twinkled. The expression took ten years from him, and he looked, she decided, relaxed and a rogue. Dangerous.

"I couldn't resist it and I'm glad I didn't. But, as I value my body the way it is, and I have seen what a good right hook you have, I think discretion will be the better part of valor here. I will now take my leave of you." David bowed and chuckled. "You might want to tidy your hair and cool down, my dear. You look thoroughly flustered."

The wretch moved away before she had a chance to react.

Josephine took a deep breath and counted to ten — twice — as she watched him disappear into the card room. Then she shook her head and, instead of going toward the ballroom as she had intended to, detoured to the ladies' withdrawing room instead. The reprobate was correct. When she glanced in the mirror she noted stray tendrils of hair had fallen from her neat topknot to trail around her face and neck. Her cheeks were flushed, her eyes bright with what she wanted to kid herself was temper and her pulse overfast.

Damn him. Why should he affect her so? It was typical of a rake, to take advantage and leave. Not that she'd wanted him to stay, of course, or take things further but…

Stop it, now. Josephine castigated herself firmly. She had to get a grip on herself. With only a few months to endure the ton before she could escape and live her own life, the last thing she needed was a gentleman, be he a rake or not, taking notice of her. It would foil everything she had put in place for her future. A future she anticipated with relish. A future where she relied only on herself and was responsible for no one's happiness except her own.

Josephine tidied her hair as best she could — lord knew it was hard to keep confined at the best of times — then patted cold water onto her rosy cheeks before she accepted a glass of diluted wine from the smiling attendant. She sipped it slowly, and did her best not to grimace. Watered wine was not her drink of choice. She regulated her breathing, even as she cursed how it sped up every time she thought of David. He had enough charm for five, and when he used it... No wonder so many female hearts went aflutter on the odd occasion he came into their orbit.

Why he had chosen to essay it on her was a mystery. Unless, of course, he saw her as a challenge, or he was bored, and baiting her passed the time. Either, she thought, was feasible. She rested the glass on her hot forehead. Why her?

Two other debs almost danced into the room and ignored her. Was she invisible? Probably, to their eyes, she was on the shelf already and thus a nonentity, not worth sparing a thought for. They sat in front of a mirror, studied their faces and began to chat. Josephine resolved to be cheeky and listen in.

"Did you see him?" one asked excitedly. She wore a fussy pink gown decorated with flounces and flowers and looked like a blancmange. "I swear he smiled at me. Oh 'twas such a thrill. I almost swooned. If he invites me to dance, I probably will swoon."

"He is so handsome," the other said. "And so well dressed." She smoothed down her yellow, frilly and furbelow-decked gown, which made her skin appear sallow, and preened. "He could not take his eyes off me. I think he is interested."

Whoever it is, he is probably wondering how you managed to get that much embellishment on that amount of material. What happened to 'debs should be demure and pale colors should be worn'? Oh dear, I sound like a cat. Nevertheless, neither gown appealed to her. Two cases of trying too hard. Josephine much preferred the adage her own dressmaker subscribed to — less is more. Although, she thought, amused, the blancmanges did attract attention, and that was obviously what the younger women wanted. Even if it was not complimentary. She herself didn't want to be noticed. With her blonde hair and curvaceous figure, men never seemed to see past the physical assets to the woman inside, and once she appeared to be uninteresting, ignored her. She intended it to stay that way. She sipped her wine and waited for the next revelation. It was not long in coming.

"I am sure no one ties a cravat as well as he," the second deb went on. "I would also swoon if he so much as looked at me. As for a dance? Oh my…I would dissolve in a heap."

That would do a lot of good. Idly, Josephine wondered who they were discussing. Hopefully she would soon find out.

"They say he is a rake," the first deb said dreamily. "Well, if he is, I want to discover more. Do you know" — she lowered her voice but not enough to make Josephine strain to hear her — "they said Lady Retford begged him to take her to his bed. Begged him, and he said no, he didn't want someone or other's castoffs. I didn't hear whose sadly," the speaker said in a regretful voice. "But the upshot was that Lady Retford was distraught and retired to the country. Her husband made her. Said he was not going to condone her making sheep's eyes at the viscount or a laughingstock of himself. No progeny yet, you know. Worrying, my mama says. But she added in a resigned sort of voice that such goings-on were all well and good as long as they weren't flaunted. Fancy that? Viscount Lyttlethorp must be someone special to evoke such behavior." The tone of voice indicated that the speaker wasn't sure whether to be delighted or scandalized. "Such a nonesuch."

David Suddards. Josephine decided she might have guessed. Not only was his dress perfection personified, he did leave a trail of broken hearts behind him. Plus, Josephine remembered, she had heard that Lady Felicia Retford was enamored with him. It seemed her attention had become too obvious for both David and her husband. To be fair, his lordship had never shown any partiality for the lady mentioned—it was well known he conducted his affairs with discretion. Some became public knowledge, of course, but in all her almost twenty-four years Josephine had never heard one of his ex-lovers, or indeed alleged ex-lovers, ever say a bad word about him. Nor any of his peers. Most praised him, and words like 'the perfect gentleman', 'generous to a fault' and 'a cracking good fellow'— depending on the sex of the speaker—were bandied around.

Even so, one thing was for certain—Josephine was positive she was not going to be one of those who showed any preference for him. She put her now-empty glass down on a shelf and slowly, so as not to draw attention to herself, stood and smoothed down her gown before she slipped a coin to the attendant and left the room. She guessed by the continuing chatter about fob watches, piercing eyes that followed you around the room — as if they had a mind of their own — and cravat pins, signets and smiles meant for one recipient, presumably the speaker, that neither deb noticed her. For that she was thankful.

Now all she had to do was get through yet another evening, and it could be crossed off her calendar. One day less to endure the ton and one day closer to her goal. After seven long seasons in the ton, where, to the despair of her parents, she had ensured she received no offers, they had agreed — with considerable reluctance, and from her mama several bouts of tears — this season would be her last.

Josephine had long known their interest in her was negligible. All they needed was each other and not to be burdened by a daughter. As a little girl she had overheard her papa saying he only wanted a son and heir, and a daughter was worthless. He had ranted that all she would do was cost him money to keep, and anything of value she had would go to said husband, not her papa.

'Costs me money to keep and I get nothing for it.' As if she were a joint of mutton. Over the years, Josephine had come to understand her parents truly had no interest in her as a person. Their idea of pushing her into a marriage was, she accepted, their way of finally getting rid of what to them was a burden and a nuisance. She guessed they had reluctantly decided, as no one was prepared to take her on, that out of sight, out of mind was the next best thing. By letting her lead her own life, they would no longer have even a nominal responsibility for her.

Come the summer, she could retire to the cottage on the Northumberland coast left to her by Lady Stenhouse, her godmother, and Josephine could hardly wait. That cottage and all it represented had been her lodestone ever since she became the owner. Almost on the beach, the snug four-bedroomed house with its acre or so of land and servants' annex would be the perfect place for her to set down roots. One day.

However, that day had not yet arrived and wait she must. Josephine straightened her shoulders and returned to purgatory, also known as the ballroom, or the debs' dinner—where debutants eyed up the eligible gentlemen as if they were the next meal. She glanced at the elegant mahogany longcase clock as she passed by its prominent position on the landing, not far from the ballroom and the grand staircase, and sighed hard enough to rustle the silk of her gown.

Only an hour or so before carriages would be summoned, but that was sixty-plus minutes too long. Once back inside the overheated, overdressed ballroom, Josephine avoided her mama, who sat along one wall with a group of other grand dames, and headed for a seat by an adjacent wall. There, she hoped her mama would not accidentally catch a glimpse of her, but she, Josephine, could see what was going on. There was something very satisfying about people-watching and seeing how they interacted with one another. Did that make her a voyeur? Probably, but she didn't care. It wasn't like she was spying. She wasn't a peeping Tom or Thomasina, just an interested bystander.

A swift glance around showed her David was nowhere to be seen. She was thankful, wasn't she?

Chapter Two

The latest news from his man of business should have made him happy. Somehow, David accepted, deep down, it didn't. Oh, he was pleased with what he had achieved but the reasons for the necessity of his actions still grated. David scowled as he shuffled the papers together and handed them back to Simmons. He made a conscious effort to remove the scowl and replace it with a smile of thanks. It wasn't his solicitor's fault it made him out of sorts to have to do what he had.

"So that's the lot?" He steepled his hands on the desk and rested his chin on the tips of his fingers as he studied the man on the other side of the mahogany desk. As young as David, Michael Simmons was a gem David didn't intend losing. "Every un-entailed Midham piece of land now belongs to me and my father has no idea? Plus there is no more that my father has to sell?" He wanted to be certain that no part of the estate that had or could be sold had been missed. "None of my tenants are facing hardship, and those in poverty who are still part of the Midham estates have been surreptitiously aided?"

Simmons inclined his head. "That is it all, my lord. The duke has no idea any of it was purchased by you, of course, which I must admit gives me a great degree of satisfaction. Not that it is my place to comment, but anyone…" He stopped and tilted his head to one side. "But I am, my lord, glad I have been able to play a small part in foiling his mean-spirited actions," he added with a defiant expression. "Far be it for me to disapprove of the actions of my elders and better, but in this case, I must."

"You are entitled to your opinion, and he is not entitled to your loyalty, so don't worry about it," David said. "You work for me, not him."

"Nor would I ever be in his employ," Simmons replied. He shook his head. "Never. I'd rather serve ale in a hedge tavern."

"Well, as I have no intention of asking you to work elsewhere, you have no need to worry." Plus, if David's life proceeded how he hoped it would, Simmons would have even more to do.

Simmons smiled. "I appreciate that. Now, as far as his grace is aware, it is a number of syndicates and such like which have purchased varying lots offered for sale, for different reasons. I made sure nothing could be traced to you. The primary acres were purchased under the name Brixham Associates." Simmons hailed from that area. "Others as you decreed. Now it is all yours and consolidated as Caldborough Estates."

David smiled. Caldborough House had been the first place he had bought when he'd come of age and, contrary to his father's thoughts, begun to invest the inheritance from his grandfather and not gamble with the money as his parent accused him. As the crow flew,

Caldborough was not that far from Midham. In attitude and ideals of the owners, a thousand miles.

"You have done all I could have wished for, and more. It fits perfectly. As you know, there is even a common boundary for a few miles with the river. Not that I intend to inform him we are neighbors. If I have been Caldborough's owner for all these years and he has never bothered to discover plain Mr. David is really me, why should I? He chooses to ignore me, I choose to let it stay that way." He smiled at Simmons. "Anything else I should know?"

"Ah." By his tone of voice, David realized Simmons was obviously torn.

"Spit it out, man. If I don't want to listen, I won't."

His man of business still hesitated. David looked at him quizzically. "What am I supposed to have done now?"

"Nothing, but, well, you'll want to listen," Simmons said. "Or you should. However, whether you will do anything about the information, I doubt. It is merely that Lady Whitcombe has admitted her babe, luckily a girl, is not yours."

"Nothing to do then. As I knew that I hadn't sired the child, it makes no odds," David said indifferently. He examined his thoughts, and was relieved to discover he really did not have any strong emotions about the identity of the father. "Out of curiosity, have you discovered who did?"

Simmons nodded. "I made it my business. It is Whitcombe's brother."

Now it all made sense. "Ah, that would cause problems, I admit." David stood up and shook Simmons' hand to indicate the meeting was at an end. "Thank you for all your help. There will be a lot more for you to do once we get to grips with the state of affairs on the various acreages, no doubt. For now, though, I intend to go for a ride to blow the cobwebs away. Then I will consult with my valet as I plan to hie north tomorrow." Even though it was still shy of nine in the morning, and he would have loved to depart that day, he had too many loose ends to wrap up first, plus his godmother's ball to attend. He'd made a promise, and the one thing he always did was keep those. "I'll let you know what needs doing first, once I get north. Will you come if I call?"

"Of course. Will you go to see your father if he is there?"

David shook his head. "You know his stance on things."

"His way or no way?"

"Exactly. And as I tore up the list of potential brides he handed me and scattered them over him like paper raindrops, that scenario is as likely as Prinny being thrifty. I highly doubt I will ever go voluntarily to Midham whilst he is still master there. I intend to see my tenants, reassure them they will not be out on the streets and decide how best to go forward." Now the new Caldborough estates were complete, he could make sure everything was as it should be. Apart from which, it would be good to get out of the capital and away from scheming mamas and their daughters. "Thwaite" — his factor — "will be overjoyed to hear he has more than Caldborough Hall and its immediate surrounds to oversee."

"Indeed."

"To that end, anything urgent send to me there, by messenger if need be." Not that David thought that would be the case. Simmons was more than competent, and now David had ensured that none of his inheritance had fallen into other hands, all should be well. "If you hear of anything I should know about with regards to Midham, you have my permission to do what you think fit, and let me know via our usual channels." It was complicated to help out and make sure it looked as if it were someone altruistic who had no connection with anywhere specific, but so far it had worked. His father might have intended that David's inheritance be a millstone around David's neck, but David had made damn sure it wouldn't be.

Simmons took his leave and David made his way upstairs to change to take the opportunity to ride before most of the ton was awake.

Satisfied he had achieved everything with regards to safeguarding his lands and people, he pondered the other problem that bothered him. It was time to look for a wife. Someone to share those lands with. Someone to help him make the estates profitable and the people on them content. And, of course, to ensure he had an heir. In his mind, that meant someone whom he chose because he wanted that person to be his wife, not someone foisted upon him.

Why did an unexpected image of Lady Josephine Bowie spring to mind? Surely she was the last person he should be thinking about. Heavens, with her in his life he'd never have a moment's peace.

But life would be interesting, and never dull. And how my papa would hate the fact that I didn't have a wife who would play false and loose, and that I was happy with someone not of his choice.

He left the house and headed for the mews and the stables. These early morning rides were his salvation when he had to endure the capital. Since his estrangement from his parents, he had unfortunately spent most of his time there, and little at Caldborough. Mainly, he knew, because he didn't want his father to find out what he was up to, and at Caldborough, as a new landowner — even as plain Mr. David there would be visitors aplenty and gossip would be rife. In London he made it seem he was following his perceived hedonistic ways. In Yorkshire it wouldn't be possible to do so.

He trotted his horse sedately through the streets to the park and managed several decent almost-gallops up the row before more people were out and about and ready to join him. David turned his horse toward the gates and was hailed by one of his cronies who, like David, also steered a much less pleasure-driven way than people thought.

"It's your godmother's ball tonight," James Dempster said once they were within speaking distance of each other. "I expect you got the 'you will attend' note the same as I?"

David laughed. "Of course, but it won't be all bad. I have promised her I will have one duty dance with one lucky — or unlucky, depending on how you see it — deb, and then it's the card room. I intend to be nowhere I can be caught and put into a compromising position. Did you hear how one chit had the barefaced cheek to follow Ronnie Phillips into the library at the Beltons' soiree and demand he offer for her? He'd gone there to wait for another deb, so you can imagine his consternation."

"Good God, poor Ronnie. What did he do, offer for the chit?"

David shook his head. "He went out of the window."

"But the Beltons' library is two stories up," James said in an aghast voice. "How the hell did he manage that?"

"Ronnie always was the one of us who could climb the best. To say they were amazed when he was found in the ballroom dancing with the Marsden chit was an understatement." And he, David thought as they parted, made sure he was never found with anyone. A state of affairs he intended to keep.

* * * *

Twelve or so hours later, with good food in his stomach and a superb brandy in his hand, David watched his friend throw his cards down in disgust.

"Suddards, damn you, you win again. If I didn't trust you implicitly, I would swear you marked the cards," James said wryly as he picked up his brandy goblet and took a large gulp. "Oh God, I know you don't cheat, straight as a die you are, but how you manage to win, I have no idea."

"I pay attention to my hand and do not ogle any sweet young thing that has the temerity to pass the card room door," David said with a chuckle as he shuffled the cards and dealt them efficiently. He took a smaller mouthful of brandy and let the fiery heat fill his mouth and trickle down his throat. It was an unconscionably excellent spirit, which he surmised had not arrived with duty paid on it. "The only way to play if you want to win."

James smiled ruefully. "True, but some of those debs are a sight for sore eyes."

"And some have wedding bells in mind. Remember Ronnie."

James rolled his eyes. "How could I forget? Enough to almost send one into a monastery."

David burst out laughing. "You? Give me strength, James. That would be the day. You'd last about five minutes."

"True, all that kneeling and no willing women who come without a ball and chain."

"No women at all," David pointed out. "A monastery is for men. Celibate men."

"Enough." James gave an exaggerated shudder. "Right, let me try and win some of my money back." He glanced at his cards and groaned. "Again, a donkey of a hand."

"Want to swap?" David offered. "You can if you think it will help you win your money back."

James shook his head. "Not now you have offered, no thank you. I'll stick with what I have."

David nodded. "So be it."

"Next time," James said half an hour later as they totted up the scores, "I swear I will sit with my back to the door and not look up even if a gaggle of ladies runs past stark naked. I make it three hundred guineas to you. I'll send it around in the morning." He kicked his chair back and crossed his legs. "Then Tatts?"

"No hurry," David said as he handed the cards back to a footman with a smile and a nod of thanks. "I doubt it would matter which way you sat, you'd still keep looking—especially if naked ladies were involved. You are not a gamester, James, which is no bad thing. And yes, I will accompany you to Tattersalls and make sure you do not buy a kicker. That would also be a bad gamble." And once more his departure for the north would be postponed. It couldn't be helped. Certain people, like James and his godmother, had always championed him and deserved his support. He would never let them down, or put his own pleasure and preference before their needs.

"True, I do not have your knack for horses or cards. Mind you, Papa was enough to put me off gambling for life." James' father had gambled a large part of his son's inheritance away before the man had fallen off his horse and broken his neck, thus enabling James to save

40

the family coffers. "Ah well." James rolled his shoulders. "If I have to lose, I prefer it to be to you. At least you will do something useful with it."

"Of course." David stood and stretched. "Still, it passed the evening reasonably well, eh? And we were not inveigled next door...ohhh lord, I spoke too soon. My beloved godmama is about to descend on us."

"That's it, I'm off. She scares me." James stood up so fast his chair crashed to the ground to be righted by a footman. "Tell her I had to see a man about a dog." He spun on his heel and walked in the opposite direction to their hostess.

"Ahhh, David, my boy," Janie Foster said in her usual boom of a voice. It was, her godchildren were wont to say, enough to scatter the ducks on the pond in the park at twenty paces. "I should have guessed where you were hiding. I need you to do your duty just one more time. Never fear, I'll collar young Dempster later. So to whom shall I introduce you, eh? Must help you find a wife." Her eyes twinkled. "One guaranteed not to disturb your equilibrium, eh?"

"Godmama, if you ever want to see me again, or for me to continue to manage your affairs, you will *not* introduce me to any more women," David said emphatically. "I came just to show face and to support you. You were vehement in your pathos that no one would turn up. I saw through that, you reprobate. No one would dare miss one of your balls. So here I am and I had duty dances with you and Lyddie." Lydia was his godmother's other godchild and they had known each other since they were in leading reins. Both knew they would not suit and therefore were the perfect foil when one or the other needed a partner for some reason. "I am not in the market for a wife, and seriously, can you see me happy with any of those witless chits? Really?"

He had no intention of explaining he was actually thinking along those lines. His wife-to-be was no one's business except his own. And, eventually, that of the as-yet-unknown lady. "Can you truly imagine me living with shrieking giggles and witless asides? Inanities, and a need for more overdecorated gowns?" He shuddered dramatically. "If you love me, you wouldn't foist that life onto me."

Janie Foster sighed. "When you put it like that…"

"Exactly." Even the thought brought him out in hives. "Therefore, I refuse to dance with anyone and raise their hopes only to dash them. I am, whatever people might think of me, not intentionally cruel. So, dearest Godmama, do me a favor and put it about I do not want to be wed, and that I would be a terrible husband."

"That'll make them all the more eager," Lady Dempster said sagely. "They'll want to be the one who changes your mind and tames you. Each and every one of them. Best just to keep using your normal avoidance tactics and hope you are clever enough to outsmart them all. Especially the mamas."

David saw a newly familiar blonde-haired lady scurry along the corridor behind his godmother and grinned. Maybe he should go against his declaration? No, that would be heartless. However… *Something to consider later.* "Not all of them are interested in me, I'd wager. Anyway, I believe it is about supper time, and I promised myself I'd lead you in. So come on, before all the crab patties are taken."

Lady Dempster snorted. "Once a rake…"

He narrowed his eyes and she tapped his cheek. "Yes, my boy, I know, but please, whatever happens, make sure you do not lose that rakish twinkle. Right then, lead on and never fear, I arranged for a plate of your favorite foods to be held back, just for you." She took his arm and let him propel her in the direction of the supper room. In the background, a string quartet began to play softly — the signal the supper room was open. "And there's a lemon confection you once commented favorably on. I'd wager there's a large portion of that hidden away with your name on it, to be on the safe side as well. My staff know how hungry dancing makes us." She winked. "Or something does."

David laughed. "Ah, Godmama, I love you so, but not even that will make me dance more. I'll just wheedle some goodies out of Cook." He bussed her cheek and she guffawed.

"Cupboard love, but I'll take it. Now let's go and find a seat and hope you do not get mobbed."

"If I do," he said darkly, "I promise I will leave you to it and go and eat in the kitchens. Mrs. Price loves me." Mrs. Price was the housekeeper. "Hence the chef's offering of the lemon confection and crab patties."

"She'll ask when you're getting wed," Lady Dempster said. "Both of them will. They want to see me dandle babies on my knee and you and Lyddie are dragging your heels."

He rolled his eyes. "Nothing worse than if we made those babies together. You know why I haven't married, and also why I have no inclination *to* marry. No one else needs to. Oh, and Lyddie and I would not suit. Mrs. Price agrees."

"Of course she does. That is for certain. You and Lyddie are too alike and would murder each other within a month," Janie said with another of her booming laughs. "Very well, I will keep mum for now. As long as you partner someone for the last waltz. Who should it be?"

He tilted his head to one side and considered the alert and intelligent lady in front of him. It was no good—he had to stir things up.

"How about Josephine Bowie?"

* * * *

Josephine stood up from the supper table where she had enjoyed a peaceful—and male-free—meal with a few of her closest friends. All had lived through several seasons, none had found any man they wanted to encourage or spend any time with, let alone marry. Each and every one intended to live their lives as they chose, and not be dictated to by others. With that in mind, they had made a pact at the beginning of the season to ensure, whenever possible, if nothing else, that they ate in peace. So far, most of the time, they achieved it. Josephine supposed the scowls one or all of them gave any male who came within five yards of them helped them in their cause. As did their habit of finding a table just big enough for whichever of them were there and no one else.

Of course, their reputations as shrews helped. It was something they all cultivated.

"Ah well." Josephine rolled her eyes. "Back to hiding until my mama decrees we may leave." She shook her skirts out to reduce the creases and surreptitiously checked her mama was involved with her cronies and couldn't see her early departure. All was well. "It cannot come fast enough for me."

Her mama appeared oblivious to what her daughter was doing, and although Josephine wouldn't have liked to wager on that point, she guessed it would be a while before any of those ladies became interested in anything other than their coterie and its gossip. As long as she got Josephine to whatever event she had chosen, Lady Bowie believed, erroneously, that Josephine would become involved in everything that went on.

Thankful as ever that her mama did not put her daughter and her daughter's activities high on her list of priorities, she left the supper room. Her mama's despair at her daughter's unwed state was not because she was interested in Josephine. Josephine understood that. It was, she had long decided, the best way her parents could really dismiss her and her unwanted intrusion in their lives. However, not even for that would she compromise, and therefore the reluctant acceptance of what she intended to do next had been given. She'd learned at a young age not to ask for help, in any shape or form, because it would not be given. She'd always be fobbed off to someone else.

Her papa's doings were a different matter in her mama's mind. Every little thing he did was important. As they were rarely apart, worry over what he might be up to didn't exercise her mother's mind to any great extent.

Nevertheless, Josephine made her way quietly toward the ballroom. Once there, she hoped to gain a chair in a corner, preferably behind a pot plant, where no one would notice her and she could spend her time watching the antics of others. She gave a heartfelt sigh as a young rake approached, paused, took one look at her blank expression and passed her without a second glance. Her not-interested, slightly vacuous expression stood her in good stead. Simply not interested would pique their curiosity. Vacuous put them off trying.

The end of the season was far too far away for her liking and every day in the capital was one day too many. Why her mama thought she needed more gowns, bonnets, stockings or gloves when the season was thankfully drawing to a close she had no idea, but when her mama decided something had to happen she was immovable as a mountain. Even though she was so wrapped up in her husband and he in her, both decreed Josephine should look her best. Not that she escorted her daughter to the mantua makers or elsewhere. Orders were given and garments produced. Josephine was expected to accept what was made and wear it. Luckily, so far, nothing truly disgusting had appeared. If it did, no doubt a clumsy hand would ensure red wine or some such stain would appear before long and render the garment useless. As her lithe and colt-like figure was unfashionable, Josephine could often steer her dressmaker's mind away from high fashion to what Josephine understood suited her.

Because her parents normally paid little attention to their daughter and this was one area where they deviated from the norm, Josephine suspected it was their way of trying to get her off their hands in a more acceptable manner than her retiring to the country. Her parents were conscious of their need to keep up appearances. Even so, it was irritating, to say the least.

Josephine's birthday was not until several weeks after they were due to remove to Brighton for a month or so. Nevertheless, Josephine had high hopes she would soon be ensconced in her own home, and ball gowns and fancy bonnets would be things of the past. She had subtly suggested it was a waste of time to take her to Brighton, and thus have to find someone to be her companion. After all, she hardly spent any time in her parents' presence when they shared a house, so she might as well be happy elsewhere as miserable there. So far her mama had resisted her pleas with an indifferent, '*You might meet someone who will turn you away from a solitary life.*' As it hadn't happened in

London, and it would be the same people in Brighton, Josephine couldn't fathom out her mother's reasoning.

Keeping up appearances again, no doubt.

Josephine had decided that as long as she kept a low profile and did nothing to give her parents any hope that she intended to make a good match, eventually she should get her way. After all, she was nothing if not dogged in her single-mindedness. Her parents may not generally pay a lot of attention to her, but she was sure the moment any gentleman showed even one jot of interest in her, they would not give her a moment's peace. It wouldn't be interest in their daughter per se, but interest in the fact that a good marriage would prove to be an 'acceptable in the eyes of the ton' way to be rid of her. She didn't intend that to happen. Therefore it behooved her to make sure she gave her parents no opportunity to think it a possibility.

With that thought firmly fixed in her mind, Josephine turned into the short corridor that led to the ladies' withdrawing room and the ballroom and met one of her contemporaries coming in the opposite direction. Harriet grabbed Josephine's arm and pulled her into a tiny alcove at the junction of where two corridors met.

"Oh, Josephine, wait with me for a moment. I am so excited." Harriet London sighed and clasped her hands together. "I do believe Lord Goffrey is to ask Papa for my hand in marriage. Isn't it thrilling? I swear, if Papa says no, I will die."

Josephine had long suspected Harriet did not have an excess of common sense. "If you die, it won't matter if your papa said no," Josephine replied prosaically. "Perhaps you better not expire before you hear what your papa says."

Harrier blinked and pouted. "Josephine, do not be cruel."

Josephine shook her head. What was it with females and idiocy regarding certain men? Lord Goffrey was a quiet, unassuming man who, as far as she could tell, wouldn't say boo to a goose and had little imagination or zest for life. What Harriet saw in him, Josephine had no idea. Perhaps it was as well everyone was different. "Lord, Harriet, do not be a peahen," she advised her friend. "He won't say no. Why on earth should he? Therefore, if it is what you want, I am happy for you." He would suit the quiet Harriet as well as anyone.

Harriet looked at Josephine with curiosity in her expression. "I want it more than anything in the world. It is what we as young ladies are meant to be, a good wife and mother."

Josephine bit back her snort of derision. "Harriet, you are deluded if you think that alone will make you happy."

Harriet stared at her in amazement. "Do you not think so? It is what we are here for, after all. I am sure you are wrong."

Josephine snorted. "In your dreams perhaps." Did she really have no more interest or ambition than that?

"Don't you want to marry?" Harriet asked, curiously. "Surely, that is supposed to be the next stage in our lives. A husband and then children."

"Not at all," Josephine said in a brisk voice. "If I married I would be a chattel. Subservient and expected to obey my husband in all things. To be ignored at will, or never have a moment to myself. I would be expected to have children who would then be cared for by nursemaids and nannies. No parental love." She shook her head. "Or, if in the very unlikely case my husband marries me for love, not convenience, he would expect me to lavish my attention on him, not our children. Either way, the children suffer. I prefer not to put any human being through that." *As I was.* In her case, her parents had eyes for no one but each other, and she and her younger brother were ignored. George had been at Eton and was now at Oxford and, when home, involved in learning how to eventually manage their estates. She thought perhaps the lack of attention hadn't affected him as much as her. Josephine, however, had spent many years in the same house as her mama and papa and still thought they were nigh on strangers. Even when at age five she'd fallen out of the apple tree and broken her arm, their attention had been minimal. Her papa had had to return to town, so of course her mama had accompanied him. Josephine had been left at home with her governess. Not that Miss Margaret Scott—Scotty—hadn't been loving and kind—she had—but just for once it would, Josephine thought, have been good to have some parental comfort. But her mama had been determined that her place was by her husband's side and nothing, but nothing, would get in the way.

The conversation she had overheard then had stayed etched in her mind for almost twenty years. *'That girl is a confounded nuisance,'* her papa had ranted. *'She's not even a beauty, so how we'll get her a good marriage is anyone's guess. Dowry I suppose. It's time she went to school. Love, if you'd produced a son first, none of this would have happened. We didn't need a daughter. A waste of space and money.'*

Her mama has said something soothing, but Josephine had been under no illusion as to what they thought of her. As soon as her arm was mobile she was shipped off to Miss Leonard's School and there she'd mainly stayed until, with considerable reluctance on both her parents' and her side, she had had her come out. With minimal input from her papa, and only what was needed, and nagging, from her mama.

In many of her contemporaries' lives it was another scenario. One where the parents had married for convenience then gone their own ways. Neither situation seemed right to Josephine. How could anyone have children and ignore them, or put all their effort and thoughts into one person to the detriment of everyone else? What if you loved your husband and that love was not returned? Or you married as you were asked to do, and were not allowed to love your children, or their father ignored them? All of those scenarios were unacceptable to her. She would therefore stay single, become an old maid and retire to her cottage.

"Oh it doesn't have to be like that," Harriet said passionately.

Having been immersed in her thoughts, to her chagrin, Josephine realized she'd forgotten Harriet. "If you say so."

"It doesn't, Josephine, do not roll your eyes like that. I love John and he" — Harriet blushed — "he says he loves me."

"Good, then let us hope your papa says yes," Josephine said briskly, tired of all the angst. "Are you going to sit with me until you know your fate?"

"Jo…seph…ine," Harriet wailed. "You are incorrigible. You have not one romantic bone in your body."

"I know, good in't it," Josephine said cheerfully. "Romantic bones sound most uncomfortable. I intend to stay that way. Emotionally unencumbered, free and single. I will grow my own vegetables, keep chickens and have cats. And a dog. Wear disreputable clothes and worn-out, comfortable boots. Be the old maid who everyone loves…or hates, who knows." She laughed at

Harriet's aghast expression and patted her friend on the shoulder. "Don't worry, it will suit me perfectly, and I promise not to be too disreputable. No corset, though. They will be the first things on my bonfire. Come on, I see two chairs by the potted ferns. A good place to see and not be seen."

"Incorrigible," Harriet repeated. "What is the point of that?"

"The bonfire? Everything, especially burning my corsets."

Harriet snorted. "I meant the chairs where they are, but you do have a point about corsets."

"I can hide from my parents, men and Lady F. in those seats. Watch who is making sheep's eyes at whom and how the recipients respond. See the beginnings of new scandals and the end of old ones. Great fun."

That, Josephine decided, was the only possible way to get through the rest of the evening. Even after Lord Goffrey very punctiliously found them and asked Harriet to dance, with such an affectionate expression Harriet beamed and Josephine blinked and stifled the pang of something unknown, she stayed where she was.

It may work for others, not for me.

Unaccountably saddened, Josephine tapped one foot in time to the music and watched between the leaves of the ferns as couple after couple swept by. Some looked happy, others uncomfortable and several bored. She was so engrossed with one couple who, although married, albeit not to each other, looked ready to commit murder, she didn't notice anyone approach until a familiar booming voice hailed her.

"So this is where you are hiding. Never mind, we've found you."

We? She looked up and silently groaned. She might have known.

Chapter Three

The poor girl looked as if she were ready to vomit, David decided as Josephine swayed alarmingly on her chair and went the color of the potted fern next to her. Throw up or throw something...or both. Really, he conceded, it was unfair of him and Lady Foster to ambush her this way, but, as he often thought, needs must.

And all is fair in love and war? That gave him a jolt. Surely this was neither, merely his sense of mischief, and a need to see if that earlier jolt of awareness when he had kissed her was still noticeable. He didn't expect it would be. Surely it had come from the unexpectedness of his action and her reaction, nothing else? David accepted that, for whatever reason, he had a deep-seated need to understand her and find out more about her, even as he wondered why he had never felt this way earlier. It was true, in general he paid very little attention to debutantes, but this stunning blonde-haired beauty had always registered, even before that last brief encounter.

He bowed and studied her features as she stood and curtsied very correctly, a wary expression on her face. Not as young as he'd first thought, but still no old maid. A coltish figure he discovered he wanted to trace, to imprint her lines firmly in his mind. Her unlined skin was a soft creamy color, her lips ripe and lush and her bosom firm and... *Good lord, I sound like one of those awful novels Lyddie read aloud to me that made me want to heave.* The orchestra struck up a waltz and she paled. His godmama, bless her, didn't give Josephine a chance to think of any reason to object to their presence, or what was about to happen. She indicated him with a languid wave of her hand.

"Lyttlethorp here will accompany you in a waltz. You both need to make an effort so you might as well make it together. Off you go." She dusted her hands together and beamed at them as David held out his arm.

"As we are directed, shall we?"

"I wonder who put her up to this," Josephine muttered *sotto voce* with a suspicious glance at his hopefully bland features as they walked to the edge of the dance floor. At least, once there, he held her very properly. "She knows fine well I do not want to draw attention to myself. Dancing with you? I might as well stand on a street corner with the town crier shouting, 'Look at me, look at me.' So damned annoying. And why call you Lyttlethorp and not Lord Suddards or... Oh, now I'm vexed."

David regarded her closely. *She means it.* It was a novel situation to be seen as an irritant, not a coveted dance partner. "She is trying to emphasize my status, not any perceived shortcomings."

Her eyes sparkled with temper. "She need not bother. I'm not interested."

"You really mean that, don't you?" Brushed off and dismissed by God.

"Well, of course? Why else would I say it?" she asked, puzzled by the question. "All I want is a quiet life and to get this dratted season over and done with. It is never-ending."

Her skirts swished around his legs as he drew her closer — but not so close as to cause scandal — as they moved in time to the music. Her perfume teased his nostrils as her silks teased the rest of body. She kept her gaze on his cravat and David knew his lips twitched. "The knot is my own. The perfection, also, but the pristine starchiness is down to Felix."

"Pardon?" She stumbled and recovered. "What are you talking about?" she asked in an astonished voice. "Are you bosky?"

"My valet." David held her steady — and a little closer. "You seem mighty interested in my cravat so I gave you chapter and verse. Now I, you understand, am still interested in why you want the season to end. Because you have no offers?" The glare she gave him made a certain part of his body want to shrivel and hide. How could he have been so insensitive? "My apologies," he said in a hurry. "I am not bosky, just rude and crass."

"Very true. Thank you for your vote of confidence," Josephine said tartly. "I now fail to see why I should share my reasoning with you."

"Because I will keep asking you until you do?" David suggested. "I'm persistent." He very deliberately moved one hand lower, just to see if his memory of the luscious curves of her bottom held true.

It did.

How tempted he was to pull her closer and caress those globes and...

"Stop that," Josephine hissed. "We are on a dance floor."

"So it would be acceptable elsewhere?" he teased her and was rewarded by a brief flash of temper and something indefinable in her eyes. His body tightened and he hoped to hell she couldn't feel just how she affected him. A certain part of his anatomy was very interested in her and showing it. "I'm happy to go wherever you so desire."

"Do not be ridiculous, of course it would not be acceptable anywhere."

But her sensual shiver and the way she licked her lips told him different. However, he needed to be gracious. "I'm sorry, I'll wait and touch you somewhere we can't be seen, shall I?" Her hand tightened on his shoulder and, for a brief second, hot temper showed in her eyes as her nails dug into his skin through his clothes. Without that protection he was sure he'd have had scars to show her annoyance.

"You really are a rake."

"No, I really am not. I'm sorry, that was quite irresistible. And you still haven't answered my question."

She sighed, long and deep. "You are a pest, there is no doubt about that. I wish I was not dancing with you, and that the season had ended, for a very simple reason. I do not want any offers of any kind. I want to retire from the ton and live my own life."

Now he was interested. Surely that was not the norm for young unwed ladies of the ton? "No marriage?" he asked, fascinated to hear her reply. David essayed a turn with smooth confidence, enjoyed the experience of her silk-clad leg brushing his evening-breeches-covered one, and decided to play with fire. "Surely all young ladies want marriage?"

"Not at all. Some are more discerning." One of those, her tone intimated, was herself. She did her best to add a few inches of space between them. With a swift maneuver and turn of hand, he foiled her with ease. He returned her suspicious look with a bland expression on his face. This dance was turning out to be so much more than duty.

"Dancing with me will spoil your plans?" David was intrigued. "How?"

"If not spoil them, it is likely to put them back. My mama will be in alt, and see me as the next viscountess. And, of course," she continued gloomily, "if she does not see us, someone else will then remark on it. Life is not going to be easy. Almost, no not almost, most definitely, I prefer it when she ignores me."

"I promise I'm not going to offer for you," David said. "It is but one duty dance." Not strictly true, but the small lie would serve its purpose if it gave her some relief. He couldn't explain his motives when he wasn't really sure of them himself.

"Thank goodness for small mercies. Will you explain that to my mama if necessary? No, do not even think of a polite demur. She would not listen."

Could he say Lady Bowie sounded even worse than the woman his own mama had become? Perhaps not a very polite rejoinder. He maintained a discreet silence as they executed the perfect turn and danced back up the ballroom. Josephine was as light as thistledown on her feet and their steps matched perfectly. David realized he hadn't enjoyed a waltz so much for an age. "Do you care to explain more?" The imp of mischief was likely to get him into trouble one day. "Let me in on your thoughts?"

"Not really. All I will say is that whatever sort of marriage anyone has, children are expected to be part of it."

David nodded. "That makes sense. All men wish for an heir if it is possible. Therefore when a man chooses a wife, he expects her to acquiesce. What is wrong with that? I had thought all women wished to be mothers."

"Not at all," Josephine snapped. "Some want to be seen as people in their own right."

That told him. "Can't you be all?" he asked, perplexed. "A wife, a mother and, well, yourself?"

"I could, but I know fine well I would not be allowed to. Therefore I'll stay single. Now can we end this waltz please, before my mama decides you are interested in me and either tries to inveigle you into giving me more attention or refuses to let me bow out before Brighton?" She sighed. "I do not want to be a wife or a mother, so why marry? Selfish of me, I don't want to have to think of others before myself."

The words did not ring true. However, before he had time to question her further, the music stopped and she curtsied.

"Thank you, my lord. Most..."

"Annoying?" David suggested as he held on to her firmly and escorted her off the dance floor. "Irritating?"

"Both of those."

"At least it got you five minutes nearer to your goal," he said as he avoided the eye of his mother — he'd had no idea she was there — and Josephine's mother, who Lady Foster had let slip was sitting with the dowagers, and tended not to pay a lot of attention to her daughter.

"My goal?" she asked in a puzzled voice. "What do you mean?"

"The time when you can go home."

"Ah yes, of course," she said, sounding relieved. "That is true."

"So as I have aided you, now you can help me."

"I can? Over what?" she asked in a bewildered tone. "I can think of nothing where I could be of any help to you. Me, a mere woman?"

"Only you, my dear," he confirmed. "Help me with regards to my puzzlement as to why you do not want children."

"Ah. That." Josephine looked around furtively and turned into a side corridor.

Intrigued, for he was sure she didn't intend an assignation, David followed her. She stopped by an alcove, half curtained off from the passageway, and took a step back so she would be hidden from anyone who walked nearby.

"We should be private for a few moments here."

David followed and waited to see what she would do or say next. It was a novel situation for him. To be so semi-private without a hint of dalliance was something he hadn't encountered before. At that moment he wasn't sure he liked the thought that he couldn't let his hands wander, just a little, just to discover if what her body hinted at was indeed true.

"It is quite simple." Josephine bit her lip, and let it go with a quiet plop.

That sent his interest — and a certain part of his anatomy — soaring once more. Why when it wasn't, or he thought it was not, intended to arouse him, did that gesture have the effect? Strange. She coughed deliberately and he wrenched his thoughts from sex and seduction to what she was about to say.

"When a couple of our…shall I say standing, have children, whatever the circumstances, the children suffer," Josephine said in a flat 'believe me I know' tone. "Tell me one family where the children come first. Where their needs and wants are more important than anything else? When their parents, both parents, are there for them come what may? Let them learn what is right and wrong, and blossom in the knowledge their parents love them and want what is best for them, even if that best goes against their own ideals."

He felt his mouth drop open. Oh yes. David understood perfectly what she meant.

She nodded, although he comprehended that what she alluded to gave her no satisfaction, just the opposite. "Exactly. In our circles it is rare. I would never countenance having a child and then handing them over to others to cherish. It seems to me, people of our class are selfish or unthinking a lot of the time. You marry for convenience, or for so-called love. You have children, also for one of the above reasons, and more importantly to ensure there is an heir. Pity the poor wife if she only has girls. For that matter, pity the girl who is expected to grow up and do the same thing." She took a deep breath. "However, I digress. The children appear. Then life changes. Either the parents are still so besotted with each other the children take a poor second place, or the parents had married for convenience and are not interested in any offspring. Even worse, one parent is interested and the other is not, the poor child has no idea why and is made to feel unwanted except for continuing the line or marrying well."

David considered how best to reply. He understood her reasoning, but surely it wasn't the only answer? "There are also a couple of other scenarios," he said quietly. "One, where the child is smothered by their parents and not given the chance to have an opinion of their own, or to learn to grow up and stand up for themselves."

Josephine looked at him for a long moment. "Very well, I thought I'd said that, but no matter, I agree. What else?"

"A happy medium. Where both parents nurture, encourage, love but do not smother."

He counted to five before she gave any indication she had heard him. Then, very daring, she put her palm on his forehead. "You do not feel overheated, or seem deranged, but where on earth did you get the idea that anything like that would ever happen?"

* * * *

The evening had been an eye opener — one she could have done without.

That dance. That damnable, everlasting, but oh so arousing, dance. Where her body had responded to his maleness once more and left her tingling and ready for something further. When he'd held her tight and looked at her as if she were the most important thing in his life. All rubbish, of course, it was a duty dance, no more, but what an unsettling one. When he touched her derrière, even through layers of silk, satin and lace, it seared her. If his handprint were outlined on her skin, it wouldn't surprise her one jot. Even the thought of that swift caress made her breath hitch and her heartbeat speed up.

Strange and unsettling.

Josephine sighed and put her hand to her throbbing head. The flickering lamps outside made her eyes hurt and she closed them thankfully. At least her mama had waited until they were in their coach before she'd bombarded her daughter with questions. Her papa, recalled from the card room, had stayed silent and just given his wife encouraging looks as she'd shot questions at Josephine so fast it was enough to make one's head spin. Josephine held up her other hand. She didn't need to glance at her mama to know what that lady would be doing. Darting pleading glances at her husband and leaning forward to emphasize her point, until her silk-clad knees brushed against her daughter. Sure enough, within a second, Josephine noticed the gentle pressure.

"Mama, enough. I told you it was a duty dance, no more," she said in a 'this should be the end of it' voice. As ever, Josephine thought with an inward sigh, her mama would no doubt choose to ignore her. "We danced. He bowed, I curtsied. He went off to wherever, and I to the ladies' withdrawing room. One duty dance."

"He doesn't do such things," her mama said emphatically. "You must have caught his eye. Now to capitalize on that. You could be betrothed and perhaps even wed before the season ends." 'And off our hands', her tone intimated.

"Not at all," Josephine said wearily. The ache in her head had begun to make her feel nauseated "Lady Foster insisted on it. You know what she is like."

"Ah, but why?" her mama asked triumphantly. "Why insist, if not because he'd asked her to."

"Now you are talking in riddles." Josephine couldn't work out what to say to satisfy her parent. She suspected nothing short of a betrothal notice in the *Times* would do that. "It was a duty dance, no more, and if I had known it would cause so much trouble, I would have pleaded the headache I now have and refused. Seriously, Mama, it was one dance, nothing else." She tamped down how much she had enjoyed it.

How for once in her life she had forgotten for a few moments where they were, who she was and what the consequences of whom she danced with could be. "I wager the minute the music stopped, he breathed a sigh of relief that he had satisfied his godmother, and retreated to the card room."

That silenced her mama for a full thirty seconds. "I still think you could have made more of an effort to keep his attention," the countess complained petulantly. "You do not make enough of yourself. You can appear quite, well, *attractive*, if you put your mind to it. Never a beauty, I'll own, but a perfect wife-to-be. Really, at times I despair of you."

When have you ever not? "Made more of an effort? Why on earth?" Josephine asked. "What would be the point?"

"Oh come along, Josephine," her mama snapped. "Do not be so naïve. He must need to marry soon. His title is a courtesy one and not as high as ours, of course. Well, until he inherits. Let's just say ours is older, but even so, what a catch."

"Of course," Josephine said under her breath. "Ours is older, and that matters to you, but not, it seems, in this case."

"However, as the heir to a dukedom he will need his own heirs," her mama rattled on. Luckily she seemed not to have overheard Josephine's mutters, or if she had, she'd chosen to ignore them. "You could do worse. You need to think about your future. We can't be here for you forever, you know."

You have never been here for me, and I doubt you are going to change the habits of a lifetime. "As you say," Josephine replied with more patience than she'd thought she could muster. "And I have my future sorted. Northumberland and my cottage. I am holding you to your promise. Before long you will no longer have to worry about me, as I will be happy in my new life. I'm sure his grace will be delighted you worry over him and his potential wife and children. Nevertheless, I will not be the person to supply them. Now please, Mama, I have such a headache, and the sway of the carriage isn't helping. Let me get home in peace and retire." *And perhaps think up some more excuses to fob you off with.* This sudden interest in her future was not pleasant, and worried Josephine. She'd needed their attention twenty-four years earlier. It was now much too late. And, she suspected, not true interest. More as to how they could use David's interest to their own ends. A horrible but, she suspected, true scenario.

"Very well, but we will continue this tomorrow," her mama decreed. "Perhaps we ought to buy you a new riding habit. In case…you know. It could be money well spent. After all, any woman should be honored to be his duchess, and it might as well be you as anyone else. I'm sure your antecedents show us in a good light." 'Even if you choose not to', her tone inferred.

Josephine sighed and closed her eyes. This conversation was going around in circles and contributed nothing to her throbbing head, and it wouldn't be polite to say that to spend money on a riding habit that would be cut down to something more wearable before that long was ridiculous.

"Please, Mama, no more."

"Make sure you take a powder."

We will continue this discussion tomorrow," her mama said again. "Make sure you take a powder."

Did the elder woman think if she repeated herself ad nauseam it would make it sound more palatable to Josephine? If she did, she was wrong.

"I rather thought we would," Josephine said wearily. "Even though there is no more to be said." All this unwanted attention was unnerving, to say the least. She thought she preferred to be ignored. Josephine gritted her teeth, wedged herself into a corner and prayed they would soon be home. She staggered up the stairs to her room and stood passively as her maid undressed her, slipped a nightrail over her head and pushed her into a chair. Then Mary unpinned her hair and gently massaged her scalp, and Josephine sighed with relief as one layer of tension was released.

"Blissful."

"There now," Mary said in a motherly, comfortable way that amused Josephine as Mary was no older than she. "I'm not going to tug at it. You just get into bed, drink the tisane I've left for you and sleep in. You'll feel better in the morning."

"I hope so." Josephine let herself be helped into bed and tucked in like her nursemaid used to do when she was a child. Sometimes it was good to be cosseted.

* * * *

It was the only cosseting she got. After a restless night, where her dreams were full of a certain viscount who kept dancing with her and telling her it was her duty to amuse him, she wasn't surprised to find all the covers in a tangle when she was woken what seemed to be only minutes later by an apologetic-looking Mary.

"Mary?" she asked, groggy from lack of sleep. "What now?" She blinked as the shutters were opened and light flooded into the room, and waited for her headache to reappear. Except for a slight thickness she could put down to her less than restful slumbers, she felt fine. "What time is it?"

Mary shook her head as she plumped up pillows and handed Josephine a mug of chocolate. "It's past twelve, and there's a note from that Viscount Lyttlethorp. He's calling in an hour to take you for a drive. To help your headache, it says. Be thankful, your mama has left to go to Richmond with Lady Pugh and Countess Derringham and your papa is, at a guess, in his club. He left with Mr. Martin an hour ago. I did say I'd let you sleep, but this is so exciting, eh?"

No wonder she was still tired – she'd not had more than four or five hours of broken sleep.

"If you say so. I'd class it as an annoyance myself. Do I have to go?" Josephine asked plaintively. "Can I not make my apologies due to this terrible headache?" Why she asked she had no clue because Mary's response was a foregone conclusion.

"My lady," Mary gasped, aghast. "He's the heir to a dukedom." If she had said 'the heir to the Holy Grail' she couldn't have sounded more reverent. "Of course you must go. Think how happy it will make your mama. She will be in alt."

"I know," Josephine said in a doom and gloom tone. "That is one reason why I do not want to. Remember, Northumberland soon. Leading my own life. No ton, no irritating rakes, rogues, or peers. No parents to upset. Anything that makes Mama think it might not happen, when I am determined it will, is just going to complicate things. Drat the man. I was better off when he, and she, ignored me. At least I knew where I stood. Now? I'm at sixes and sevens and have no clue as to what might happen, and rue the day he decided to annoy me. He and my mama are each an unstoppable force in their own right, but together? Lord almighty, what chance do I have? It was better when they paid no heed to me."

"Ah but surely this is preferable?" Mary opened the wardrobe and took out a smart riding dress in a deep cherry red that suited Josephine's fair coloring. "I can't think of a finer man to court you. After all, he is one that most look up to. Now I've drawn you a bath and, once you are ready, I think this is the one. With the hat with the two feathers, and your new kid half boots. Perfect."

"Not from my point of view it isn't." Josephine pushed the bedcovers back and swung her legs over the edge of the mattress. The words 'court you' put a nasty taste in her mouth and a disagreeable flutter in her stomach. Or she told herself it was that and not pleasant anticipation of what might come to pass on the outing and afterward. "None of it is," she added, more to convince herself than Mary. "It is too bad. I was going to walk in the garden, then have a leisurely afternoon visit to Hatchards before I prepared for yet another boring and uncomfortable evening, this time at Lady Salmonds' musicale. The only good thing about that is few men attend, it is seen as too tame for them. Now you have upset it all."

"Not me — his lordship," Mary said as she shook out the riding habit and laid it on the bed. "And it is an honor."

"You have a point with regards to his meddling and not with regards to the honor." Lord, why was all his attention directed at her? Why not at someone who would appreciate it? "Very well, as it seems I have no option." Josephine sighed deeply. "I suppose the red will do."

* * * *

David wondered what his reception would be. He understood how high-handed he had behaved and had debated as to how she would respond. At least it hadn't been a note saying 'Go to Hades', which, if he were honest, he had half expected. Instead, a terse 'Thank you, I would be delighted' intimated more in what it didn't say than in what it did. He suspected delighted was the last thing she would be, but his mind was made up. Lady Josephine Bowie deserved more attention from him. It had been a long while since someone had intrigued him as much as she, and it behooved him to act on that. If it annoyed her, so be it. As he was certain the interest would decrease once he got to know her better, she would not be inconvenienced for long.

Hold on... This is all me, my and me. The fact he might hurt her had never occurred to him, she was so adamant she wasn't interested. No, she would curse him to the devil, show her impatience and no doubt do her best to ignore everything she chose to, and merely heave a sigh of relief when his attentiveness waned as it surely would. Which led to the knotty subject of why he was doing what he was. Surely this heightened inquisitiveness was due to two things. One, he had acquired all his un-entailed inheritance without his parents' knowledge, and secured it — and his future — and two, he had not pursued a woman in an age.

With that sorted out to his satisfaction in his mind, David tossed his reins to his tiger and took the steps to the Bowies' front door two at a time. It opened as he approached it and Josephine swept out, clad most elegantly in a deep red riding habit and a matching hat with two jaunty feathers over one ear. She looked, he decided, ravishing. Why had he never seen how alluring she was before? He looked her up and down and grinned. The glare she gave him made him bite his lip to ensure he didn't laugh out loud. She certainly looked as though someone — no doubt him — had ruffled her feathers. He couldn't resist ragging her.

"A sight for sore eyes indeed, my dear."

She harrumphed and stepped past him. "And you are not a sight for a sore head. In fact, you are more likely to increase the pain. Can we go before anyone sees you here?" She stood by his curricle and tapped her foot impatiently on the pavement. "That would at least alleviate one of my worries."

"Why? After all, they will see us in the park." He bowed very extravagantly and chuckled. "This is where I say your carriage awaits, my lady."

"That is another thing set to annoy me. You are," she said as he handed her up and moved around to take the reins, "so very trying. Stop attempting to be pleasant. You are also one of the most aggravating, irritating people it has been my misfortune to meet."

"One of the nicest things ever said to me." David waited until his tiger jumped up and set the vehicle in motion. "You, meanwhile, are one of the few who are not sycophantic."

"Well, why on earth should I be — Hold on..." Josephine thought over his words. "You said the park?"

"Yes?" He glanced at her. "It is the perfect temperature." He raised one eyebrow in interrogation, even though, of course, he knew exactly what she was getting at. "Are you cold?"

Josephine rearranged her skirt until not even one boot-shod toe was visible before she tutted and gave him a disgusted look. "Of course I'm not cold." She looked up at the sun. "That is not what I'm talking about."

"No?" He hid his grin and checked the horses as a stray dog took exception to their presence and rushed toward them snapping and snarling. His tiger jumped down and shooed it away until a grubby urchin grabbed it by the scruff of the neck and dragged it away. Henry, the tiger, re-boarded and David turned the equipage in the direction of the nearest entrance into the park. "Five minutes and we will be free of this traffic."

"And into the gossiping type. Why, oh why are you doing this, my lord?" Josephine demanded. "You do not take up young ladies for rides in the park. It is well known."

"Didn't. I'm a reformed character," he said in a complacent voice. "Well, to the extent that I now will take up one certain lady to ride in the park, no one else. I look forward to discovering what it all means."

"For goodness' sake."

Her tone didn't inspire confidence in him that she was about to be an amenable and interesting companion. Anything but.

"Why reform with me?" Josephine asked in a voice full of long suffering. "Why not pick someone who appreciates it?"

The verbal sparring was more than enjoyable. It made David wonder how she would cope with sexual badinage. Probably thump him as she had done Lord Percy. That was not the scenario he aimed for. His privates clenched at the thought they might be attacked.

Even so…he had to say it.

"The thrill of the chase," he said as they approached the queue of traffic waiting to enter the park. Already, interested glances were being thrown their way. He wondered if Josephine had noticed. "And the result, of course."

"So just to appeal to your jaded senses, you will mess with my intended future. I am not a pheasant for the plucking," she said *sotto voce.* "And people are staring."

"I know, but you are so much fun to rile." They maneuvered through the gateway and began to move steadily up the track. "No, do not pucker up or make a fist like that, you'd break your fingers if you used it on me."

Her fingers uncurled and then re-curled in a different way, and he chuckled. "Much better. Smile at Lady Jersey, she is on your right."

Josephine gritted her teeth and made a facsimile of a smile. She dipped her head and Lady Jersey, with a knowing grin, responded similarly.

"Now she will tell the world and his wife, including my mama, we were here together. My papa will be deciding how to word the notice to the papers. You are an unmitigated nuisance."

That told him. "Really? All you are doing is taking a turn around the park. Perfectly respectable and the perfect day to do it on."

"Pshaw."

He'd never heard it expressed so perfectly or by someone so young. "If you say so."

"My lord, please, do not patronize me. Perfect? Not at all. For some reason you have decided to single me out. I have no idea why unless it amuses you to upset other people's lives. If so, why the — why on earth did you have to choose mine?"

David steadied the horses as they came to the end of the track and all the carriages in front slowed to execute the turn and go back the way they'd come. He followed the others and they picked up speed again. Should he be honest?

Why not? What have I to lose, apart from my manhood? "You interest me. I need a wife. I feel we could suit." Now where on earth had that come from? His subconscious? He examined his mind. His father would hate the partnership, and think her not suitable. He would expect a curvaceous diamond of the first water, who would defer to her husband, give him an heir and do as she was told — or someone who would defer to him, the duke, and make sure David did so as well. Not a slim, pretty, albeit alluring blonde with a mind of her own. Perfect. However, there was a lot more that drew him to her. A lot more. None of which he was able to voice at that moment. Not if he didn't want his face — or worse — rearranged. "Shut your mouth, my dear. You look like a fish."

"I feel like one," Josephine muttered. "One you are very skilfully reeling in. But remember, between reeling in and catching, a lot can happen. Now take me home." She glared at him, smiled sweetly at a young matron in a garish green dress and dipped her head at a bosom-bow of her mama's. "Now," she snapped. "Or next time we meet, my hat pin will be in my hand and aimed at you."

Her expression decided it for him. As he had suspected, she was in no mood to listen to him or his other reasons for his behavior. "Your wish is my command."

"If it was, we would not be here," she said tartly and rolled her eyes. "That's really done it. Mrs. Sedgefield is over there in that dark brown barouche. She is a particular friend of my mama's. The gossipmongers will be at it immediately, all vying to be the one to share the news. You are a nuisance and a menace and I am sick of you."

"Oh, why not tell me exactly what you mean." David was rapidly losing his temper as well. Did she not know the honor he had bestowed on her? To break his rule and drive her in the park and to intimate he wanted her to be his wife? And all she could do was rail at him.

Oh my, listen to me. What do I sound like?

"Careful," he warned. "If you are not on guard, you will get a reputation as a viper."

"Better that than to be known as someone you are dallying with," Josephine stated. "Who wants to be seen as your light skirt?"

"Hell's teeth, woman," he hissed as they exited the park and drove away from the all-knowing eyes of the ton. "I am not bloody dallying with you. I want you to be my wife, though why on earth I do, heaven only knows. You are the most infuriating woman I have ever met."

She sniffed. "I'm so glad heaven does, because I have no idea either. Let me get this straight and into your thick mind. We. Would. Not. Suit."

That wasn't what he thought. Not even after that exchange. David held his tongue, and they drove back to her parents' house in an uneasy silence. Once there, he gave the reins to Henry and moved around to assist her to alight from the curricle. It was like holding a lump of wood as he helped her down and she punctiliously took her leave.

David watched until she entered the house and climbed back into his curricle. *Time to plot the next stage.*

Chapter Four

"What is this I hear?" Lady Bowie burst unceremoniously into her daughter's bathing chamber as Josephine tried to relax before dressing for the soiree. "Why didn't you tell me? Oh my goodness, a ride in the park. Why, it is as good as a declaration. You will soon have your own establishment. When will he call on your papa?"

"Never." Josephine stood up and waited until the water streamed off her before she stretched out to reach for the towel. This newfound notice by her parents was unwanted, unwarranted and damn worrying. "And I have my own establishment ready and waiting in Northumberland. Now, if you do not want to be dripped on, I suggest you take a step or two back." She waited until her mama complied, got out of the bath and stood on a towel placed on the floor for the purpose. "Thank you. Now, Mama?" she went on conversationally, "I have no idea why his lordship has decided to toy with me, but take my word for it, that is all it is. He means nothing by it. It is, I suspect, a way for him to pass the time until the season ends and he moves on to his next ploy. Yes, we went for a drive, yes, I know until today he never took a woman up beside him and yes, I know you have at last remembered you have a daughter, but no, it does not mean I am about to become a viscountess. I'm sorry to upset your plans." *No, I am not, but I am too polite to tell you what I really think of your belated attention.* "Nothing is further from the truth. Do not get that bee in your bonnet, Mama, for it will sting you."

Her mother put her hands on her hips and shook her head in sorrow. "What did I do to deserve a daughter who does nothing to better herself?"

Ignore me, perhaps? Forget you had a daughter until now, when it is almost twenty-four years too late?

"I have no idea, Mama, but there it is. I'm sorry I'm such a disappointment to you, but, sadly, life does not always go according to your plans." She patted herself dry and shivered. Now she was out of the hot water, her body had cooled rapidly. "If you want me not to sneeze my way through the evening, I suggest you let me get dressed. Are we not due to leave within the hour?" She walked past her open-mouthed mother and into her bedroom. Her mama followed her.

"Really, Jose— Argh, why did you not tell me? I must hurry." She swept out of the room.

Josephine sank onto the bed and began to laugh. It was that or cry. "Oh, Mama, you have only ever heard what you want to hear." Weary to the bones, she finished drying herself and rang for Mary to help her dress. At least the soiree should be irritating rake free.

It was, and even though Josephine steeled herself to be on the receiving end of a lot of questions, they were in the main good-natured and not too intrusive. A couple of the younger debs gave her envious glances from under lowered lashes, and the looks that passed between them made her mentally chuckle. It was obvious they wondered what on earth the viscount was doing with someone so ordinary and nearly on the shelf as her. It would have been fun to confront them and inform them she also had no idea. However, whatever the circumstances, she could not do that to her mama.

To her everlasting thanks, Harriet wasn't in attendance, so she was spared what she was sure would have been more intimate and searching questions than those half-heartedly offered by the other attendees. Whoever had advised people not to annoy her by being too inquisitive deserved her heartfelt gratitude. She could hopefully get through the evening without showing her ire.

Even with the lack of intrusive and in-depth queries, keeping her temper was at times a close run thing. After one elderly dowager had blatantly used her age and title to ask what came next, Josephine had to count to ten before she replied.

"The harpist, a quartet, supper and then Miss Jones on the piano," she said with a composure she didn't feel. "So, if you will excuse me, I will go and find somewhere to sit." She curtsied and turned away before anything else was said. As soon as they'd arrived, her mama had behaved as usual and left Josephine to her own devices, so there was no one to call her out for her undoubted rude behavior.

Josephine took her seat to listen to the harpist and sank into the music. A rustle and a penetrating whisper interrupted her concentration.

"If it were me, I'd have ensured everyone noticed me," someone said. "And be certain it happened again.

If Viscount Lyttlethorp is after a wife, I'll make sure Mama invites him to her end-of-season ball. After all, I would be perfect."

"So you say," someone else replied. A few hissed *ssshhh*s meant nothing else was forthcoming, until the harpist finished and took her bows.

Josephine clapped along with the rest of the audience and carefully turned her head to see who had spoken. The two young girls who sat behind her colored and looked away. She leaned back over her chair. "I'll pass on the information so he knows you want to be put on that list."

"The list?" the speaker asked. "What list?"

Josephine smiled and patted the girl's shoulder. "Did you not know he has two lists? One of those who want to be the next Viscountess Lyttlethorp and another of those who will never be considered? I, of course, have no way of persuading him upon which list any particular name should go." She stood up, leaving both girls slack-jawed, and, unrepentant, she made her way out of the music room to where supper was being served.

She chuckled at their opened-mouthed expressions as she left them. That was the most satisfactory part of this whole sorry affair.

Or non-affair.

Josephine contemplated the repast spread out on the table before her, chose a patty and an apple and found a seat in a corner. She was unsettled, and hated it. So many people were interested in her and her life was uncomfortable and unwanted. Drat Viscount Lyttlethorp. If he'd been there, she would have used the paring knife she held and pared him, not her apple.

As he wasn't, she amused herself by imagining ways he could suffer. Nibbled by ducks or chased by a swan. Had to walk home when his horse cast a shoe. Made to listen to inferior poetry with no way out. Forced to dance with one of those drooling, simpering, idiotic debs who would do anything to be his bride. Trapped between an epergne and a table with one. And she would chuckle as she watched.

However, she was realistic enough to know none of that was likely to happen. Instead, no doubt he would just charm everyone to do his bidding then go his own way. Plus now she had told him what she thought of him, he would surely leave her alone and head for an easier target. Why did that thought not comfort her as she had expected? Was she truly wondering what it would be like to be properly wooed by him? Wooed because they both wanted it, not for propriety or necessity. She mentally shrugged. It was unlikely to happen to her.

To anyone else it could, just not her.

With that thought uppermost in her mind, Josephine got through the rest of the evening and the drive home. Whatever the morrow brought, it would be better than that day.

* * * *

How on earth could she be so wrong so often? For the second day in a row, she was woken by Mary at an hour much too early for coherent thought.

"My lady, your mama wants you in her sitting room as soon as possible. She says not to bother dressing, but to go down in your robe."

That woke her up. "Eh? Not dress? Has someone died?" Her mama was a stickler for decorum.

Mary shook her head. "I don't think so. No one is in black at any rate, and we've not been told to decorate the knocker in black crepe. I'd say your mama looks unaccountably pleased with herself."

More attention? It was unnerving. Worse than no attention at all. Josephine threaded her arms into the sleeves of the dark blue robe Mary held out to her. At least it matched her nightrail and was presentable, she decided as she tied the sash. She couldn't be faulted in that way. A nasty trickle of dread slithered down her spine. "If she is pleased about something, it cannot have anything to do with me. I couldn't please her if I tried."

"Unless you married the viscount," Mary said as she swiftly brushed out Josephine's hair, plaited it and pinned it in a loose coil near the nape of Josephine's neck. "There, that's better."

"And as marriage is not going to happen, it isn't me who has put her in a good mood. Let's hope she keeps it when she sees me."

* * * *

"Godmama, you are a gem. A veritable diamond." David bowed, grinned then kissed his godmother's hand in a very flamboyant way. "Whatever would I do without you? I will owe you forever."

Lady Foster laughed and patted his cheek, one of her favorite ways to show her appreciation. "Oh you will, but fear not, I will think of something as a fitting repayment. That woman is one of the most miserable, self-centered people I know." She paused and tilted her head to one side as she thought over her words, and waved her be-ringed fingers in the air in a circular motion. "Well, not exactly self-centered, more immersed in her husband to the exclusion of everyone else, including her poor children. It is no wonder Josephine is wary of any sort of intimacy, when the closest marriage she has observed is that of her parents. If you consider that, you immediately should accept she had an unhealthy relationship to use as her guide."

"Hmm, so what do you suggest?" David asked in interest. He hadn't understood just how bad it was, but it did explain a lot with regards to Josephine's attitude. "That I ignore her and change my mind? Focus on someone else? Because, as far as I can tell, that is very unlikely to happen." That thought had surprised him when he had realized he was in no way jaded or bored of his—his what?— possible intended's intentions to ignore him. Although he had been at Waterloo, fought hard and understood the value of careful planning and expedition, this, he thought, was a campaign like no other. Whatever the outcome, he intended to enjoy it. That was not something he could say about the carnage of Waterloo.

"I thought not," Janie Foster said. "Very well. I will give you five days, no more, or you may have to find me someone to defend me on a murder charge. Or rootle out another pipe of brandy, because if anyone is sure to drive me to drink, Drusilla Bowie is. She is a stupid woman. She and her husband deserve each other, and not their gorgeous children."

"I hadn't been aware you knew them so well."

"I don't, not really," Janie Foster said. "For which I am ever thankful. But I know people who do, and I am a great observer of human nature. That couple do not head my list of good people. So, as I say, you owe me."

"We have a deal." David stood up and stretched. "A five-day house party, with the Bowies amongst the guests. Lord, I ache."

"Late night on the tiles?" Janie winked. "I might be old but I do remember some interesting times when…" She broke off and colored. "Well… Anyway, enough about me. What about you?"

David laughed. "I wish that were the case. It would be my own fault. Not that it is any other soul's fault. This was planning and plotting so I could come to you cap in hand and ask for your help. There was no one else I thought could pull it off."

"You are such a sweet talker, David," Janie said in appreciation. "What you really mean is no one else is as stupid as me. I hope she gives you a run for your money."

He inclined his head in acknowledgment. "I am almost certain you will get your wish. Now, I must take my leave and let you get your arrangements sorted. I myself need to head north and make sure all is on order up there before I join you in Derbyshire. I have a barn to make watertight and a schoolteacher to interview."

"You are setting up a school? Seriously? You, my dear man, have hidden depths beneath your hidden depths. Where and how, if I may be so bold?"

"I made sure of a school as soon as I bought Caldborough," David said. It had been one of his first priorities. "However, it is incredibly well-attended and the numbers are so large now we need another teacher. It seems my agreement is needed as to whom. So to Caldborough I must go before anything else. I promise to be with you the day before your impromptu and oh so select house party assembles."

"Harrumph. You better not be late," Lady Foster warned him. "This is a very large favor I am bestowing on you. That woman is enough to bring me out in hives, and to add insult to injury, to ensure her husband is entertained I'll need to invite Freddie to make up the numbers. No doubt the old goat will take it as a sign of encouragement, damn him." Lord Aitken, the old goat, had pressed his suit on Lady Foster for more years than David could remember, and the long-widowed Janie had ignored his pleas for equally as long.

"Do you want to renege?" he asked quietly. "For, if you do, I will understand."

"Ah, men. Who could ever understand the way your mind worked?" Janie sighed. "No, you fool, I am looking forward to seeing what sort of a dance she leads you. All I ask is that there be a ring somewhere at the end of it."

As long as it wasn't through his nose, David thought, he could agree with that sentiment.

* * * *

"You what?" Not very polite or grammatical, but it was the best Josephine could manage at such short notice. She'd been roused and made to dress and come downstairs to hear this? Before breakfast? "You think we should do what?" Surely she was in the middle of a nightmare, which she would soon wake up from?

"Not think, do listen," her mama said testily. "We are going to go to Lady Foster's Derbyshire home for a house party."

You never do anything with me. Why now?

Definitely a nightmare. Unfortunately, it looked as if it were a living nightmare, not a dream. There was more to it than a personal invitation to a house party. Her mama was not on those sorts of terms with Lady Foster, surely? Who had put the idea into Lady Foster's mind?

She could easily guess.

"Enjoy yourself. I will go to Northumberland." *And enjoy every second of my freedom.*

"You will not." Her mama sounded appalled. "You will come with us."

"Why?" Josephine asked baldly. "Why us? You hardly know her, and I am sure to be an encumbrance."

"Rubbish," Lady Bowie said, somewhat unconvincing in her denial. "She is a long-standing friend." Josephine noticed her mama said nothing about Josephine herself. Perhaps lying there was one step too far, even for her parent?

Acquaintance, Josephine mentally substituted. A very slight, merely to nod to acquaintance at that.

"She says, as the weather seems set to stay fair, a few days in the country might be pleasant, and she is just asking a few special friends if they would like to attend," Lady Bowie carried on in a hurry. "A very informal affair."

"And you are one of them?" Josephine cursed the skepticism in her voice. She was lucky her mama either didn't hear or chose to pretend she hadn't. "Who else?"

"Just us and a few of her close friends and family, I believe. I'm not sure who. After all, she is under no obligation to share that information with me.

Especially if she is asked not to. Josephine had a good idea who could have requested *that*.

"It is an honor for us to be invited. Of course, I said we would be delighted to attend. Such a thrill, I believe her gardens are second to none. And as for her hothouses, they are said to be spectacular. We will all have a perfectly amazing time."

"Hmm." Josephine was not so sure. There must be a reason—a large rake-shaped reason, perhaps?—why her mama was so cagey about the other guests. "Why me?"

"What do you mean why you? Why on earth not?" her mama said pettishly. "I swear, you are awkward just for the sake of it. You never used to be so intransigent."

As you rarely saw me, you never gave me the chance. As for why not? She could give her mama chapter and verse but knew it would do no good. "When," she asked, resigned to her fate, "is this due to happen?" *How long have I got to prepare?*

"Ah, from Thursday next week, for five days. So we arrive on the Thursday afternoon and leave on the Tuesday." Her mama clasped her hands together as if she were about to pray. Josephine looked heavenward. If her mother was praying, could she herself ask for divine intervention to prevent the visit?

She sighed. Probably not.

"I declare, a few days in the country will be very pleasant," her mama said in the sort of tone that just dared Josephine to argue. As her mama much preferred the town and often said the countryside made her sneeze, that was an obvious mistruth, but Josephine was aware there was no point in saying so. She curtsied, wondering as she did why she gave her mama so much unwarranted respect.

"I'll make sure Mary knows what to pack."

Please let me get out before I explode.

"There might well be an informal dance on one evening, so pack the green," her mama instructed. "And the lilac as a standby."

That stopped her in her tracks. "The green for an informal dance?" The green was more suited to a formal ball, not a dance in the country. Even the lilac was, to her mind, too fancy for anything other than a town engagement. She made a mental note to insist that her cottons and lawns were included. "Who else will be there?" If she asked often enough, would she get an answer?

Probably not.

"You need to appear your best," her mama said defensively. She didn't look Josephine in the eyes. "Who knows who will be there?"

"Exactly so. Who knows? Perhaps you had better tell me."

Her mama colored. "I'm sure I have no idea," she replied unconvincingly. "Lady Foster said it is a select few people and I would not be so uncouth as to ask who."

And if you expect me to believe you, you are deluding yourself. It was easy to guess who had done the selecting. Lady Foster would not have acted alone, and Josephine would bet her new diamond pin she knew who else had been involved.

"If you think Lord Suddards will be there, then make my excuses now," Josephine said with a snap as she stood by the door, ready to make her exit. "I am not going to be paraded before him." *Or give him a chance to do anything else.* She was beginning to understand how a deer felt when it was being stalked.

"Why on earth would I think that?" Her mama twisted the fringe of her shawl around her fingers and could not look her in the eyes.

"You tell me, Mama."

"This is ridiculous," her mother blustered. "I need to get ready to meet Lady Craddock, and if I do not hurry, I'll be late. Just make certain you know what to pack and get Mary to ensure everything is ready when it is needed."

Would it be counted as readiness if she included a dagger?

* * * *

David rode out from Tansy House, Lady Foster's country home, early enough to enjoy a gallop along the local bridle paths and be back in time to bathe, dress and appear presentable for the Bowies' arrival after luncheon. Those first few minutes would be crucial to the success of his campaign to woo and wed Josephine. Her parents would not be a problem, except for interfering and trying to coerce Josephine into accepting his proposal. At the thought of their daughter as a potential duchess, they would be in alt. Her papa had beamed when he had asked permission to address his daughter.

"But I have to say, the girl is a mystery to me. She's seen off enough suitors over these last years to give every new debutante a husband twice over. Don't understand it myself, but for every one who approached me, not one ended in an offer." Her papa had paused and shrugged. He hadn't met David's eye. "My poor Josephine. Who knows why, but it must worry her."

Why had his interest in his daughter appeared false? Even if he hadn't been privy to some of her thoughts, her parents' attitude would have struck David as odd. Almost as if it were a prepared speech.

"Or, maybe I should say, not one ended in an offer that I heard about," Lord Bowie had added. "For all I know, she cut them off before they got started. Now she's got this crazy idea in her brain that she's had enough and is retiring from the ton to live in the wilds of Northumberland. Even if her mama's ancestors hail from that area, it is no excuse to hie there as soon as she is old enough. Her poor mama is in despair. Well, I tell you, my boy, if you can dissuade her from that, you'll have my eternal gratitude. Save us worrying about her."

As worrying about their daughter was something David reckoned the Bowies never did, he'd chosen not to answer in any great detail but had merely nodded his head and replied with brevity, "I will do my best." Not what he'd really wanted to say, but to tell your prospective father-in-law he was a disgrace to all men was not the way to ensure a positive outcome to your wooing.

That had led to the invitation to Tansy House.

Even though he had reiterated that any interference and he would back off, he knew there would be some sort of parental pressure exerted, and he intended to limit it as much as possible. He wanted Josephine, but only if she wanted him, not because she was in some way forced into accepting him. He didn't bother to ponder the knotty question of why her and no one else. David had no idea why she affected him so. However, he wanted to discover what made her tick. Plus, if he were honest, to find out to what degree she was aware of him and ascertain if he could increase that awareness to a level where she yearned for more. It certainly hadn't been propinquity, she had made sure any meetings were minimal, but something about her called to him. He was equally as certain it was not just that he was ready to wed and was on the lookout for a suitable wife. He had always known whoever he married would have to be a certain sort of person to satisfy him, and hadn't held out a lot of hope of finding her. However, it seemed Josephine could be that person. It wasn't just because she would be everything his father thought wrong in a wife, although if he were honest that did play a part. It was also that if there was one thing he did know, it was that lust could and did strike anywhere and at any time. So it surely followed that more than lust could do the same.

Only with Josephine. Where did that come from? David blinked. What else had he decided?

More than lu — He stopped that thought short. Was it more? How the hell would he know?

Lust or whatever apart, if he had a chance to get to know her better, and she him, he was certain he'd be able to bring her around to his way of thinking. He mentally jumped. No, he wasn't at all certain. She seemed to be the only woman immune to his charm.

David put his heels to Pegasus and let the horse have his head for five glorious minutes. When he slowed, they were both breathing heavily, and he was ready to face whatever the day would bring.

'You are a nothing, you will end up in gaol or deported. A blight to our name.' Why had that taunt from his father all those years ago re-emerge now? His scars throbbed again, and he deliberately let himself remember just

one of the many whippings the man had seen fit to administer. The last one.

On the hot summer day over twenty years earlier, David hadn't broken the window of his godmother's prize hothouse. He'd been nowhere near. The fact that he had been playing in the river with some of the local lads, an activity strictly forbidden as 'beneath his status', had kept him quiet. Those few snatched hours had been precious to him, and had given him friends he would otherwise not have had. However, his parents' arrival at Lady Foster's house had coincided with him walking across the lawn and Janie Foster's head gardener telling his employer about the smashed panes. His father had snatched the whip from his coachman and laid about David without waiting for explanations.

The sharp slash of the whip over his shoulders had brought David to his senses with a jolt. Up until then, he could have agreed that some punishments were deserved in that he had committed a misdemeanor or other. But this violation, given without cause or justification, had been one too many. With a roar, and the strength of an almost adult youth, he had snatched the whip from his father. Instead of returning the stroke across his parent's body — something in his red haze of rage and pain he could easily have done — David had found strength of mind and body he didn't know he possessed. The whip had been broken in half and thrown onto the ground in front of the duke.

"Do not ever try anything like that again," he had said in a voice devoid of any emotion whatsoever. "Or it will be the last thing you do. Even hardened criminals get a hearing. You have played judge and jury and found me guilty — wrongly — once too often."

Lady Foster had started toward David. He'd waved her away. He hadn't wanted her to see just how scarred his back was, and how the new injuries would just add more scars in time. "Now please excuse me, whilst I wash and make myself presentable for my godmother's table." He'd bowed toward his mama, who'd stood at the carriage steps, white and shaking, smiled at his godmother and ignored his father. As he'd left them, he'd heard the tremulous voice of the head gardener.

"A branch fell from the apple tree, m'lady, and broke the pane. I never had a chance to tell you."

His father had never mentioned anything more about the incident. His parents had left the following day, and David had stopped in Derbyshire until he'd gone back to school. After that, his visits to his home had been as infrequent as possible. He saw his mama when he could, saw his papa when he had to and spent as much time as possible wherever his parents were not.

Strange that those memories should come back so clearly. Why was he out of sorts? Because so much rested on those next few days? Not just to show his papa — if the man cared or even discovered what his son was up to — that he had a mind of his own, and wasn't afraid to use it but also because he wanted, really wanted, to learn more about Josephine. Plus show her he was not a lightweight and was a good and upright citizen who would be a perfect and loyal husband, true only to his wife and family. Who would love and cherish his progeny, whatever sex.

David took a deep breath and let his pulse slow and his mind become calm. It would do no good to rush his fences. He needed to be cool, calm and collected. With deliberation, he let the peace of the countryside fill him.

This part of Derbyshire was hilly, wooded and picturesque. He'd visited it as man and boy and knew it intimately. Each time he returned, he was struck anew at the sheer size of everything. Not dissimilar in some ways from his beloved Yorkshire, and in others as unlike it as it could possibly be. He skirted a large outcrop of rock that he'd climbed many times as a boy, although it had seemed ten times higher and twice as daunting in those days. He scanned the area with a keen eye and noticed the nearest cave to the house was now fenced off. Probably too many local lads doing as he had — exploring without sharing their destination.

He'd had more than one thick ear from Lady Foster due to that sort of behavior.

David glanced at his watch and noted with a shock he'd been out longer than he'd realized. Somewhat reluctant but knowing he had no option, David turned Pegasus back toward Tansy House and gradually slowed their pace. When he trotted into his godmother's small but perfectly presented stable yard, he was happy and satisfied he was ready to face anything that the next few days — and Josephine — could throw at him.

He handed his horse over to his groom. "I hate not being able to rub him down myself, but time got away from me. I'll need to get a move on."

"Indeed, my lord, I believe there is but a half-hour until luncheon. Never fear, I'll do right by him."

"Good man." David clapped him on the shoulder. "Thank you. I know you will." He walked quickly toward the house, stripping off his gloves as he made his way to the back entrance and the minor stairs that would take him to within a few yards of the room always allocated to him. It was situated across the gable end of the house, at the end of one corridor, and he'd occupied it since he'd first ever visited. The views of the moors were vast, and the old tree nearby, with branches that tapped his windowpanes, had long been his own personal entrance to the house. He wondered idly if the ivy and oak would still take his weight. Not that he intended to discover that fact, of course.

Tansy House was not overlarge, having a mere ten bedchambers, but it suited Lady Foster perfectly. And for David's purpose it couldn't have been better. Each wing of the house had five bedrooms with their own sitting rooms and bathing chambers.

As soon as he arrived in the house, Lady Foster waylaid him.

"Ah. I wondered where you were." She wrinkled her nose. "I might have guessed you'd be on horseback. Lucky thing. I could do with a ride to blow the cobwebs away."

"I bet you managed to sneak out earlier before anyone was around," David said. "I know you."

"I…" Lady Foster spluttered and held her hands out in supplication. "What can I say?"

David grinned. "Nothing. Don't you go and apologize. I'd have done the same thing."

"Thank goodness, and to be honest, I did the cobweb thing the other day. Now, as to your guests…" She winked and informed him that as he, Josephine, Lyddie and a hopeful James Dempster were the only 'young things', she'd put the others close to him in the east wing. "But not," she declared, "with either gel next door to you or young Dempster. That would not be acceptable. He's next to you, the gels are on the other side of the corridor."

Which meant, due to the position of his apartment, one of them had to be next to him, albeit with their bathing chambers separating their accommodation. No doubt it would be Lyddie, for his godmother would have no intention of making things too easy for him.

"The rest of us" — herself, the Bowies, Lord Aitken and the Hansons, the other couple she had invited for the occasion — "will occupy all the rooms in the west wing. Mind you, if the Bowies hadn't been determined to share a room, and the Orchid room wasn't so large, it could have been different," she said as she and he sat in the snug family dining room and began to eat lunch. "But I have put them in there and hope they like it. So what happens now is up to you. I've done my bit."

"You have indeed. So who is due to arrive when?" David helped her then himself to a slice of salmon and some salad. "I know James will be here within an hour or so. He was to stop overnight in Chesterfield with Brampton. He promised to arrive before two."

"Then he'll be the first. Lyddie is to drive over with the Hansons as they live near her parents. The Bowies intimated they would arrive by four. Freddie Aitken arrived when you were out, but decided to take a nap and eat in his room. Suits me, that's one less meal I have to endure with him." She gave her infectious guffaw. "He'll be up in time for a snack before dinner, even though we keep country hours. Can't let him go without regular snacks. He's convinced he'll fade away."

"Why did you invite him if you feel like that?" David asked with interest. Lord Aitken was a jovial, rotund gentleman who did indeed say at regular intervals he needed to keep his strength up. "Why not someone else?"

"Better the devil you know," Janie said. "Ah, he's fine really, but when he is tired he is a nightmare. Best he rests and is refreshed for later. I'll need him to stop me telling Drusilla Bowie what I think of her."

That sounded fair enough. David applied himself to his meal, and the conversation became general. Replete, he pushed his chair back as a commotion sounded in the hall outside.

"James," he guessed.

Janie Foster snorted. "Bound to be. You and he were always the ones to make the most noise." She paused and winked. "And mess."

The door opened and a caped and dusty-booted James Dempster entered and bowed over Lady Foster's hand.

"Excuse my dirt, but Birtwhistle" — the major-domo — "said if I came in there might be some food left. As Brampton's chef walked out yesterday, something to do with ingrates who didn't enjoy good tripe, we had to partake of dinner in an inn." He shuddered theatrically. "So no sumptuous meal, just basic fare. I'm fair clemmed, as you'd say up north."

David laughed. "Exaggerating as usual."

James grinned, not a whit abashed. "Well, just a bit, but a bite to eat would be most welcome. As Brampton is still chef-less, breakfast was uninspired to say the least. So yes, if you don't mind me sitting down in my somewhat disheveled state, any food to feed me will be gratefully received."

"Whenever is food not," Janie Foster asked rhetorically. "You better fill up before you fade away. I'll leave David to entertain you. I'm off to check my chef hasn't bolted. Mind you, as when he heard I actually had visitors due he beamed and began to decide on his menus, I very much doubt it." She whisked out of the room in a flurry of skirts and, within moments, her booming voice could be heard asking some servant or another question after question.

"So what's the plan?" James mumbled as he stuffed his mouth with a hot pork pie, homemade mustard and some ale. "This is good — Durham mustard?"

"Derbyshire, made by the chef, who, even if he is French, loves Godmama enough to make her his take on the English version. Thank the Lord you are here."

"Well, if you chose to thank him, so be it. When does everyone arrive? In fact, who is everyone else?"

David filled him in on details as James made short shrift of the pie, several slices of rare roast beef and the rest of an apple pie and cream.

"Trying your hand at matchmaking, are you?" James asked as he studied a fruitcake and cut himself a generous slice.

David raised his eyebrows. "Me? Of course."

"That's all right then," James said dryly. "I wish you luck, and do not involve me."

"As if I would. Lady F. has done that instead. She's invited Lyddie."

"The —" James spluttered crumbs and glared at David, just as David heard the rumble of carriage wheels.

"Come on, I wager that is the Bowies. Support me and help me look innocent."

James swallowed his cake and wiped his mouth. "Impossible."

Chapter Five

Josephine looked around her with interest as the carriage rumbled around the semicircular drive and pulled up in front of a large house built of warm gray Derbyshire limestone. It had been a long, at times boring drive, interspersed with obsequious innkeepers and the blessed relief of a room to herself and Mary, and no parents making her feel she was an insect under a microscope's lens. They had dined in their room, and taken a separate carriage, something she was well used to.

Each evening after dinner, Josephine had relished the way she was able to sit in restful silence, as Mary had sewed and she, with a mental apology to each and every tutor who had tried to make her embroider tidily, had sat and read.

Now, as her parents' coach pulled up behind them, Josephine collected her thoughts and mentally prepared for whatever was to happen next.

The large imposing doors opened and servants rushed out to mill around the vehicles, hand her parents and herself out and retrieve the luggage.

Lady Foster sailed — there was no other word for it — down the three wide and shallow steps and embraced her mama and her in turn. "So glad you made it, and in such good time, eh? You've even beaten the Hansons and my goddaughter. Not so Suddards and Dempster, though." She indicated David and James Dempster, with whom Josephine had a mere nodding acquaintance. "They have been reacquainting themselves with their surroundings."

She ignored the two men and rounded on Josephine. "Now then, I'll show your parents to their room, Josephine, and let these two youngsters take care of you. The green room, David. Lyddie, when she arrives, is in the gold room. You'll be fine, my dear," she said firmly, and patted Josephine's hands. "They know how to toe the line."

Josephine shut her mouth. She hadn't been going to argue, just to proffer her thanks, but 'know how' and 'will do' were two very different things.

"We don't stand on ceremony here," Lady Foster finished as she began to herd Lord and Lady Bowie toward the steps. "Just relax and enjoy ourselves, eh? No pomp."

It seemed not. Josephine watched as her parents left her — as usual without a backward glance — and walked into the house with their hostess. They were arm in arm with each other — also normal behavior from them. Their interest in her had waned over the journey, and the last exchange had been merely to warn her not to disgrace them.

"So much for parental affection and concern," she muttered, before she turned to David. "What next?"

He grinned. She mistrusted the wicked glint in his eyes as he bowed, took her hand and audaciously kissed her inner wrist. Josephine gasped and James coughed theatrically.

"Don't mind me," James said in a humorous tone. "I'll go and inspect the rhododendrons if you like." He bowed, almost, but not quite, she decided, as elegantly as the man who still held her hand. "James Dempster at your service, my dear. Although, as I value my body in the shape God gave me, not too much at your service."

The remark, accompanied with a wink, made Josephine splutter and David growl. "James, go and walk in the lake."

Josephine ignored David, turned to James — not an easy task, while David still held her in a firm grasp — curtsied and smiled. "I will remember," she said gravely. "So who else is part of this alleged party?"

"Allegedly, a select few," James said solemnly. "As in, you, me and this reprobate here. Lydia Frewitt, for my sins, the Hanson couple who are dry as a desert and as boring as well…take your pick, your parents and Lord Aitken. And Lady F., of course."

It seemed a strange blend of persons. "That is all?" Surely a house party should have more guests to ensure a good mix? "It seems so few people."

"The house is nigh on full," David said. "It only has ten bedchambers. And as I will freely admit, in front of a witness, so there is no mistake about my intentions, this was arranged purely so I can get to know you better. And you me."

Raven McAllan

She gaped, she knew she did. How on earth could he say something so outrageous with a straight face? "I…you…er…" *Get a grip.* "Do not be ridiculous."

The thought gave her a curious sense of satisfaction, even though she wished it were not true. The last thing she needed was his attention, or indeed that of her parents.

Her parents definitely not, but the rest? That sense of satisfaction turned into more of an inquisitive need for discovery. Just what was in his mind? Why and how did he intend to do whatever it was? *Oh, how complicated this appears. Why me? Why here? Why now? In fact, just…why?* As she had spent so many years ignoring men and turning their interest away from her, Josephine discovered she hadn't the first idea how to find out. "You are being ridiculous," she reiterated.

David smiled. "I'm not. Though once Godmama agreed, I rather think she added some machinations of her own. Hence James and Lyddie and the Hansons."

James choked. "Do not add me into all this. Lady F. would not try to throw me and Lyddie together."

"You think not?" David said quizzically. "You poor, deluded soul. The elders here can never be said to be the sternest chaperones in the world, unlike Lyddie's parents, who luckily were promised elsewhere." He sounded relieved. "They put the fear of God into my soul merely by looking at me and showing they find me lacking. I have no idea why."

"Grass snakes and teacups, I expect," Jamie said. "Their summer fair?"

David patted Josephine's hand. "Ignore him. It was a worm, and I was only giving it a drink. I was eight," he explained. "I thought I was helping it."

Josephine laughed even as her mind whirled. Lydia Frewitt and James Dempster? That might take some of the attention away from her and David. Josephine was under no illusion that David meant every word he spoke. That, she was certain, plus his charm when he decided to use it, made it very hard to dissuade him from any direction he had chosen.

"Sometimes, my lord, you infuriate me to the edge of reason."

"Only sometimes?" James, whom she had forgotten was listening avidly, said in a dry tone designed to amuse. "He must be slipping."

"Enough," David said. "I will begin to feel maligned otherwise. Josephine...no, don't pucker up, we surely have got to the first name stage by now, and if we haven't, it is time we changed that status quo. Let me show you to your room. Within the boundary of politeness, of course. Then perhaps we can take a walk in the rose garden until tea."

"Won't you need to be here to greet the others?" Josephine said doubtfully.

David shook his head. "No, James and Lady F. can do that. My job is to keep you entertained until the gong goes to dress for dinner. Which I have on good authority is to be informal. As in no tiara and pearls. And we can discuss our strategy."

His tone intimated that he hoped they didn't do that. Presumably because he was certain it would not meet her approval.

Josephine chuckled as she thought he had intended. Any strategy would be hers. "Just as well. I forgot my tiara and I do not suit pearls."

"No," David said thoughtfully. "Sapphires and Blue John."

"Blue John?" She had never heard of him. "Who is that?"

"Not who, but what. A lovely local semiprecious stone. Godmama has a vase made of it in the aptly named blue room, I'll show you later. It is a beautiful piece. You can get necklaces and brooches and such made from the stone. If we plan our days well, we might find time to ride to one of the caverns where it is mined. I think you would be interested. There is only one hill in the world where you find this exact stone, and fortuitously it is within riding distance."

An outing like that would fill in some time nicely. "I'd like that."

"Then we'll let James work his wiles on Lydia and make up a party."

"Why work his wiles?" she asked, interested to hear more about his friends. It struck home how little she really knew about him or indeed most members of the ton. Perhaps she should have paid more attention, then she might not be in the present situation. "What do I not know?"

"Do you ride?"

"What?" What a strange question to ask a young lady such as she. "Of course I do. Stop changing the subject."

David chuckled. "No flies on you, my dear. Let's say James is interested in Lydia and she will not indicate if that interest is reciprocated. Now, enough about them, they are old enough to sort their own lives out. So you would be up for riding to the caves?"

"Is it possible on horseback without upsetting any arrangements made for us?"

"Godmama will be happy to accommodate our plans. It is easy if we are all accomplished riders. We will start early and have lunch in an inn nearby."

"Then I think that sounds perfect," she replied and smiled to herself at his self-satisfied smirk.

"Then that is settled. Now, we go this way."

Josephine didn't demur as David led her around the side of the house and along a graveled path that meandered through shrubs and bushes. "I thought you were going to show me to my room?" she said as he seemed to direct them nowhere nearer the house.

"After." He turned off the main path into a narrow grassy trail, which was only just wide enough for them to walk side by side.

"After what?" she asked as they reached a tiny circular clearing, surrounded by rhododendrons. In the middle was a curved stone bench, with its flat seat of polished local stone and its stumpy legs ornately carved. David towed her to it. "Please rest for a moment." He put gentle pressure on her shoulders until she sat down with a thump and carefully arranged the skirts of her traveling dress over her knees and legs so it covered her ankles. She bit back the oath hovering on her tongue and waited with less composure than she hoped she conveyed.

David looked down at her and frowned. "Where do I start?"

"By not towering over me, perhaps? Sit down, do. As my old governess would say, you are making the place look untidy." Josephine shuffled along a good foot to enable him to be seated without crowding her. "For goodness' sake, tell me what on earth your intentions are."

David sat down and twitched his buckskins into place. "To woo you. To make you mine?"

Before or after the wedding? Good grief, I hope I didn't say that out loud. She sneaked a glance at his face. As no glee or amusement showed, she was hopeful that stray, and erroneous, thought had not been uttered. "But why? You keep saying that, but not why."

How on earth could he put his emotions, his needs and his wants into words without scaring her? How could he explain his situation without showing what his parents were like? Would she even believe him? David understood anyone would have a hard time accepting that parents would behave in such a manner. In fact, he had found it difficult to comprehend. Now, with the wisdom of distance, David would admit that it had taken him a long while to understand that his father was a thoroughly unpleasant person who took a delight in subjugating people. Who enjoyed inflicting pain on innocents, had no vision and no way to see anyone's opinion except his own. In the man's mind, there was his way or the wrong way and nothing in between.

David took a deep breath. He had no option but to be open and honest. "It is a long story, and probably not one we have time for at the moment. Once I start, I will really need to carry on until I get to the end. The rest of the guests should be here within the hour and then it will be a cup of tea, a snack and get ready for dinner. What I will need to share shows certain people in a bad light, and, well, it is not an edifying thing to hear." How difficult it was to be so open and say those things he had kept inside himself for so long. "I would be doing both of us a disservice if I do not tell you everything. Perhaps this evening? We are housed close to each other. Your sitting room once everyone has retired?"

It was an outrageous suggestion, but in one way it made sense. Not too far for him to navigate unseen, and once everyone was in bed, no one was likely to disturb her. However, would she see it like that?

Josephine looked at him suspiciously. "Be warned, if this is your idea of entrapment, and someone oh so conveniently finds you there, I will tell you straight, I will flatly refuse to have anything, and I mean *anything* to do with you, or any of your plans for my future."

"You wound me."

"Do I? If so, have my apologies."

She sounded as if she didn't care one way or the other if he accepted them or not, and it riled him.

"I wouldn't inveigle you like that," David said in a flat tone that, he decided, indicated he was holding on to his temper by a thread. "By wooing, by showing you what we could be, yes. By underhand means, no, never, I swear. I have had that done to me and it stings. This is above board."

She stared at him for a long moment. Could she see how sincere he was and accept what he said was true?

"Very well, I am inclined to believe you, but woe betide you if you aren't telling the truth."

"I am." He wasn't used to having his integrity questioned—except by his parents. "My word as a Suddards and a gentleman."

"You're an aristocrat," Josephine pointed out. Her tone indicated she held no truck with the word of such a person.

"Exactly. Therefore also a gentleman. You can trust my word. If you need to, feel free to ask my godmama. She has always called a spade a bloody shovel and would never lie to save her own skin, let alone anyone else's."

"Then, I will agree with you, and say when the house is put to bed," Josephine said. Her demeanor was so composed she could have been saying she wished for a cake for tea, instead of agreeing to an assignation, which, although innocent, could have serious repercussions if it were discovered. "In my sitting room, which I have yet to see. Perhaps you should show me? I really must wash the grime of the journey away before tea."

David inclined his head, relieved she'd agreed to his suggestion without too many protestations. "Follow me. Do you need any help?"

"Only in directions to the room."

"Pity. Ah well."

He was all innocence and she mistrusted him.

"Then let's go in the back way," he suggested, straight-faced. "After all, we better not let your mucky person be seen in the front hall, eh?"

His expression was so earnest, Josephine just stared at him. Then he winked. "That got you wondering, did it not?"

"Ohhh…" She tried to look angry and failed miserably. "You wretch. I will remember. Beware the next time we find ourselves next to a puddle. I will show you mucky. However, in all seriousness, I better tidy up a bit or questions will be asked. Ones I suspect neither of us would know how best to answer."

"Then this way." She followed him as they skirted the edge of the rose garden and took another grassy track toward the house. Once there, David opened a narrow door in the wall. "This leads to what my godmama calls the back passage. Not the most savory name but it serves its purpose."

Josephine bit her lip to try to stifle the giggle that threatened to engulf her. "T-true," she managed. "Where does it come out?"

"At the bottom of a staircase. Which in turn leads to the floor where our bedchambers are situated. Halfway along the corridor."

That is convenient. "You know it well?"

"I did." David stood to one side to let Josephine climb the stairs before him. "I'll say it now, the chief reason to put you in front of me was to save you if you slip. A nice bonus is that I can watch how your body sways beneath your gown, and indulge in the most amazing fantasies."

She almost missed the next stair tread. "You…you…wretch."

"Careful, you do not want to fall." The blighter sounded not one whit repentant. She would have to watch her step with him, and not just on the stairs.

"If I did, I would make sure my heel came into contact with a certain…delicate part of your anatomy," she remarked before she realized what she had said and to whom she spoke. *He deserves it, he is baiting me.* "Now where is my room?"

David stretched past her to twist the knob of the door that led into the corridor. Without a word, he put his hand to the small of her back and turned her slightly to the right. Even through her traveling dress, she could swear she felt his handprint on her skin. It was a strange sensation.

"Here." David opened the large, wood-paneled door and took a step back to let her precede him into the delicately furnished room. He waited in the doorway and watched while she swiftly scanned her surroundings. Elegant, expensive but not overwhelming. The delicate perfume of freesias assailed her nostrils and she took a deep, appreciative breath. She loved them and the chamber.

"Your sitting room," he said. An unnecessary comment — it was obvious. "The door on that adjoining wall along the corridor is my sitting room, the next my bedchamber. And in case you are interested, our sitting rooms do have an internal adjoining door as well. You may have the key if you do not trust me, although that door will be useful later on, when we have our discussion. Very convenient."

She gawped. It was a lot to take in at once.

David grinned and tapped her nose. "Once again, I offer you my apologies, my dear. You are far too easy to tease. Everything I said is true, but the way I said it could have been less annoying, I agree. But, in my justification, I did offer you the key to our mutual door."

"Hmmm." She drummed her foot on the parquet floor and stared at him until he ran his fingers under the edge of his cravat. "But not proffer it. Will you knock when it is time to go down for tea? Hopefully by then the key will be in your hands for you to give to me." She shut the door in his face and smiled as she heard a guffaw through the wood panels. She needed to keep her wits about her when he was around. Josephine suspected it would not be easy. However, if nothing else, it meant life would never be dull.

Was he really serious about this marriage silliness? She washed her face and hands and let Mary help her into a pretty afternoon gown.

"I hope this will do for dinner as well," she said, as once more Mary anchored her fine hair with an excess of pins to hold the simple plaited knot in place. "All this changing is so irritating. Why is it necessary? Do not shake your head like that, Mary. You know what I am like. What have you heard?"

"That not dressing doesn't mean a simple country tea gown but a town tea gown, if you get my meaning."

"Tarnation. Semi-formal then."

"It seems so. Which gown?"

Josephine considered the wardrobe she had with her. "The gold, I imagine. With the sandals to match and the shot silk shawl."

"Yes, that will do perfectly," Mary said with the gravitas of someone twice her age. "I'll help you into your gold when you come up at the gong. I'll get those pretty sapphire clips out to go with it."

"Perfect. Ah." There was a double *rat-a-tat-tat* on the door. "That must be his lordship. Will I do?"

Mary gave Josephine one swift but comprehensive glance. "You'll do, my lady. You will indeed. I'll have everything ready for you, when you come up."

Josephine flashed her a grin as Mary moved to the door and opened it. "My lady is ready," she said portentously, then spoiled it with a hastily smothered giggle.

David eyed Josephine with an appreciative twinkle in his eyes that Josephine mistrusted. All rakish innocence.

"I agree," he said suavely. "Perfection."

Josephine firmed her lips, took one look at David and swiftly turned her scowl into a cough. There was no need to upset him unnecessarily. Better to save any annoyance for when it was really warranted. "That is a label never before applied to me," she said as she joined him. "Perfection. And I do not believe it is applicable now, either. Adequate will do. I am no diamond of the first water and I know it. Pretty, maybe, but the adjectives most often used by gentleman are 'insipid' and 'uninspiring'. 'Ornery' and 'imperfect' are more usual from others. Ask my parents."

"I prefer to make my own decisions." David tucked her arm in his. "And I say perfection." His tone dared her to argue.

Did he not know how their stance would look when they made their appearance in front of the others? Josephine did her best to tug her arm away and he tightened his grip.

"Stop it, you will hurt yourself."

"Then let me go. This will look much too intimate."

"Really?" He shrugged. "I would say get used to it, but as I don't want you to start railing at me, I'll say they will soon get used to it."

"Argh..." Josephine checked they were as yet unseen and brought her heel down on his instep as hard as she could. As he still had top boots on and she wore soft slippers she doubted he felt the pressure, but it did her good. "I say it again, you are the most annoying, infuriating, irritating, damnable person I have ever had the misfortune to meet."

"Careful, your impartiality might start to show," David said with a droll expression. "No, please, do not pucker up. I promise to behave. Look." They reached the top of the stairs and he rearranged her arm so her fingers rested on his sleeve. "There, we can go and practice being Miss Prim and Proper and Mr. Perfect Escort. Ready?"

It was becoming a habit to mutter, 'As I will ever be.' Josephine curled her fingers into his sleeve and they paced so stately down the stairs she was ready to giggle again. The man might infuriate her, but he amused her in equal portions. She guessed the next few days were about to confuse her. Which David was his true self?

"Ah, I thought you might have got lost." Janie Foster appeared from behind the drawing room door, like a jack-in-the-box. "The others have just arrived and Clutterby is about to bring in tea. I suspect you might prefer ale, David?"

"You suspect right, Godmama." David ushered Josephine into the room and bowed to the Hansons before he bussed Lydia on the cheek. "Hello, Lyddie, you are looking well."

"Thank you." Lydia turned to Josephine. "Hello, I've seen you around, but sadly never had the opportunity to make your acquaintance. Lydia Frewitt."

"Josephine Bowie." They smiled as the teacups were handed around and conversation became general. Apart from a few covert glances at her, and David who sat by her side, her parents generally ignored her. Much to her relief. James and Lydia sat at right angles to her and David, and it seemed a straightforward case that the occupants' ages divided the room.

"Shall we take a turn on the terrace?" James suggested once the cups were empty. "Plan tomorrow and try to make some space for dinner?"

"Good idea." David stood up. "The others seem settled until the gong goes." The three older ladies were clustered together, and as they watched, the men got up and made their way out of the room. "The study or the billiards room, I'll be bound," David said as the four of them walked out of the long window and onto the terrace. "Luckily there are two billiards rooms, so we won't miss out if we want a game."

"Billiards," Josephine said with confidence. "For my papa anyway. I think it is his only pastime that doesn't involve my mama."

David raised his eyebrows.

My runaway mouth.

"I did not mean that," she said indignantly. "You know I didn't."

"I do, of course." He slowed their steps as James and Lydia moved ahead and went down onto the lawn. "It's that imp of mischief again." He nodded to where the other two were fast disappearing. "Do you mind if we do not join them? We can plan tomorrow later."

"What?" she asked, puzzled. "Oh, tomorrow is fine, and this perfectly respectable. But, why?"

"Because I want to talk to you, alone but in full sight." He turned slightly so no one inside could see his face. "Make sure your door isn't locked when you retire for the night. I'm a darned sight too old to climb the ivy, and I'd bet your maid has found the key for the internal door and used it."

"What?" she said again. *Good lord, I sound like a parrot.* "Used it how?"

"To lock the door and keep me out. And the tree branches don't stretch to your room, only mine."

That was a statement designed to intrigue. However, before she had a chance to inquire more, a hail from Lady Foster, inside the house, called them back to their surroundings and duties.

"Will you?' he asked as they turned to walk back to the house.

"Yes, all right," she said rapidly as they climbed the terrace steps to be accosted by Lady Foster.

"Didn't you hear the gong?" that lady demanded as they approached the house and the open French

110

window Lady Foster stood by. "A good five minutes ago. Where are the other two?"

"Ah." David scanned the garden. "They came in by the far door."

Josephine blinked and his eyelid drooped for a split second. Evidently, damage control was in force, just in case.

"Hmm, well, you better hurry. Freddie Aitken is a stickler when it involves his stomach. Dinner will be at six-thirty prompt. No dressing." She turned and walked in her usual brisk fashion out of the room.

"I do hope she doesn't mean that literally," David murmured as they followed her. "The thought of all of us in our birthday suits, making sure we do not drop soup on any sensitive areas, does not bear thinking of."

Josephine was glad she had not been drinking when he said that.

Chapter Six

Josephine's parents were, to David's mind, people who did not deserve children. Apart from a brief searching glance from her mama, who proffered her cheek for a very unemotional kiss and whispered something that made Josephine scowl, and a gruff hello from her papa, they ignored her and sat close together on a long, cushioned seat. They were approached by the Hansons and began to chat in low voices.

David watched Josephine as she straightened her shoulders, looked around the room and, after a brief hesitation made her way toward Lydia, who sat on one of the window seats. He forestalled her, and bowed.

"Very fetching, my dear. I wonder if you can help me? What is that flower under the bush?" He lifted her hand onto his arm. "Follow my lead."

"Pardon?" She swallowed and closed her eyes briefly.

"Ignore them." They were the sort of parents any right-minded person would give thanks not to have. "Just pretend they are not here and you are enamoured with me. That you can see or hear no one else when within my vicinity."

She coughed and her lips trembled as he steered her toward another window embrasure. "I wonder if you can help me. I'm not up to scratch on my plant recognition. That one." He pointed toward the garden. "What is it?"

"A weed," she said dryly, but so softly that no one else would hear. "Ah," she said more loudly, "I can't really see from here. I fear my eyesight is not as good as yours."

"Never mind, look at that. Such a pretty bird." He surreptitiously put his other hand on her wrist and squeezed it in sympathy. "Always appears alert and interested in everything."

"What?" She looked up at him in confusion. "Why?"

"Just nod and relax," he said in a low voice. "They do not deserve you, nor you them."

"I agree." She nodded and raised her voice. "Yes, you are right, it never fails to amaze me how some creatures are so different to others." She sighed. "You never truly get used to it, do you? Generally it doesn't bother me, in fact I prefer it, but on occasion it hits me. They really do not have room in their lives for anyone other than each other."

David understood. "Not at all." He paused before he continued in a normal voice, pitched slightly higher so his words could be heard all over the room, "The differences can be noticeable. The cuckoo, for instance, farms its offspring out as soon as it can and ignores them. Luckily, some other bird takes it in and nurtures it. Some others keep their offspring close until they are well able to fend for themselves. Teach them everything they should know." Would she get his hidden message? With every moment they spent together he became more and more certain she was the perfect partner for him. Not just the fact his body tightened when she was close and his senses cried out to learn more about why, but also because deep down he knew she wouldn't bore him, or he, he hoped, her. The problem would be, he understood, to convince her of that. "It is easy to see who is the better parent, and from that learn a lot of what is right and wrong."

Josephine sent him a quick glance. "Indeed, I agree."

"What would you be?" he asked quietly. "What would you want me to be?" David almost held his breath. All of a sudden, her answer was the most important reply he had ever needed. He had a deep-rooted desire to hear her reply.

"I think…" She hesitated and David fancied he could almost see the way she turned various responses over, ready to answer as best she could. He held his breath as he waited.

"What can you see?" Lady Foster called across the room. "Birds? Anything unusual? Nothing awful, I hope?"

David cussed in his mind. Just as he thought he might get the chance to discover more about Josephine, Lady Foster foiled him. Although judging by the way Josephine stiffened, perhaps it was not a bad thing. *Take it slowly. Four days slowly at least.* He turned his head so Josephine didn't have to. "Not really. Just passing the time." He watched his companion out of the corner of his eye as she collected herself, gave him a swift and grateful smile and moved so she also faced inward.

"I'm hopeless at naming plants and so on. I recognize a daisy and a dandelion and not much else," he added. "Lady Josephine was giving me some tips."

"Both weeds," Lady Foster said in disgust. "I hope you can't see any down there?"

"Fear not, Godmama, evidently your lawn is weed free."

"Such a lovely garden, it is a joy to spend time discovering something so interesting, until dinner is served," Josephine responded in a composed voice. She coughed and lowered her voice so only David could hear. "And not be anything other than myself."

Lady Foster gave her a searching look. "It behooves us not to ignore anything that matters to us, be it human or of the rest of the world."

"Including our stomachs," David said to lighten the tone. He didn't want Josephine to become uncomfortable with the innuendo. "I swear there were some interesting aromas emanating from the kitchens earlier. Very tempting."

"Ah yes, you men and your need for food at regular intervals. Any minute now to go in, I should think." Lady Foster narrowed her eyes as she stared at first one of them then the other, as her butler entered and cleared his throat. "Freddie looks ready to start a two-minute countdown."

The butler, well used to Lord Aitken, ignored that comment and bowed. "Dinner is served, my lady."

"Good show. We won't stand on ceremony," Lady Foster declared as she proceeded to organize things to her satisfaction. "David, you take Josephine in, please. I'll grab Freddie Aitken, or there could well be an undignified scramble." Within seconds, she nodded. "Right, come along." She turned on her heel and led the exodus from the room.

David turned to Josephine and offered his arm. "Shall we? It never does to cross my godmother. She has a long memory, and always gets her own way in the end. It's much easier to give in immediately, and save yourself a lot of energy and effort."

"I am beginning to realize that." Josephine essayed a swift grin that lit up her face and relaxed her tense expression. "I have come to accept she is quite a character, with an indomitable will."

He chuckled. "People soon do. I learned very early on to give in and let her have her way. Or at least not let her know when I went against her edicts. Much less wearing on the nerves. Ah, I believe we are supposed to sit here." David indicated two empty chairs, held the seat for Josephine and waited until she was settled before he took the place next to her.

Dinner was a pleasant affair. Whether it was the informal atmosphere and seating, or because there were so few of them, intercourse had to be general. David wasn't sure which held sway, but conversation was wide and varied, and everyone added their opinion on whatever was discussed.

By his side, Josephine was at first subdued but as the meal went on and conversation became less stilted, he watched as she gradually relaxed, offered a quip or comment and appeared less stiff. When at one point she leaned forward without any hesitation and calmly but with deliberation contradicted something her papa had said, her matter-of-fact manner made him want to cheer her. With every hour, he admired her more.

Just admire? It was a sticky question. He took a mouthful of wine and contemplated his emotions. Why her? He had no easy answer. Why now? That was perhaps easier to define. He was at last free to move forward, his people, lands and heritage secure. His mind had begun to roam over the various scenarios that could potentially be part of his future when he was brought up rudely by a sharp dig in his ribs from Josephine.

"Listen," she said without moving her lips. "You need to reply."

What on earth was she talking about? He looked across the table into James' eyes. Luckily they had been friends long enough for James to recognize his plea for help.

"Don't you think so, David?" James looked at him earnestly. "We need to put our own country in order before we do anywhere else. Parliament, schooling, health. All take priority."

Thank goodness for friends who found a way to explain a question they knew fine well you hadn't paid any attention to. David smiled, wrenched his thoughts back to the present and answered clearly, giving his views without heat. He didn't want to upset anyone but neither would he compromise his ideals.

"So you believe in schooling for your workers?" Edward Hanson said. "That it will help your, or should I say your father's, lands?"

David nodded, conscious of Josephine's keen interest in his reply. He ignored the comment about his father's lands. That was no one's business except his family's. Although, perhaps, soon it could be Josephine's as well. He would explain it all to her if she wanted to know more about him.

If. Such a tiny word with enormous consequences. Whoever had said 'if only' were two of the saddest words in the English language had been correct. David hoped he would never have to use them in a negative manner. Now, though, it was time to show his hand, just a little.

"I think it is essential," he replied. "Knowledge is power. I want my estates to be run as efficiently as possible. For that we must be informed. Must know what is best for the land and understand it. I believe education is the key."

"You, young man, are very outspoken, but we need to make sure everyone knows their place, eh?" Hanson leaned back in his chair. "A fine line. Can't do with people thinking they are better than they really are, you know. Where would we be then, eh?"

David bit back what his instinctive reaction was—to give the man an earful. He began to count to ten under his breath and got to seven before, after one swift glance at his expressionless features, his godmama broke into hurried speech.

"I trust my godson to do the correct things every time, Edward. One of which is to escort me into the drawing room." As senior gentleman present, it was the done thing. "Tonight we are not standing on ceremony, but I reserve the right to collar him for that. The port will be passed in there and I intend to have a glass myself." Her tone dared anyone to comment in the negative. "It is time to relax and not worry about convention or correctness. This is a small party of people who I hope will soon be firm friends."

Of course, David thought, amused for the umpteenth time how no one ever dared contradict her. He stood up, walked to the side of her chair and bowed. "My dear, shall we?"

"We better, I don't want anyone to think I do not mean what I say," Janie Foster said in an undertone. "There's enough stuffy old men who think they can overrule me without me giving them ammunition. How's your campaign going?"

Lord, she was incorrigible. "A good general never divulges what he has achieved and what he needs to attain, until he's secured the lot. I'll just say slowly, as I intended."

Out of the corner of his eye, David watched James hold the back of Josephine's chair, and the others turn to whoever was nearby, ready to escort, or be escorted into the dining room. Josephine's parents didn't seem enamoured with the idea of partnering other people, but he assumed they were much too polite to dissemble. Her mother smiled — if that forced expression could be called a smile — at Freddie Aitken, while her husband went across the room and bowed to Lydia. His face reminded David of that of a particularly disgruntled schoolboy. What a peculiar response from them. Perhaps they had thought small and informal meant they wouldn't need to pander to such niceties as mingling.

Lady Foster turned away from the dining room. "That's sorted some people out," she murmured as she let David lead the procession from the dining room, along the corridor to the pleasant, sunlit room where an array of drinks had been set out. "I swear that your beloved's parents will send me to Bedlam before this house party is over. They know the rules."

"Which they also know you will disregard if it pleases you."

"Well, of course. My house, my house party, my intentions hold sway. But don't worry, I will behave."

David laughed. "May I have that in writing?"

"Of course not." Janie did the little pat on his cheek she favored. "Now get me my port and go and rescue Lydia and ask her to get my shawl from the dining room. It's there on purpose because I thought Bowie might cut up rough and I might need to give someone an easy getaway."

David relayed the information to Lydia, who sent him a grateful look before she curtsied to Lord Bowie. "If you will excuse me, my lord?"

"Of course, my dear." He looked at David. "Nice young lady, no overenthusiasm there." 'Not like my daughter', his tone inferred. "How are you getting on with Josephine, eh? Any headway?"

Drat the man. David's heartbeat sped up as he tamped down his rapidly increasing ire. Lord Bowie had an unfortunate way of riling him without any effort.

"If at any time I have any information that I decide is in anyone's best interest to share, I will, at my own discretion, do so." Good grief, he sounded as if he were pontificating in the House of Lords. "Until then, I will keep my own counsel, and I suggest, my lord, in the interests of a harmonious house party, you do the same." He bowed in the most punctilious manner. "Let me fetch you a port?"

Whatever Lord Bowie's wife chose to suggest, David was the senior peer. Therefore, it was no wonder Lord Bowie stared at him goggle-eyed. "It is an informal evening," David added. "We are not standing on ceremony, *as* my godmother so recently intimated. A nice touch, don't you think? Seeing as we are so few." The word 'godmother' felt alien. He much preferred the less formal 'godmama', but in that instance decided formality was needed.

"Ah, yes," the older man stammered. "You are, of course, correct. Thank you for your offer. So kind of you, your grace, but I best go and see my wife settled first."

As if she were a poor wilting flower caught among a large bush of thorns instead of one woman, one grown woman, in a room of only ten people, David thought in disgust as Lord Bowie scurried off. David turned to Lydia.

"Lyddie, how about you?"

"Port, please, and I shall help you." She smiled at the rear of Josephine's father. "Poor Josephine, what a horrid man. He spent the whole two minutes pontificating about how I must move or I'd be on the shelf. What's it to him? I held my tongue, but it was hard. Very hard. I need a drink." She walked swiftly across the room to Josephine and James. "Port for you both?"

Josephine met David as he caught up with Lydia. "What has my darned parent been up to now?" she asked, resigned to hearing the worst. No doubt railing at her old maid status. How embarrassing. "Do I need to apologize on his behalf?"

"Never," David assured her. "He is old enough to apologize for himself when needs be. And on this occasion there is no need. He merely escorted Lydia in and said he had to make sure your mama was settled."

Josephine noted the startled look Lydia gave him before that lady muttered, "Port. Come on, James, you may aid me, I cannot carry four glasses." Lydia took hold of James' sleeve and almost dragged the poor man to where the decanters were. "I'll say that Lady F. remembered she'd put her scarf on a chair in here if anyone questions me."

"I'm sure he did say something," Josephine replied quietly once they were alone. "Along with other things that embarrassed Lydia and annoyed you." She'd watched their faces until they had taken their leave of her papa, and quietly seethed. What had her parent commented about? "I'm so sorry for whatever it was that put that look on your face."

"Smile and nod," David said. "We are being watched. As I intimated earlier, we will talk alone, once we can. If you still trust me?"

"What?" She smiled as directed and managed a noise halfway between a laugh and a groan. "Oh dear, now people will wonder what you said to me." The dratted man had a way of making her seem a tongue-tied, simpering idiot. Worse than any young deb newly out. It was aggravating to say the least.

"A risqué suggestion?" David raised one eyebrow and stroked his chin. "Well, if you want me to…?"

Josephine wondered if she had heard aright. "A…?" She spluttered and rocked on her heels. "Er well…" How eloquent, but really, would she even know what a risqué suggestion was?

He winked again. "There, that worked, didn't it. You now do not appear to despise me."

"I never have despised you," she hissed as she went hot, cold and hot again. "Stop it now or I will…well, I don't know what I will do until I do it, but no doubt it would embarrass both of us. I am not known for thinking then acting, more the opposite."

David inclined his head. "Your wish, my dear, is my command."

"I wish it was, however, I know better." He might give lip service to that idea, but she'd bet her new reticule that was all it was.

"Are you two arguing?" James asked as he handed a glass over to Josephine. "Don't bother, Josephine, he always wins. I just ignore him and do as I prefer."

"Liar, you try, and then come to discover I was correct all along."

James laughed. "Sadly, that is true."

Lydia joined them and passed a glass of port to David. He took it and grinned. "Lyddie, he is maligning me."

"Someone needs to." Lydia turned to Josephine, who was somewhat taken aback by the banter. "I swear he is as ornery as a pig at times, just because he can be."

How Josephine wished this ability to rail and tease were something she had experienced. However, her life so far, and her intentions never to marry, had made it difficult to make that sort of friends. She smiled. "No doubt I'll discover that over the next few days. I shall stand on his toes, hard, if I think it necessary."

Lydia giggled and James guffawed as David tried, and didn't succeed, to look hurt. How good of these three friends to include her in their circle. For the first time in forever, Josephine experienced the warm satisfaction of belonging.

"Lydia, my dear, will you play for us?" Lady Foster called across the room. "Maybe you and Josephine could take turns."

"Duty calls," Lydia said in a resigned tone. "Shall we do it, Josephine, and get the required entertainment over and done with?"

Josephine nodded. One more thing she soon would not need to do.

She could hardly wait.

* * * *

The latter part of the evening had passed pleasantly, David decided a short while later. Lydia and Josephine had played the pianoforte, and both he and James had been called upon to sing. He would normally have called it purgatory, but knowing his comrades felt the same as him had helped to alleviate the pain somewhat.

It was a pleasure to listen to Josephine's playing, and also her firm refusal to sing, due, she'd said with a laugh, to a voice like a crow with a sore throat. Instead, he'd accompanied her with a couple of airs, then handed over to James.

As the tea trolley arrived, the four of them exchanged relieved glances and moved to serve their elders. As most people had spent considerable hours on the road to reach Derbyshire, once the cups of the aromatic brew were emptied, the company dispersed.

David looked at James as the ladies all declared they would head to bed, and the older gentlemen decided they would retire to the library with brandy. "I'm for bed myself."

James fluttered his hand over his chest. "Did I hear aright? David Suddards to bed before midnight? Are you ill?"

David laughed. "Funny man. No. I have a lot to think about, and very little time to put any plans into action."

"Josephine?"

"I have no idea if she has plans to act on or not. I'm not privy to her thoughts," David replied, as bland as possible. "Only to my own, and believe me they are enough." He clapped his friend on the back, conscious of the way James stared after him.

An hour later, David looked at the clock on the mantel of the drawing room of the suite he had been assigned, and mentally counted down to the time he thought — hoped — the servants would be abed and the house silent. The clatter and footsteps of various valets and ladies' maids had died down several minutes before. James had come up not much later than David, and now the only noise that emerged from his chamber was an occasional snore.

David checked his appearance. He'd deliberated what to wear. Once he had ascertained that indeed the connecting door was locked and the key missing, he'd debated whether to pick the lock. A swift perusal of the door made him decide that he'd need it oiled first. It probably hadn't been used in years. The corridor it would have to be, for this visit at least.

If he was discovered in the corridor—not that there was any reason why he should be—he needed to have a plausible excuse, look the part and not get anyone, i.e. a servant, into trouble for forgetting to do something—like leave him brandy. Thus he was still in shirt and breeches, without a cravat, waistcoat or jacket, and wearing house shoes. He carried a book he'd borrowed from the library earlier. He'd decided, if need be, he would be on his way to the library to change it or back from said room with the book. The age-old explanation of 'can't sleep', 'need a book, drink, or walk in the gardens' was well used and probably never believed, but difficult to dispute.

As it was a mere ten steps or so from his chambers to hers, he made it unchallenged. With utmost care, David turned the handle and eased the door open. He had no idea if the main door hinges were kept well oiled on the doors of rooms not in common use. In many houses, those apartments would have their contents shrouded in holland covers until needed, and door furniture might not be quite up to scratch. On more than one occasion, he had heard of attendees at some house party or another being caught out in their nocturnal wanderings by an unoiled hinge or noisy floorboards. Another reason why he had discarded the lock-picking idea.

He should have known that his godmother, in common vernacular, was up to snuff, and her housekeeping exemplary. No floorboard would dare squeak, and the hinges behaved as only those that were attended to on a regular basis could. He slipped inside and shut the door behind him.

Josephine looked up from the armchair next to the glowing embers of the fire. It might not be the coldest month of the year, but here in Derbyshire, a fire was often needed to take the chill out of the upper rooms. She had remained dressed — he couldn't imagine she would have done anything else if he were honest — and had a fine paisley shawl around her shoulders. Old houses had a lot to answer for.

"I didn't know whether I should light the lamp or not. I'm not *au fait* with assignations."

David hadn't seen the meeting in that light until then. In his mind it had been more a declaration of intent. "Do you mind?" he asked. "Is this going to make you uncomfortable?"

"Not at all," Josephine replied in a calm manner. "I have a good left hook, and evidently precise aim when needed. Nor would I be afraid to defend myself if I had to."

David grinned. "So I have heard — and seen."

"Yes, well." She colored. "Some so-called gentlemen are anything but, and need reminding of their manners."

She was correct. David inclined his head. "Not I. I know my manners and generally abide by them."

She smiled and her face lit up with amusement. The change was enough to make his body tighten. That carefree, innocent but cheeky look appealed to every part of him.

"I'm glad to hear it."

David added more coals to the remains of the fire and stirred them into a cheerful blaze. "If you close the shutters, I will light the lamp," he said as once more the room was filled with flickering shadows. He'd have liked to have kept it that way, but it was too reminiscent of a scene for seduction to be comfortable. "Then, once we can see without squinting, with your permission, I'll sit and explain everything." He waited until she nodded and did as he'd asked and within a few minutes both were seated in armchairs, on either side of the fireplace, with a glass of watered wine. He did his best not to shudder. Why anyone would think such fine wines as his godmother offered had to be diluted he had no idea.

"Urgh," Josephine said suddenly. "I hate watered wine." She put her glass down. "I don't suppose you brought any brandy with you?"

David shook his head. "Sorry, no. Why did you ask for watered wine if you dislike it so?"

She chuckled. "I didn't, I asked for wine. Period. I imagined if I asked for brandy I would blot my copybook and create a scandal. To be honest, I suspect this is my mama's doing. Why she seeks to interfere in something so trivial when she pays no attention to anything else, I have no idea, but it is very annoying. For years I was ignored, and now, just as I am about to escape, she notices she has a daughter. So damned irritating. Oh well, I do not have to suffer it for much longer."

"You mean you will accept my offer?" His pulse jumped as a certain part of his anatomy recognized all manner of arousing things that could and would occur. It, of course, reacted in a predictable fashion and went from flaccid to rock hard. David strove not to look down as his staff strained the material of his trousers.

Why did she look aghast? What else could she mean? Surely she hadn't reacted like that to his erection? In the position in which he sat, it wasn't that noticeable to an onlooker, just to him.

David pressed on before she had a chance to protest or disagree. Riding roughshod, perhaps, but she had to hear him out. "Thank you. You have made me a very happy man." David leaned forward and took her hand in his. "Good lord, your hands are freezing." As frozen as her expression. He began to chafe them. "I must make sure you don't have cold hands in future, eh?"

"No wonder, I've just had a shock." Her jaw dropped and she paled. "Say that again. Not the cold hands bit, I always have cold hands, the ridiculous bit."

Ridiculous? Not a good sign. David took a deep breath. "I don't remember anything of the sort. You said you wouldn't have to suffer your parents' interference much longer. I assumed that meant you would remove yourself from their sphere of influence, and thus our betrothal was secured in that manner." Hell, he sounded like a pompous old man. "After all, you know that is what I desire."

"Well, you couldn't be more wrong," she snapped. "What about what I desire? You made no mention of that. You, my lord, sound like every other male I have had the misfortune to know. All what they need, want or intend. Never what anyone else has a yen for."

That told him. David's erection disappeared as swiftly as it had appeared and he felt two inches tall. "I…"

Josephine silenced him effectively as she leaned forward and put her palm firmly over his mouth. Her scent, of roses and something he couldn't identify, surrounded him. He waited, more amused than irritated now, to see what happened next. If — *that word again*, if — he ever persuaded her to accept his offer, life would never be dull, that was certain.

"Let me finish, please," she said in a less aggrieved manner. "You have had your say, it's my turn now. I'm afraid you misunderstood me. I meant that in six weeks, I reach four and twenty, and my parents have promised I can retire from society. I intend to hold them to that promise."

That was a blow he hadn't expected. Not only did he have to convince her he would be a good husband, he also had to prove life with him would be preferable to the one she had chosen.

And all in a few weeks, with only these next days to really press his cause. It wasn't going to be easy.

Chapter Seven

Josephine swallowed and moved her hand from his mouth to her lap with an insouciance that was assumed and showed nothing of the turmoil she experienced. He appeared taken aback by her response to him. "You do understand, don't you?" she asked. "After all, I have never intimated I would be happy to accept your proposal of marriage, have I?"

Why was he staring at her in that way? Intent and considering. A strange combination, and one that made her uneasy.

"Not in so many words, no," David replied in such a reasonable tone that she bristled.

Was he not in the slightest bit affected by her reply? Had she imagined that brief expression of hurt?

"But you haven't told me you wouldn't," he added.

"Well, how could I? It's not the sort of thing a young lady can broach, is it? But never have I intimated you are more than an acquaintance." She didn't add a thoroughly irritating one, but she hoped he heard the unspoken words. "And after all, you would have to speak to my papa to ask if you could approach me and he would then..." All of a sudden, things fell into place.

The bloody man.

"Oh lord," she groaned. It was that or throw something, and she didn't think that destroying the nearest thing to hand — a pretty Meissen dish — would go down well with her hostess. "You have, haven't you?" Unable to contain herself, Josephine jumped up and began to pace the room. "No wonder I've had more attention from them these last few days than in the rest of my life." David also stood and she waved him back into his seat. "Sit down and give me room."

He subsided back into the chair and crossed his legs. Such a confident, male thing to do. It raised her annoyance level even higher. "Why do men always sit like that?" she asked. *Gah, such a crosspatch I am. Maybe when he sees how glimflashy and peevish I become he will change his mind.* However, it was not her normal self and she knew that. "Lord, you bring the worst out in me, my lord."

"David," he said. "'My lord' makes me think I'm about to be quizzed on something."

"What?" What was he going on about?

"If you want to rail at me, use my given name," David said in a patient voice. He grinned and shrugged. "Everyone says 'my lord' in such a dismissive manner, I ignore it. If you call me David and then ring a peal over me, I am more likely to listen."

"And take heed?"

"Well, no," he said apologetically. "Not necessarily. But I will make a considered decision."

Josephine snorted. She supposed it was a small concession but it did not go anywhere near far enough.

"You are the bane of my life. I suggest you watch my lips."

His mouth twitched and his expression immediately changed from innocent to predatory.

Oh, lord, I let myself in for that. Drat him.

"Not like that."

"How then?" he asked in an innocent, what-on-earth-have-I-done-wrong voice.

"Argh." She flung up her hands. "You infuriating man. Listen well. I do not want to marry. You or anyone. Whatever you may have been told to the contrary, I intend to stay single and hold my parents to their word. Before the next season starts, I will be ensconced in my own house and running my own life. Any mistakes I make will be mine alone, any friends will be of my own choosing and anything else because I want it. Do you understand?" She listened to the way her voice rose and swallowed hard. Getting overemotional was not the way to show how determined she was. "I am not the sort of person any man would want to marry. I am opinionated, ornery and hard-headed. I couldn't be a woman who agrees with everything her husband decrees. Not wife material at all."

"You really think that, don't you?" he said in amazement. "You really think you have nothing to offer a man."

The seriousness of his voice surprised her. No teasing, no enticement, just amazement.

"I *know* that." A coal sparked and spat in the grate and one greeny-blue flame flared and died. She jumped and all the fire went out of her. "My papa has said it often enough in my hearing. Why are you doing this, David? Why me?"

"Because we suit."

Not 'would', she noted, nor 'might'. Was he so confident of getting his own way? Surely he wouldn't do anything underhanded to achieve his goal? No, she did not believe that of him, but she did believe he would do everything he legally could to get what he wanted. "A woman with no womanly wiles or allure? Hardly. You are mistaken."

He inclined his head. "Not at all. We will fit. In every way. Me into you, you into my life. Into each other's lives — and into my bed."

"David!" His frank words curled around her heart. Children. Little humans to love and cherish and... No, it couldn't happen. "That is not something you should say to me. Stop it."

"Why?" he asked in a tone she was certain he'd chosen to goad her. "You insist you're no young impressionable deb. Surely it doesn't embarrass you to talk about such intimate things?"

Now she accepted he was provoking her on purpose. Josephine hoped her cheeks were not as warm as the rest of her and gave him a sickly smile. "Not at all," she said in a deprecating way. "If I were interested, it would be something we would have to clarify. As I am not, we need not discuss it."

David laughed. "You do the schoolmistress face and voice so well, my dear. But I can see through it. You are scared."

"I am not." She knew she didn't sound as certain as she should. He, dammit, was correct. She was worried she might discover she wanted something other than that she had previously set her heart on.

"Yes you are, scared what I could say will worm its way into your brain. Make you think and wonder 'what if'. Make your body respond, your mind work hard and your intentions alter." He smiled. "Ache to experience my hands on you. Yearn to touch me. Have to back down and admit I am correct."

Josephine sat with a thump. Her heart beat erratically and her hands were clammy. Tiny black dots danced in front of her eyes and she prayed she would not faint. "It would not work."

David took both her hands in his and stroked her palms. "Lord, you are icy cold. Should I risk nipping to the library for some brandy? I forgot to have any sent up to my room." The rough tips of his fingers showed he was no overseer, but a landlord who took part in maintaining his lands.

I don't even know where they are or what they are. I know nothing about him, other than hearsay. Do I want to? Dare I?

"No, I'll sip this disgusting wine and water." She took a few swallows. "That's better."

"Then if you are so sure," David said softly as he continued his unexpected, arousing caress, "that you know what you want, why not let me try to persuade you to the contrary?"

It was nerve-wracking, he admitted to himself, to wait as patiently as he had it in him, until she gave him her answer. As a man who hadn't needed to be accountable for his actions, apart from to those who relied on him for their livelihoods, it was an unusual and uncomfortable position to find himself in.

It was several minutes before she stirred in her chair and lifted her gaze from their joined hands to look at his face. "I wish I knew why you fixed on me. I'm not viscountess or countess material, believe me. I hate the ton and all that goes with it. I've told you my ideas on marriage and children and still you persist. Why can't you leave me alone?" It was a cry from the heart and it struck him hard.

"Because I think we could want the same things, albeit we approach them in different ways," he replied honestly. It was time to bare his soul. "I need to tell you a little about my life these past few years. However, if I do, I must ask for your promise not to let the details go any further."

She looked at him skeptically. "It has been well documented, my... Very well, David."

He sighed. "Actually, no, it hasn't. The only things you have heard were what I chose to be known. Mainly, I confess, to annoy my father, and to pull the wool over his eyes. Do I have your word this will go no further?"

She tilted her head to one side and bit her lip. Damn her, it was arousing. David wanted to laugh at himself. Such little things sent his libido soaring when she did them. From others it would have provoked no reaction whatsoever.

"Very well," she said as the silence stretched far enough for David to scream at her to answer him.

And that would have done him no good. Such a female reaction. He inclined his head. "Lord, I wish we did have brandy." He had an idea. "Why on earth didn't I think of this earlier? May I go through your bedchamber and bathing chamber?"

"Through them?" She sounded puzzled. "Through them how?"

"It completely slipped my mind that both our bathing chambers have a door leading to a common service stair."

"So?"

"So, I have brandy. My hip flask is in my room." Why he hadn't remembered that earlier he had no idea. Probably because he had been musing over more alluring things.

Josephine grinned, stood up and, with a swish of skirts that allowed him a brief glimpse of her trim ankles, walked across the room, thence to open a door with an extravagant flourish and curtsey. "Both my bed…" She paused and waited for his riposte.

David said nothing. He'd wondered how she would proceed. With aplomb, it seemed.

"And bathing chambers are at your disposal," Josephine added without a blink. "Another thing. While I think of it, why did you not come this way?"

"I am an idiot. I forgot all about it."

However, now he had remembered it, it would serve not only to fetch the brandy, but also to use as his unseen entry and exit to Josephine's accommodation. If she let him. Her rooms reminded him of her. It was the scent she wore, he realized. So enticing, and so incongruous on a woman who said she had no interest in attracting a man. Of course, there was no reason why she should not wear it for her own enjoyment, but it was a fact it was pleasurable to him as well. He inhaled deeply and chuckled to himself as he registered what he had done, before he made his way to his own rooms.

So much depended on her reaction to what he was about to divulge. David found his hip flask—luckily still over three-quarters full of brandy—and two goblets and made his way back the way he'd come until once more he was in Josephine's sitting room. She smiled as he held the bottle aloft.

"My hero."

"If I had realized that was all it took, I would have bribed your maid to let me leave a bottle here."

Josephine shook her head. "I'd like to see the way your head rang as she boxed your ears for your temerity. Mary, my maid, is not bribable. She is loyal to a fault. However, if you pleaded with her, explained to her that to your mind, my life would be empty without you, and only you can make me a happy, fulfilled woman, she would champion your cause. She says she despairs of me."

"I wish I'd known." David poured brandy into both goblets and handed one to her. May I?" He indicated the chair he had so recently vacated. "I'd feel less conspicuous and on trial if I were sitting comfortably, so to speak."

"Don't be daft, you are not on trial. Sit and do that silly leg-crossing thing if you want."

He laughed and did as she said. Then sipped his brandy and let it warm his throat. Her gaze skittered to his torso and away again, only to return a few seconds later and watch him drum his fingers swiftly on his thigh. The gesture screamed he was nervous. He prayed she saw it as a good sign, not a pathetic one.

"Right, in confidence?" he asked quietly.

"Of course."

"Then let me explain who I really am to you." David turned what he hoped to say over in his mind. He didn't want to show his parents in too bad a light, but if he ignored their place in it all, it would show him in a bad – if not to say unacceptable – light instead.

Josephine nodded, and held her hand up in the wait-a-second gesture. "One moment. You say that what you are about to tell me is confidential?"

David nodded. "Very."

"Is it illegal?"

"Not in any manner." What a strange thing to ask, he thought, when he was about to divulge what it was. Unless, of course, she was worried he'd killed someone and she would then be in the horrible situation of having knowledge of a crime, and she'd promised not to share. "It shows some people in a less than flattering light, that's all."

"Very well." Josephine nodded. She sat back, wriggled a little, presumably to make herself more comfortable — which had the opposite effect on him. It was all too innocently arousing to make him relaxed. She cleared her throat. "I think I'd better say this first. I do not want you to think whatever you tell me will have an effect on what my eventual decision will be. I promise to think about your proposal without a preconceived idea on the outcome." She smiled and shook her head. "Actually that doesn't make sense, does it? I'll have to think about whatever you choose to impart, I wouldn't be human otherwise. But I want you to know that I owe it to you for being so open, that I will listen without prejudice. How does that sound?"

"As good as it could be." It was a concession he hadn't expected. "I will add, before I start on the confidences, that I want a wife to be my partner, a mother and my lover. The one person I turn to in every circumstance. In sickness and in health, for better, for worse, will be said and meant. I do not want a sycophant, or someone who looks elsewhere for pleasure. I intend to be a faithful husband."

She looked contemplative. "That gives me more food for thought. If, I suppose, I ever did think of marriage, I would want all of that and act accordingly, and more."

She didn't explain what that 'more' was.

"But to know that is not enough for me to say yes," she finished.

He hadn't imagined for one minute it would be. "You need me to woo you?"

"Woo?"

"Court, pay attention, escort you."

"I know what woo means," Josephine said with dignity. "I hadn't even thought of that. No, for a start, I need you to do nothing that might encourage my parents to assume an announcement will be made. If you spoke to my papa, he would have told my mama even if you asked him not to. They cannot keep anything from each other. It is very frustrating. However, in a case like this, for a brief moment all their attention is fixed on me, which is even worse than being ignored. They will scrutinize every little thing we do whenever they spy us together. Then the interrogation will begin. I can't cope with that and think about my future as well."

"Then I suggest we remain at a friendly distance when in company, and spend an hour or so each evening here, and get to know each other that way. I promise to make sure we have brandy." He could not say he would never speak to her father. If things went well, he would have to do so again before he formally approached her. It was only honorable. "What do you say?" He waited and half expected her to dither. She didn't. Instead she tilted her head to one side for a second or two then nodded decisively.

How had he never noticed how long her eyelashes were? And not the soft blonde of her hair but duskier? Combined with her smoky eyes and rosy lips, it was irresistible. Strange how he had never before been attracted to blondes. All his lovers had been brunettes.

My wife will be different. Hold on, am I not getting ahead of myself?

"Very well." Josephine's crisp tones brought him out of his reverie. "Now tell me your deep, dark secret and let me get some sleep," she said. "As I have been told we are going for a ride at some early hour, I better have some rest so I don't fall asleep on horseback. But not until you have divulged what I need to know. Oh and I'll have the other brandy you were about to offer me."

David laughed, as he was sure she meant him to, and refilled their glasses. He had to explain and he could have no input on the outcome. "Here you are. Right. So I need to go back to when I was a lot younger. When I did as all young bucks and kicked over the traces. However, contrary to what my father and most of the ton imagined, I gave up somewhat earlier than most others. My grandfather died and left me a rather nice nest egg." There was no need to say just how much. "I discovered the enjoyment of the stock market. Of investing, buying and selling and generally making money. Oh, as a new boy, I made mistakes, but I learned fast and amassed a considerable fortune. It came in handy." He shrugged. "You will see, when I explain more, that it still does."

He sipped some brandy to relax his tight throat. This was proving harder than he'd thought. The interested expression on Josephine's face gave him strength to continue.

"Around a year ago, Lady Whitcombe put it about that I had sired her unborn child. A lie, and one I suspect said in malice as I had turned down her hint that she wouldn't be averse to a dalliance." He grimaced. "On more than one occasion, and once rather crudely. I did say this showed some people in a less than favorable light."

"I had heard," Josephine said diffidently, "that the child was her brother-in-law's. As Whitcombe is unable to do the necessary."

The prosaic way she said it made David choke. "I did not expect to hear that from you."

"No?" She raised her eyebrows. "I might be a spinster, but I do have a reasonable knowledge of the world we live in. Plus, people look through me and forget I can hear all they say. That nugget was imparted by two dowagers who should know better than to chat in an anteroom that adjoins the ladies' withdrawing room. Sadly, I cannot now add that I know what else you might be about to tell me, other than what we discussed at your godmother's ball, and what you assured me was exaggerated. The gossip about you is very limited. All I ever heard was you were up to every lark going and ready to do anything for fun. Plus, if you deign to ask deb 'a' to dance she will swoon, and deb 'b' swears you looked at her and her heart stopped beating. So far no one has reported the state of their health when you actually do ask them to dance."

"Good lord." It was the first he had heard of it. "I never ask a deb to dance unless forced to by my hostess. As most of them know me, and understand that to be coerced into doing something I don't wish to do will result in any more invitations being refused, that now rarely happens."

"You, my lord, are spoiled," Josephine told him in a severe tone. She then ruined it by smirking. "I'd love to have seen some certain people's faces when you told them that, though. A couple of people who need bringing down a peg or two spring to mind."

"Only a couple?" This verbal sparring was exhilarating. David realized he had not enjoyed himself so much in an age, even with the knowledge of the revelations he had yet to share.

"I am being polite."

"Ah, love, never hold back for me. I am unshockable, you know."

"I am not your love."

"Yet."

"Argh." She scowled and narrowed her eyes. "Just carry on with what you have to say and stop baiting me."

It was a fair enough request. David inclined his head. "I wasn't baiting but saying what I predict. However, yes, to get back to my confidences. With regards to my other supposed excesses, I best formulate my defense. I did very little but made it seem as if I did a lot. As he never thought I was worth anything, I was determined not to let my father think any good of me." He moved uneasily in his chair and waited for his scars to ache. To his surprise, that telltale sign of stress — or reminder — didn't appear.

Had he finally turned the corner from excessive bitterness, through reluctant acceptance, and come to terms with his unhappy childhood? Was he now able to move onward with a clear mind? He hoped so. "It seemed that, with regards to my father, I succeeded, and no one ever discovered how things stood between us. We have now been estranged for several years. As for young chits? Never, and now I am glad. I can think of nothing worse than to be always aware of their eyes on me, of being besieged."

"Exactly. How uncomfortable. For both you and the recipient of your favors. I fear young impressionable debs get sillier each year."

"Just so, and I don't ask anyone to dance. Present company excepted, and that was because I wanted to."

Her eyes widened. "Wretch."

David grinned, his heart light. "More than likely."

His prosaic reply made her roll her eyes. "Do you know the trouble you caused with that? My mama was all for booking the church and arranging for the appropriate notice to be worded so it would be ready to send to the *Times* as soon as you formalized things. Then this invitation arrived and she was in alt. My life has been impossible. I much prefer when they ignore me. At least I know where I stand then."

"Again, my…actually no, I will not apologize," David exclaimed. "I want you here. So where was I? Ah yes. La Whitcombe. Well, after that fiasco, my esteemed papa, with the unusual backing of my mother, decreed I must marry within a very short timescale or he would sell all the un-entailed land and ensure I got as little as possible. Which would mean that workers and staff loyal to the dukedom would be cast off, and there would be extreme hardship for a lot of people."

"What a horrible man. How on earth can he be your papa?" Josephine burst out, then blinked. "But you are unwed. So you must have had a plan. I do not believe for one moment you would let your people suffer."

"You know?" David said honestly. "That means more to me than anything and you are correct. You have shown more faith in me in this short time than they did in all of my thirty-five years. They were so sure of me, and not, I believe, because they thought I was concerned about our people, but instead that I was concerned about money. Thus my father gave me a list of suitable women and told me to choose one. My mother agreed with him."

She gasped, then chuckled. "Was I on it? I doubt it."

"I have no idea. I tore it up and scattered it over him before I walked out. We haven't spoken since. How the ton have never found out we are estranged I have no idea but I can only be thankful. Once I left their house, I got Simmons, my man of affairs, to set up different businesses and accounts to buy everything my father offered for sale. He was as good as his word. Every last un-entailed building and piece of land was offered within a few weeks. Even so, it took the best part of a year for me to acquire it all, for he was determined to show me what I had lost. I got details, in an unsigned missive to my club, for every transaction made. Little did he know that I knew about every one. Not one acre went elsewhere, no family lost their home and no worker lost his or her job."

"Oh, how perfect. What did he say?"

"I don't think he knows. I made sure none of the transactions led back to me until everything was signed and secure."

"I like it. So now you have land." She appeared pleased at the outcome so far. "Plus loyal workers."

That gave him courage to continue. "I had land anyway," David said. "The first thing I did when I came into my inheritance from my grandfather was to use some to buy a small country estate called Caldborough, in Yorkshire. It is big enough to enable me to learn how to manage lands and people but not so large as to draw attention to myself. Even though, to all intents and purposes, the absentee landlord is a Mr. David. My staff there are loyal and do not mention my comings and goings. A petty attitude concerning my sire maybe, but I had no intention showing him I was not all rake."

"Good. He sounds a perfectly horrible man. The sort who would pull wings off of butterflies and whip children..." She gasped and David cursed. He knew he'd paled.

"He did, didn't he? The...the bastard," Josephine said passionately. "How I wish I could give him a taste of his own medicine."

How tempting it was to say, 'Marry me and you will.' But that would be unnecessarily cruel, and David understood it was no longer his reason for wanting Josephine as his wife.

"The last time he tried, I broke his whip and suggested I might do that very thing if he attempted such an act again," David said quietly. "He never did."

"The last time? Oh, David. I wish you hadn't given him one more chance."

David shrugged, pleased she called him by his given name. He'd do his best to ensure she continued to do so. "I refused to stoop to his level. Because, you know, for all he was so full of his own worth, my father never attempted to listen to me, believe in me or allow me to be shown how to manage the dukedom. So Caldborough, with the guidance of a good estate manager, and Simmons, my man of business, became my education. So much more satisfying than university. Strange to tell, Caldborough has a short common boundary with Midham. Typically, my father never attempted to discover anything about his new neighbor and it was when I was not an unwelcome and unmentioned son, but still his heir. You know? I waited to see what he would say when we met. It never happened."

"But you want to marry and guarantee the dukedom? Why, when there is no love lost between you?" She sounded confused. "Why not just protect your people?"

"It is my heritage. My duty and my future. I love every inch of it all and I owe it to my people to make certain they are safe. To do that, I must secure the future of Midham. I can't do it alone. I want a wife to stand by me, to be part of me and to help me continue the line. What do you say? Will you be that person?" He held his breath. It was oh so clear to him that they could make it work. Why was it not the same to her?

Chapter Eight

It all made so much sense. Not enough for her to agree to be his wife but, she owned, at least enough to see how they got on over the next few days, and do it without prejudice. For, much to her surprise, the idea of a husband who wanted a wife as an equal partner — or as equal as could be — appealed more than any other idea if marriage ever happened. Her problem was to decide whether it was better than the single state that had been her goal for so long. Plus fathom out if what she wanted was truly what he desired. Then came the knotty question of deciding if it were at all likely to happen. So much depended on trust, and that had to be determined via the head, not the heart. Josephine was honest enough to accept the sticking point would be his attitude toward his — and, if they married, their — children.

"I can understand that you do not wish to do it alone." Josephine was tired and, she admitted, confused. So much to think about, and so little time to do it. Four days left. Four short days when they had to act like friendly acquaintances and also learn everything there was to know about each other. It wouldn't be easy. "If I can't get my parents to let me go to Northumberland when we leave here, I'll be in Brighton," she said, apropos of nothing. "Where will you be?"

"It depends. On whether you think we might have a future." David grinned but she saw the stress in his eyes, the weary shadows on his face, and understood how much the last minutes had taken out of him. He had shared his family's awful history, and had to hope she was honorable enough not to spread it.

"My plans are adaptable," he added.

Josephine considered how best to answer him. "I promised to consider your offer," she said slowly. "And I will do. But I will not be pushed into making any hasty decisions, one way or another. I will take these few days to deliberate whether I think there is any reason for us to take our friendship further. Then I will no doubt have more questions."

David inclined his head. "I suppose I can't ask for anything more."

"No, I suppose you can't." She yawned and put her hand over her mouth. "Oh, goodness, I'm sorry. How crass. In my defense, it is late, I have a lot to process, and…" She trailed off. "And I need to think."

"Then I will leave, and I will meet you here each night before we retire. Just in case you have more questions that need answering to help you make up your mind, or at least point you in the right direction. First, though…" David tugged her to her feet and took two steps closer to her so they were almost touching. He grinned, a cheeky, devil-may-care twist of his lips that made his eyes sparkle.

"David Suddards, you are not to kiss me." Her skin tingled. That was happening a lot these days. It was a peculiar sensation, almost as if someone were tracing a pin lightly over her body. It was neither good nor bad, but indicated that her body was alive and waiting…if only she could make her mind up for what.

"Why? You need to discover how much you like it. Then you can tell me if there is room for improvement."

He was incorrigible. Try as she might, Josephine couldn't find it in her heart to be downright rude. "No. Go away, now. I can't think when you are so close."

"Good. Don't think, just feel." He moved closer, put his lips to hers and, as she relaxed, teased his tongue into her mouth.

Never mind thinking, she now knew what that deb meant about her heart stopping. Josephine's gave a pitter-pat and missed a beat as his arms went around her waist and he caressed her. Even over her gown, she fancied, his fingers seared her skin. She moaned deep in her throat and she oh so tentatively let her tongue mesh with his. It was agony and exciting. Arousing and worrying. Nevertheless, it was so easy not to think, but just to let her senses take over. Josephine relaxed against him and into their kiss.

David tensed as she leaned against him. He tore his mouth away. "Sweet lord." And moved back in to kiss her once more.

She exulted in the agonized groan he gave. She, wallflower Josephine Bowie, she with, according to her papa, nothing about her to attract a man, affected this man in the way he affected her? All thought of whether she was being fair or not vanished as David slowly gentled the kiss and moved back an inch.

She felt the loss like a blow. When he lifted his head, his breath as harsh and uneven as hers, the loss of his heat so close to her was as if someone had opened a window to let cold winter air in. Josephine sighed. "Why did you stop?"

"I forgot you are an innocent," he said wryly. "It could have been oh so messy, not to say unfair, to take you deeper and then to get to a point where to stop myself making love with you would have been nigh on impossible. I promised I wouldn't take advantage of you, and I intend to keep that promise."

"Even if at some stage I want to go further?" she asked, amazed at her temerity and her lack of anger at his frank words.

He really wants me. But how, and why? That is the crux of the matter.

"Even then, if you do not have my ring on your finger. I am no seducer of innocents."

"Just a seducer of your wife-to-be?" The dichotomy intrigued her.

"Not even then…" David sighed. "Well, maybe then. But we're not at that point, are we? Not even near."

A rake with morals? But then, he had admitted his reputation was far from the real him. "True. Therefore you stopped?"

David nodded. "Therefore I stopped." He kissed her nose. "Now, do you need help with your buttons or laces?" He winked. "That is one part of a rake's duties I excel at. It's on page three of the rake's notebook. After how to make extravagant gestures. I ignored that…and how to check for escape routes. I took extra note of that page, although I swear I never had cause to use it. The unlacing now… That is another story."

Josephine couldn't help the heat that rushed into her cheeks and she shook her head as she laughed. He was incorrigible and this unforced, natural side of him appealed to her more than she cared to admit. "No, thank you. I wore this dress on purpose. It buttons up the front."

David examined those closures and clapped his hand to his forehead. "That is a dangerous thing to say."

She glanced down at his lower body and blinked. Was that bulge what she thought it was? "So it seems," she blurted before she could stop herself. *Oh my. Where is a hole to hide in when you need one?*

David followed her gaze and shrugged. "Ah, well. That is what banter and kissing does. A rake would ask what you intend to do about it. Be thankful I am no longer a rake. I will pretend it isn't there. Hard, but still."

"Hard? Oh yes. Oh my, oh… Enough." She put her hands to her heated cheeks and closed her eyes. What on earth had she said? *My damn talk-first, think-later mind.*

David roared with laughter. "Oh, love, you really did drop yourself into the mire there, eh? I'm sorry to tease you, but to think you noticed enough to discover that is indeed a positive thing for me to dwell on."

She had to get a grip on her wayward emotions. "Perhaps, but my answer is still no, thank you."

"Spoilsport."

"Maybe so, and now I intend to spoilsport even further. Good night, David." She made flapping gestures with her hands. "Go to bed. Your bed."

"Organizing woman. I'm going… Before I forget, do I knock on your door to make sure you are ready to ride? Help you find your way to the stables?"

"As I suspect you will go via the breakfast table, I think not. I'll see you in the stable yard. Now shoo."

He shooed.

* * * *

The morning was fresh with a hint of a warm day ahead. Perfect for riding. Lydia and James were ahead of her as she walked briskly across the cobbles, which led from the side door to the stables. They turned as she approached the yard. Several equine heads showed over the half doors of their stalls, and more than one animal whinnied a greeting. Josephine drew a deep breath. Weird or not, she loved that aroma of horse and straw.

"No David?" James asked in an innocent, butter-wouldn't-melt-in-his-mouth way, as Josephine greeted him and Lydia.

"I suspect he is at the breakfast table," Josephine said with a smile. "But as I haven't seen him, I wouldn't know. Do you mean you didn't partake before you came here?"

James blinked as Lydia blushed. "Ah, no. I thought I'd work up an appetite. I did beg a pasty from the chef though. Apple at one end and meat at the other. Known as a clanger, and very tasty it was."

"A clanger?" David had joined them without Josephine realizing. "Singular? Chef's last job was in Bedfordshire where the clanger originates. He's made them Godmama's favorite. And it seems yours, James. A pasty indeed. Make that four. I was lucky to commandeer the last three. Here." He passed one each to Josephine and Lydia. "Just to stave off the pangs. Are we ready?"

Josephine smelled the enticing mix of herbs, apple and pork and salivated. She took a healthy mouthful of warm, buttery pasty, nodded and swallowed the food. "Delicious. I agree with your godmama. Ah, look, the grooms are about to bring out the horses."

The clatter of horseshoes on the cobbles showed she was correct. Within five minutes, the pasties were consumed, and after a brief discussion, each of them were comfortable and mounted on horses to suit them. The four rode out of the stable yard and toward a long, low, nearby hill and some crags just beyond it. Josephine hung back a little while she got the measure of her horse. It had a soft mouth, which she didn't want to spoil by excessive tugging on the reins because she wasn't in command. She was a good rider — sadly not a very awake one at that moment.

Truth to tell, she hadn't slept that well, her mind full of all the new information she had assimilated with regards to David, and she wasn't at her most alert. The evening had brought more questions than it answered. She stifled a yawn and blinked to try to wake up. Her mount, a spirited filly called Ruby, would no doubt unseat her if she didn't pay attention. Not what she wanted.

"If we head toward Wylane Crag and come back via Stern Hill that should be perfect," David called as they trotted in single file around a field of crops. "James, you lead along the track until we reach open ground. You know the way. If we ride at a sensible pace and don't stop too long to look at the view, we might reach the village in time to have a drink before we head home and be back in time for a late breakfast or luncheon or whatever Godmama chooses to call it today."

James waved his crop in agreement and cantered down a bridleway toward the hill with Lydia following him. David slowed to a walk, and as the bridleway opened up a little, stopped until Josephine caught him up. "We might as well enjoy the peace for a moment or two. And let those two work out their problems."

"They have problems?" Josephine let her horse keep pace with David's larger, more powerful mount. "I thought they were just friends."

"To be honest, I'm not sure they are even that now," David said thoughtfully. "A year or so ago, I was certain we'd have a betrothal between them. Then all of a sudden there was a frosty silence if I mentioned either of them in the other's company. I know Jamie is keen, but Lyddie is keeping her own counsel."

"Then let them work whatever it is out by themselves," Josephine suggested. "There is nothing worse that well-meaning people interfering when you're trying to solve a problem," she said in a pointed manner. "Especially one that might involve the emotions."

David shot her an intrigued glance. "As you are?"

He had her there. "In a way. Although I dare say my parents are wary of saying too much." At least she hoped so.

"So me trying to press my suit isn't counted as meddling? Thank goodness for that."

They navigated round a tree that split the bridleway and began the steady climb to where the dark craggy outcrop of rocks was silhouetted against the blue sky. Happy now her horse was under her control, Josephine risked a quick look at him. "Did I say so?"

David appeared so startled, he let his hands drop, and his horse broke stride. For the few moments it took him to get it back under control, Josephine enjoyed the knowledge that she had the capability to surprise him. He swore under his breath and gentled the horse until once more it was in step with hers. Then he laughed.

"I suppose I deserved that."

"I think so. Although I'm sorry if I'm impudent. I couldn't help myself. You sounded so smug."

"My own fault then, so I will change the subject. Look, you see the darker shadows on the crag?" He pointed with his crop to where a pattern of light and shade stood out. "Caves. Not only on the crags themselves, but also under them. Caves and potholes. The area is riddled with caverns. I spent many an hour exploring them as a youth. I'd go off with a couple of local lads, two or three candles and a tinderbox and a ball of string. We were convinced that there had to be Blue John around here, and were going to prove wrong all the experts who insisted it is only in close vicinity to Castleton, and thus make our fortune. We never did, of course, but we had so much fun trying. We'd tie the string to something at the entrance and explore as far as we could. You know, until we came to the end of the string."

Josephine shivered. "How unpleasant. I can think of nothing worse than being underground in the dark. What if the string broke or the candles went out? What then?"

"We were lads. We didn't think of things like that. It was an adventure. We'd come out filthy, strip off and wash in the stream and go home starving and happy. I adore Lady F., and my time with her each summer was something I looked forward to from the moment I returned to school until the time I arrived back at Tansy House. Here I was just David, not the heir to Midham who had to try to learn, with no help from his parents. Just David doing what young boys should do. Riding, hiking, fishing...simple things that give the most pleasure."

To hear him speak so naturally about how he'd spent his youth was enlightening, and information she relished. "And your companions?"

"Will Bonsall and Bert Killer," David said in a reminiscent tone. "Now both respectable adults. Will is head groom for Godmama and Bert, head gamekeeper. I confess we still meet up for hunting and fishing."

"And caving?"

He laughed. "On occasion. Although we mark our way with chalk and nicks in the rock these days, as well as stronger string and lanterns. We might be adventurous, but age and responsibilities have tempered it somewhat."

"It sounds perfect," Josephine said wistfully. "I was generally ignored and left in the care of my governess. Oh, she was lovely, and did her best, but my parents didn't pay much attention to me or welcome visitors and so I suppose I was not encouraged to make many friends. Until I went to school to learn to be a lady, at much too young an age, I admit I was lonely. But, if nothing else, it showed me I could be happy with my own company, and that it was best never to rely on others."

"You can rely on me."

Josephine inclined her head. "Thank you." It was time to change the subject before she began to blubber. "Which direction?" They had come to the end of the bridleway.

"Left and hold on... Stay here." He dismounted, threw his reins to her and strode toward the thorn hedge that separated the common land they were on from the field to one side. Josephine grabbed the reins and soothed both horses as she watched him bend down and wriggle under the wicked-looking thorns. His torso, his rear — which she couldn't help but notice was nicely rounded and firm — and the top half of his legs disappeared from view and she contemplated the soles of his hessians for several seconds before he began to emerge. When he finally stood up, to her surprise he held a squirming bundle in his arms.

"A puppy?"

"A puppy," he confirmed. "It was in a sack. I saw the sack move and knew it wasn't here when I rode by here yesterday. Some bastard, excuse my language, couldn't do the decent thing and ask around if anyone wanted a dog — they had to try and kill it this way. Well, when I get my hands on them, they will wish they'd thought differently."

"You'll find out who it was?"

"Of course. It's a close-knit community. Easy to find whose dog has had pups, where not all the pups are accounted for. Godmama will also add her mite, and that, believe me, is a lot scarier than anything I can do." He examined the shivering pup carefully. "Nothing broken, just hungry and thirsty. We'll soon sort it out once we get back. Can you hold her until I remount? We'll catch the other two up and get it some food and water at the inn. They might even have an idea whose dog whelped."

"To find out who needs whi — given what for is an incentive to hurry." Josephine bit back her first thoughts and altered her statement. She checked her mount was settled, passed David his reins and made sure she had a hand free. "Give him, or is it her, to me." She hadn't had a chance to look.

"Her." David lifted the liver-and-white bundle into her waiting arms. "Only just old enough to leave her mama. Someone will pay." He mounted in one fluid motion Josephine envied—side saddles and skirts had a lot to answer for—and held both his hands out. David squirmed in the saddle to face Josephine.

His horse never moved as he maneuvered himself to the position he wanted. How she envied that.

"I'll take her," David said. "It will be easier for me."

As much as she would have loved to have said she could manage, it would have been a lie. "Very well, but I reserve the right to first cuddles."

David settled the pup on his lap, held her steady with one hand and gathered his reins with the other. "And first widdles no doubt."

She giggled. "And that. But she could be easily trained. If someone offers to have her, of course."

David looked at her suspiciously. "Are you suggesting...?"

"Me?" She opened her eyes wide as she urged her horse to match the easy pace of his. "What makes you think that?"

"Elementary, my dear. The look of innocence, the lack of pleading, the sighs and, when you think I am not looking, the longing in your eyes."

"Oh dear. Am I so transparent?" She supposed she was. How she envied him. She had always yearned for a puppy. Something to love and be loved by in return.

"'Fraid so," David said cheerfully. "You want her."

"Of course I do, but I can't. So will you? If no one comes forward to claim her? Will you keep her?

Because if you don't, what will happen to her? I would be so grateful if you do."

David sighed. "You know I will, and without even asking how grateful. Not even mentioning betrothal grateful, or a kiss grateful. But if you married me she would be ours."

"I am not getting married just to be joint owner of a dog, even one as entrancing as this."

"Of course not. Whatever gave you that idea?" He winked. "I suppose you'd like to name her. If I keep her."

"Of course you will keep her," Josephine said with confidence. "No one else deserves her. And I will name her Gaia, which means earth, I believe. I do appreciate you not asking for something from me to show how grateful I am."

"I thought you might," he grumbled. "I should have been less accommodating."

"Don't be a crosspatch. Is that James and Lydia ahead?" Two horses with riders waited beneath the crag.

"Yes, they will have wondered what kept us." David urged his horse into a faster walk.

"Where on earth...ah...David the animal rescuer," James said as the four of them became reunited. His animation seemed forced to Josephine, and Lydia looked stonily ahead. Evidently, things were not happy between them. Josephine felt for the couple but held her counsel. It was up to them to sort their problems out. She had enough of her own.

"What have you there?" James asked.

"A puppy," David replied. "Tied in a sack and thrown under a hedge. I am informed that she is now mine, and her name is Gaia."

"Her owner? Or should I say ex-owner?"

"No idea. Let's head to the inn and discover if Riggot knows anything about her."

"Riggot?" Josephine queried. "Who is that?"

"The landlord. A wily old bu — soul who is not averse to a bit of poaching, but would never stoop to this. He has his finger on the pulse of all that goes on in this part of the county. If this is down to someone local, he'll know who it is."

As one, they headed toward a long, low, stone building in the distance. The sun went behind a cloud and the crag became dark and menacing.

Josephine shivered as she averted her eyes from the dark gray screes and slopes. "It's eerie."

"It's Wylane. Around here, they say it has a mind of its own. It can be storms here and sun in the village not half a mile away. At night, it gets dark earlier and stays that way longer."

Josephine could well believe it. She wouldn't want to be here by herself during daylight, let alone at night. "And you played in the caves around here? You must have been crazy."

"Not crazy," David corrected her cheerfully. "Ripe for adventure. Three boys with too much energy and imagination."

"Whatever. I still think you were foolhardy."

"Oh undoubtedly," David agreed. "But don't worry, I'm older and wiser now."

They reached the inn as a stout, gray-haired man bustled out. He took a step back when he saw whom his potential customers were. "My lord? You're about early." He blinked as he saw the bundle in David's arms. "What have you there?"

"An abandoned dog, callously left in a sack under a thorn hedge. I could easily have missed it, which is what, I suspect, the person who abandoned her hoped for. Plus three thirsty friends. Ale, watered wine" — he winked at Josephine — "plain water and perhaps something puppy suitable, and anything easy and swift to eat. We are later than I'd hoped."

"Ordinary wine for me, please. Not watered," Josephine said firmly. "Or I will have cider." She laughed at David. "Even ale, for I enjoy ale once in a while."

"Of course, my lord, my lady, at once. I have my own cider and Mrs. Riggot has a nice raised pie just out of the oven, and some fancies as well." Riggot waited until David had swung down from his horse. "It's a spaniel, eh? I don't know anyone around here with a dog that just whelped. Where did you find it?"

"Not far from Wylane, where the bridleway ends. Can you hold her a moment whilst I help Lady Josephine down, please?"

Josephine chose not to mention that she'd been dismounting unaided for years. She rather liked the idea of his hands at her waist. What a contrary creature she had become.

David passed the puppy to Riggot. The man's dour countenance softened. "What a beauty. What are you going to do with her? I'll take her off your hands if you want. The missus sore misses our old Shep who passed three months back."

Josephine cast an agonized glance at David as he helped her to the ground. His hands did feel good around her waist, but she was far too agitated to give the experience the attention it deserved.

David smiled at her reassuringly before he turned his attention back to the landlord. "I've promised the lady that the pup will be mine, but if you do hear where she might have come from, I'd be obliged if you would let me know. Someone needs to learn how to respect all creatures, be they big or small."

If her heart hadn't melted just a little before, it did then.

* * * *

David tied his cravat for dinner and looked down at the slumbering puppy at his feet. "You are happy to turn my life around, aren't you?" he mused as Felix his valet helped him into his jacket.

Gaia yipped and her nose twitched. "Chasing rabbits in your sleep? As long as you don't bring them indoors half mangled, we will cope. Not you, Felix. Gaia. No doubt she will howl the place down, but she cannot come to dinner."

Gaia opened one eye and emitted a doggy sigh.

"You have had food," David said and did his best to aim for a no-nonsense tone, although he felt somewhat uneasy lecturing a dog. "And a bone, which I believe is under my bed."

Felix smiled. "No need to worry, my lord, the bone is now in your sitting room, along with her bed. I'll take her out to do her business, then I'll make sure she's comfy. I've taken the liberty of putting your worn shirt in her basket. A day shirt, my lord, not an evening one. That'll make her feel better. I wouldn't suggest you try to put her in the scullery. She's fair taken with you. A one-man dog, I would say."

The one-man dog shut her eyes again and rolled close enough to put her head on the tip of David's house shoe.

David nodded. One less shirt. He might need to make a visit to the nearest town for a couple of daytime garments, if Gaia took charge of much more. Naturally he had clothing for a month or more with him, but he would hate to be caught out for any reason.

"And, of course," Felix went on as he gathered up used towels, "I'll be around for a while."

"Thank you, Felix. What would I do without you?"

"Mangle your cravats and have a howling pup?" the valet said with a smile.

"The pup I agree with, the cravats I do not. When have I ever mangled one of those?"

Felix raised his eyebrows, very much in the manner of an old and beloved retainer, and David laughed. There were only a few years between them, but Felix and he went back a long way and didn't stand on ceremony when they were alone. "All for show, I assure you. My love life has not been very active these last years. Very few ladies to crease it to perdition as they strove to get me naked."

"I know, my lord, so I wondered why you tried to show me different." He bowed and went into the bathing chamber.

David shook his head in amusement as he checked his appearance in the cheval mirror his godmother had obtained from France as a young girl. He'd long admired the sheer elegance of the piece and, with a laugh, she'd arranged for it to be put in his room. "The darned thing shows me as I really am, not at all flattering," she had said. "I prefer one that slims me and forgets to acknowledge my age."

He, on the other hand, was glad it showed him as he really was, and he was satisfied with the result. With a final tweak to his shirt cuffs and a mental prayer of thanks that ruffles were no longer in fashion, David carefully moved Gaia off his foot and put the pup in her new basket. Gaia snuffled and let out a tiny howl.

"Now that is enough. You have my shirt, that will have to do for now." David smiled as the pup let out a big loud sigh and closed her eyes. He left his room just as Josephine closed the door on hers. She looked at him with suspicion.

"Were you waiting for me?"

"Strange as it may seem, no, I was not," David replied. "I was ensuring Gaia was happy snuggled up with my second-best shirt and a large bone. Felix is in charge and she will be spoiled. Although it is fortuitous because now I can escort you to the drawing room for sherry before dinner." He held out his arm. "Shall we?"

"I hate sherry." Josephine put her hand very properly on his arm and they walked to the top of the stairs. "It tastes like the linctus the doctor used to give me for a chesty cough. Horrid."

"Then feed the pot plants."

She shot him a swift and astonished glance and giggled as they descended the wide shallow-stepped staircase to the lower floor. "They'd die."

"Not at all, my godmama does it regularly. She says they thrive on it." David paused until Josephine looked at his face, and winked. "She hates sherry as well."

"Then why on earth does she serve it?"

"She says to remind herself she is not the only person in the world she has to please. Plus, she adds, it leaves more port and brandy for later."

Josephine made a noise somewhere between a snort and a snigger, and changed it to a hasty cough as they approached the drawing room door. "I find myself liking your godmother more and more with each passing hour."

"She says she is getting rather fond of you as well. Now brace yourself. Smile sweetly at anyone who looks interested about us, and if your parents are so crass as to query how we came to enter together, pass them over to me with one of those stupid comments silly young debs make."

"I'm not a silly young deb. I never was."

"No, but I bet you've heard it said often enough. The" — he changed his voice to a falsetto — "ohh, I really couldn't say. Perhaps you better ask his lordship…" He chuckled at her astonished expression and reverted to his normal deep tone. "Or some such thing."

Chapter Nine

To her pleasure and surprise, several hours later, with her hair down and a warm shawl around her shoulders, she saw David had remembered the brandy. As he entered her sitting room — presumably as he came from her bedchamber, via their bathing chambers and the servants' corridor — she saw he also carried a wriggling bundle that woofed and tried to lick Josephine's face as he put it on her lap.

"Gaia missed you," he said as he kissed her cheek and proceeded to pour them each a drink. "Your bathing chamber reminds me of you."

Josephine stroked Gaia's silky, baby-fine hair. The puppy wriggled in ecstasy. "Damp?"

He chuckled. "No, it is redolent of your scent. Roses and something else."

"Mr. Pears soap."

"Ah, it can't be something so simple, surely? I was thinking of all sorts of exotic things."

"Sorry, Mr. Pears it is." She waved him to a seat next to her. Gaia immediately slid off her lap and did her best to climb David's legs.

"Behave and do not snag the knit of my unmentionables with your claws, dog." He lifted the pup into his lap. "Well, I will have to thank him. Along with the roses, it suits you."

Josephine laughed and indulged in a swift sideways glance at the unmentionables he'd mentioned. A contradiction in terms, surely? They fit as snug as a glove and outlined every contour and… Oh no, no more of that. Goodness knows what her wayward mouth would utter if she let her mind dwell on all the garment covered. Not that she knew, exactly, but even so…

"Thank you, I think." She dragged her mind back to perfumes and soap. "I have never been told a bar of soap suits me before. It is a novel compliment, if indeed it is a compliment."

"Oh it is, and don't forget the roses."

"As if I could. Or this." She sipped the brandy. "I watched Lady Foster. She poured two glasses of sherry away. What a waste."

"If you like the stuff. How many did you discard?"

"Just the one. I sipped, tipped and nursed what remained until dinner was called. Then I forgot the glass and left it on the mantel. Or so I hope people think."

"Clever. So on another subject, did you enjoy the day? Was my company acceptable?" David regarded her over the top of his goblet. "Did I behave as you preferred?"

"You know you did." She sipped her brandy with appreciation for its velvet smooth taste and the way its fiery warmth spread through her. "I enjoyed our time together. Then when you disappeared to play billiards, Lady Foster saved me from my mama's inquisition and bore me away to admire her rose garden, where she regaled me with stories of your youth and untruths of your adulthood. It passed an interesting hour or two, which could have, if I hadn't already accepted a lot of what is said about you is a pack of lies, put you in a whole new light."

"Enough to accept my offer?"

"Ah, sadly no." Oh how she wished she truly knew her own mind. It would have been so easy just to say yes, and wonder if she had done the correct thing. If nothing else, she had no intention of doing that to herself, or David. "We have two more days left, and I intend to use them to decide my response to you." She leaned forward and fondled Gaia's ears. "If I said you are the only person who has ever made me think I might change my mind, it is true. But only *might*. It's a big decision, and one that will affect both of our lives, whatever it is. It behooves me not to make it lightly. And, I must add, I have certain things to ponder over."

"I can see that. I do hope, though, that Janie...Lady Foster didn't sway your decision in the wrong direction."

"So do I— What?"

A peremptory knock on her bedroom door had made her jump. David put his finger over his lips, stood up and gathered goblets, decanter and dog together. "Are all the doors to the corridor locked?" he asked in an undertone.

Josephine unscrambled her wits. "Yes, why?"

"Because I need to get me and the pup out of here, and I'll have to go via the bedchamber."

She nodded and led the way. The knock came again. "Josephine? If you are asleep, wake up, I need to talk to you."

"Mama."

"Answer and say just a second. Damn, you're dressed. You can't pretend you were asleep."

"Never mind, I'll think of something. Shoo."

Gaia chose that moment to yip. David rolled his eyes. Josephine grinned. "Perfect, give her to me and go. Now." The dog changed hands, and, although she wriggled as David walked swiftly and silently into the next room, Gaia chose not to complain too much but lick Josephine's cheek instead.

Josephine took a deep breath and walked to her bedchamber door. She'd checked that the key could move silently and had just turned it when the handle moved and the door opened. She took a hasty step back and stared at the intruder.

"Mama? What on earth are you doing here at this hour?"

"Why aren't you asleep?" her mother countered as she peered around the room. What did she think was going on? That David was in the wardrobe? *As he could well have been.* Josephine bit back her smile and stared stonily ahead.

"At this hour," her mama added. "It is late."

It was going to be attack, was it? Josephine was well versed in counterattack where her parents were concerned. "Well, if I had been, I wouldn't be now, would I? What do you want? I'm ready to go to bed."

"You're dressed," her mama pointed out.

"So are you."

"Do not speak to me in that tone," her mother said icily. "Do I not deserve respect?"

Dare she say no, respect had to be earned, not expected?

Gaia took objection to her mother's tone of voice and growled.

Josephine bit back a grin as Lady Bowie took a hasty step back. "What is that?"

"*That* is a *she*. The viscount's pup, he found today. She was crying. As I came upstairs, his lordship's valet was about to go in search of his lordship." Good lord, how much more pompous could she be? "As I believe his lordship is playing billiards, I offered to have her here with me. She's no trouble except for needing out. Which I was about to do."

"You can't go wandering through the house at this time of night," her mama said in an outraged voice. "It's not right. Where is your maid?"

"She's in bed, where I told her to go. I can undress myself. And why can I not take the pup to do her business?"

"Well, because," her mama said lamely, "you'd be alone."

"You came to my room alone."

"I am married. It's different once you are a wife."

Josephine couldn't fathom out the sense in that statement. "So come with me."

"What?"

If Josephine had suggested they go for a swim in the ornamental lake, her mama could not have sounded more scandalized.

"Come down to the garden door with me. Make sure of the proprieties."

Her mother gawped at her. "Do not talk nonsense. Ring for a servant to do it."

"No, Mama, it's late and I'm perfectly capable of doing this," Josephine said in a voice that she hoped dared her parent to argue. "Now did you come for anything particular or can it wait until the morning?" She opened the door and took a step into the corridor. Her mama perforce had to follow. "For if there is nothing more, I will do what is necessary and then get that sleep you insist I need."

Her mother hovered, and opened her hands in a 'well, if you insist' gesture. "I wondered how you and the viscount were getting on."

Aha, so now they were getting to the crux of the matter. "Fine. Why? He is most amiable to everyone, don't you think? He looks after his godmama so well, and is punctilious in his attentions to her." Josephine began to walk to the stairs. Her mama trailed behind. She would have to walk past them to get back to the room she shared with her husband.

"Ah yes, but... Oh." Her mama squeaked the last word as David came up the stairs, saw them and bowed. Josephine hoped her mama hadn't seen the brief wink he'd shot in Josephine's direction.

"Ladies."

Gaia, on hearing his voice, yipped joyfully and squirmed in Josephine's arms. She passed her to David. "She needs to go outside."

"As ever," David said wryly as Gaia tried to clean his ear. "Enough, you monster." He held the pup firmly and turned slightly to face Josephine. "My thanks, my lady, but why are you inconvenienced like this?" The mirth he strove to contain was almost her undoing, and enough for Josephine to firm her lips.

"She wouldn't settle. I heard the commotion and came out to see what was going on. F — your valet was setting out with her to find you." She'd almost called his valet by name until she remembered she wouldn't generally know it. "As she seemed happy to see me, I offered to take her into my chambers. He was to leave you a note. No doubt you will find it on your mantel."

"Such a thoughtful girl," her mama interjected.

Josephine rolled her eyes but kept her mouth shut.

"Just so," David murmured. "My thanks, my lady. I'll take it from here." He bowed to them both and turned on his heels to retrace his steps downstairs.

"Now, Mama, as it is well past the time either of us would normally retire, and you have seen for yourself how his lordship sees me — as nothing other than a fellow guest — I suggest you go to your bed and I to mine," Josephine said in as even a tone as she could. "Papa will be waiting for you."

"Well, really, you could at least try to hold his interest," Lady Bowie replied crossly. "You must make an effort."

"Could I? Must I? If you say so, but I choose not to. Good night." Josephine made her way back to her room before her mama had a chance to remonstrate any more. Once inside, she leaned back on the wooden panels with a sigh.

What next?

Next was a commotion in the corridor that made her sit up, push her hair out of her eyes and wonder what was going on. Someone shouted and there was the sound of running feet. Weak moonlight showed behind the curtains. She always chose not to close the curtains if possible. Josephine hated total darkness. It might have something to do with the thick curtains that had been used at her school, where they'd helped to keep in the warmth but had made everyone feel they'd slept underground.

Not a pleasant experience.

She found her robe and slippers and, with an enormous yawn, fumbled with the door handle to open the door and peer into the corridor.

David strode by in buckskins and a thick thorn-proof jacket with an anxious expression on his face, Gaia running as fast as her legs would let her to keep up with him. He checked when he saw Josephine and for a brief second let his desire for her, and his admiration for her attire, show. Then, just as James caught up with him, David's face was a blank canvas and he was all business once more. He scooped up Gaia and thrust her at Josephine. "Here, look after her."

Josephine took the dog from him without a second thought, and held the wriggling pup firmly. "Why? What's all the commotion about?"

"Two young lads went out late yesterday afternoon and have not been home since." He grimaced. "They were last seen heading for the crag."

Josephine stared at his closed expression. His words sank in and her heart sank with them. "To go caving?"

He shrugged, the action at odds with his manner "We don't know. It's too late for birds' eggs, too early for foraging. All I know is they finished their chores and went off with fishing nets. Allegedly to go to the river. A search found their rods."

"Oh lord, where?"

"Not near the river."

That was one positive thing, Josephine thought. "So at least you don't need to search around water?"

He shook his head. "But as it's young Sam Bonsall and Freddie Killer, I'd wager somehow they've heard of our exploits as youths and thought if their fathers did it so can they. But we were older, if not a lot wiser, and we went equipped. We've no idea what they have with them. Look, we must go. We're meeting the others in the stable yard as soon as it's possible to see clearly. That's not long."

"No, then you must away." She hesitated, then, unheeding of James, stood on tiptoe and kissed David's cheek. "Take care."

"If there's more where that came from, I will indeed," he said as his concerned expression lightened for a second. "I'll see you anon. With two young boys in tow, I hope. Why the hell I wasn't called out earlier I do not know." He shook his head. "Ah well, too late to change that." He and James clattered down the stairs two at a time.

Josephine watched them go thoughtfully. She wasn't going to be able to get back to sleep, and would wager the staff were up and about. Maybe there was something she could do, even if it was just to walk Gaia.

It seemed strange no one else had heard the commotion. She walked to the top of the stairs and looked down them and along the corridor to the other wing. Not a soul.

She turned around and almost collided with Lydia, who was dressed similarly to herself.

"What's going on?" Lydia asked in a sleep-filled voice. "I heard noises."

"Two boys missing. David and James have gone to help find them." It was not the time to worry about formality. "I'm about to get dressed, take Gaia out and see if I can help anywhere."

Lydia nodded. "Good idea. Give me five minutes and I'll join you back here. If you have stout shoes and a thick walking dress, it might help. After all, I don't suppose you are any more likely than I to sit meekly in the morning room and wait?"

"Indeed not."

* * * *

"Why didn't you call me earlier?" David asked as he stood in the middle of a circle of Lady Foster's staff just outside the tack room of the stables. It was just about light enough to see the outline of each man, well muffled up and with stout sticks in their hands. What did they intend to do with those? Beat the bushes or the boys?

He would love to rant. Ask if they didn't trust him, or thought him too lofty to be called upon to help before then. However, it wasn't the time or the place. Instead, he counted to ten under his breath. "How long have you known they were missing?" After all, he could be doing them a disservice by thinking they hadn't thought of him at once.

"A bit now, but not over concerned until now. Not really. Our Sam said he was going to have supper with young Freddie, and Freddie said he were comin' t'ours," Will Bonsall said in a voice of doom and gloom. "This time ut year they often fish after supper. Well, you do, don't you? We did, eh? So, wasn't 'til well on and we wondered why Sam weren't 'ome. Me and Bert met halfway atween the 'ouses. Light nights and we wondered if they'd not realized the time and were still fishin'. Nowt a sign at 't river. So we went home and checked barns and so on. Then" — he drew a deep breath — "then we got some of the others, and Jem Walker said his youngster heard them talkin' about

Wylane. So we spread out, found the rods and decided we needed to ask you if you'd come to the caves. You were allus the one who kept us right."

David didn't have the heart to remind him just how many years it was since they'd ventured underground. Instead he nodded. "Do you have everything we need? Food and water?" He had to say it. "Rags for bandages?"

Will went white and shook his head.

"Someone go and ask Lady F. for some, then follow us," David said. "She's in the kitchen. Lanterns, candles, ropes? A tinderbox?"

Will nodded. "Tommy, off you go, eh? Rest of stuff we should be right, and her ladyship said to make free with the cattle so we've saddled up as many 'osses as we might need."

"Can everyone ride?" Every man nodded. "Then let's be off."

David set a sensible pace. The last thing they wanted was the horses to stumble and be injured. Until it was full light, no one could see all the rabbit holes and boggy areas that occurred. Bert rode up beside him and James dropped back to facilitate the man's move forward.

"I'd like to skelp the young buggers, but are they any worse than we were?" Bert asked as the sun slowly began to make itself known and lighten the predawn sky to something more friendly. "Exploring and mischief is in a boy's nature. Well, one with any spunk anyhow."

"We never stopped out later than we were told," David said grimly, even though he accepted the words. "And we went equipped. However, I daresay you are right. Let's hope we have some way of discovering which cave they might have chosen to explore."

"Ah, not gonna be easy, is it." Bert sighed. "His mam is worried sick. He's our only lad."

David didn't know what to say. He was under no illusion as to how difficult it could be to find the boys. Wylane was riddled with caves and potholes, some they had explored as youths, but a lot more they had not. It was going to be as difficult as trying to discover the proverbial needle in a haystack.

"Let's see what we can find," he suggested as they came to the end of the bridleway, near to where he'd found Gaia. Had it only been the previous day? It seemed like much more than twenty-four hours had passed. He waited until everyone had arrived. "So, now we have goodness knows how many caves to cover. I suggest we start with the more obvious ones." He named half a dozen or so, with the nicknames they'd been given by him, Will and Bert all those years ago. "Any more?"

Will shook his head. "After that you have to walk a fair way to get to the next crop."

David thought rapidly. "Then we'll split up. James, it is a lot to ask, but can you stay here so there is a central point and be a man to report to?"

James sighed. "It makes sense, but it galls I can't be in the thick of things. Very well. I'm the point of contact and reference."

David flashed him a grateful smile. "I appreciate it. For the rest? Three teams, and each one of us leads a team." He noticed the worried look that passed between Will and Bert. "What?"

"The thing is, m'lord, we're not that sure we'd be able to remember what to do, like. We're happy to go a few yards but then?"

David sighed. "Fair enough. Then let's start with the nearest one. I'll need at least one of you to come down with me and two of you to stay by the entrance. Do you think we can have someone at least shout down each cave? Just in case they can hear us and shout back?" He didn't add his worry that perhaps they were in no fit state to reply.

"Aye." Will split the men up and, once they had set out, turned back to David. "I'll go down and Bert and Jem will stop up top."

"Then let's get what we need and start."

* * * *

Josephine and Lydia walked into organized chaos in the kitchen. At one table, Lady Foster was calmly kneading bread, while by the stove the under chef was stirring a large pot of something aromatic. In one corner, several young children sat in a circle, sandwiches in their hands as an older child told them stories. Servants dashed hither and thither, filling water containers, asking for advice and showing rags rolled up — presumably for bandages.

It was no surprise to Josephine that her mama was nowhere to be seen.

Lady Foster looked up and smiled. "I didn't think you two would be long. I've sent the Hansons back to bed and told them they'd be better to get some sleep so they can be of help tomorrow if need be. Freddie is supervising the footmen, who are up in the storerooms to find anything I imagine we might need." She didn't mention Josephine's parents. "Can you relieve young Winnie over there for a while? She needs to eat, and the youngsters need entertaining. All their elders are busy, either here or out with David. Once she's eaten, you two can. I think her need is greater."

"Of course." Josephine, followed by Lydia, made her way across the enormous room. "Half each?" she asked. "Surely it will be easier that way?"

"I'd say so."

Winnie stood up as they approached. "I'm mighty glad to see you, my ladies. 'Cos not only am I famished, I need, well, you know…"

Josephine nodded. "I know. Well, we're here now." She was 'mighty glad' she'd had the foresight to use the commode before she ventured downstairs.

Within a few minutes both she and Lydia were answering questions from children to whom shyness meant nothing. Josephine realized that even though she had had very little interaction with youngsters before, it was no hardship to hold their interest with a good story. Except for one little girl of around seven or eight years of age. She sat silent and brooding, and didn't meet anyone's curious glances.

"Lydia, can you keep an eye on them all, please?" Josephine asked her new friend in a low voice. "I think that little one might be worrying about something. I'll try to get her to talk." Lydia nodded and Josephine made her way to the child and sat down on the floor next to her. The child stared and gulped.

"Miss, your dress'll get dirty."

"My dress will dust down," Josephine said. "That's the best thing about a thick material like this."

The little girl fingered the woollen skirt and nodded. "Me ma has a dress like this. Not as fine, but she says it's good and thick to use for work."

"Your mama is a wise lady. And therefore, I have no doubt, so are you. What's wrong, sweetness?"

The little girl bit her lip. "I think me brother's gone to get Boy John's treasure, and it's guarded by a dragon near a castle."

"John? Your brother?"

"Nah, Sam, me brother. I heard him and Freddie Killer saying if they got it then we'd all be rich."

"Did they say where it was?" Josephine asked in a gentle voice. "Or who John is? The dragon's castle?"

The child bit her lip and looked ready to cry. "Not really, miss, and I dunt think it's the dragon's castle just near him. I dunno who Boy John is. I follered 'em a week or so ago, and I reckons I could finds it." She nodded. "Once I see the dragon."

She sounded more certain by the second. Josephine made her mind up. "Then would you come with me and we'll see if we can find the dragon together?" Something niggled her about dragons but for the life of her Josephine couldn't remember what. No doubt it would come to her when she wasn't thinking about it.

The little girl studied Josephine for a moment and nodded. "I think so. Mind, it's a bit away. I was almost late for supper."

"Then we'll go now." Josephine stood up and took the child's hand. "And take something to eat with us. If someone else finds your brother, we will have a feast."

The girl's face lit up. "Ah, and serves 'em right, eh?"

"Exactly. What's your name, lovey?"

"Rose, miss."

"Then let's tell Lady Foster, Rose, and we'll go. Can you ride?"

Rose shook her head and her lips trembled. Josephine gave her a swift hug. "No matter, because I can, and you can come up in front of me. I won't let you fall. All right?"

Rose nodded and smiled, somewhat shy but no longer looking as if she were about to burst into tears. It was progress of a sort.

The two of them walked over to Lady Foster, who had been watching them with interest. Josephine relayed the news and her intentions.

"Are you sure?" Janie Foster asked. "Can you do it? Does Rose know the way? There's no men around to help."

Josephine smiled. "I'm sure, and Rose is fairly certain where we need to go. We'll head towards the crag and then...then I don't know yet. Rose will show me. So perhaps if you give me some rags, I'll use them to mark the route."

Lady Foster nodded in a decisive manner. It was evident she did not subscribe to the idea that women were the weaker sex and needed to be protected from unpleasantness or actions. "Very well. Go with my blessing. Damn. Now who can I send to tell David?" She shrugged, a somewhat awkward gesture as her hands were covered in flour and dough. "No matter. Get whoever is in the stables to come and see me once you've got everything you need. Oh, and I'll fob your parents off with something innocuous if they realize you're not around."

"Ah, thank you." She'd forgotten about them. "I doubt they will." After all, why would they change their habits of a lifetime at that moment, when they had never seemed inclined to do so before? Lady Foster tutted and Josephine smiled. Her parents' attitude rarely had the power to wound her anymore.

Apart from my attitude toward marriage? Even that was no longer as clear-cut as it had been.

Josephine waited while Rose executed a wobbly curtsey and ushered the little girl into the courtyard.

Ten minutes later, she looked around the tack room and sighed. Why was everything so high up? She wasn't tiny, but she would have a problem reaching even the lowest pegs. The youth who had been left behind when the men went to look for the lads stared at her. "You want what?" If she had asked for a diamond-encrusted coach, he couldn't have sounded more surprised.

"A saddle."

"A side-saddle, my lady?" The lad pushed his cloth cap back from his crown and scratched his head. "These are all men's saddles. I'll go and get one from the other side of the stables, shall I?"

No, that wouldn't do when she had Rose up in front of her. "A regular saddle on a fast but not overspirited horse would be best. Do you have such an animal? The filly I rode out on yesterday, perhaps? If she will take an ordinary saddle?"

"Ruby? Ah, she's here, but, my lady, I don't want to be rude, but have you ridden astride before now?" The youth sounded worried. "It's a bit different-like."

"Of course I have," Josephine lied. There was, after all, a first time for everything, and it seemed this was one of them. "Now please make haste so Rose and I can get away." She was convinced that every minute counted.

Within a few moments, Ruby was saddled and Josephine led her to the mounting block. "Avert your eyes," she said firmly to the youth. There was no need to advertise she preferred lace-trimmed petticoats even under an everyday, less than glamorous gown. "And when I say so, hand Rose up to me," she instructed him. "She will sit in front and show me the way."

Skirts were a confounded nuisance. She mounted easily enough—she was reasonably agile—but even in a serviceable walking gown there was way too much material, in all the wrong places, to sit elegantly. Josephine arranged her skirts over her legs as best she could and decided that showing off her ankles was the least of her worries. "Now, Rose," she said. "If you swing her up, I will catch her."

The youth turned around, looked anywhere but at Josephine's legs and handed Rose up. Rose giggled as Josephine put her snugly in front of her. "Comfy?"

"I think so." Rose wriggled a little and Ruby shifted. Rose let out a yelp and Josephine held her firm and close.

"That's just Ruby making sure you sit just how you want to."

Rose drew a deep breath and patted the horse on her neck. "I'm right settled now, Ruby. You can move proper anytime."

"Then in that case it's our turn to have an adventure," Josephine said gaily. She prayed the worry that gave her butterflies in her stomach didn't pass to Rose or the stable lad. "Why should the males have it all?"

Rose laughed. "Me dad say's tis way of t'world."

"Ha. Not here today, it isn't. We won't allow it. Now, which way? Towards the crag?"

"Yes, that way for a bit then to the dragon and the castle thing."

Josephine turned the horse and spoke to the youth. "Make sure you inform Lady Foster and anyone else who arrives back what is happening. We are heading towards Wylane," she told him. "To look for a dragon."

The lad blinked. "A dragon?"

"Evidently. And a sort of a castle. And treasure."

"Boy John's treasure," Rose added. "In a castle."

"There you are, Boy John's treasure, in a castle," Josephine repeated for emphasis. "Once we get out of the bridleway, I'll mark our route with rags. Lady Foster knows that, and will arrange for someone to send the news to his lordship. She asked for you to go to the kitchen once we were sorted. That's us ready now, so we'll go and do our part and let you do yours."

He touched his cap. "Aye, miss, er, m'lady. An' what do you want me to do with the pup?"

Gaia had arrived unseen, and wove her way around them with excited yips. Luckily, the horse was unfazed and ignored her. Rose giggled, for once the sort of carefree child Josephine hoped she would normally appear.

"Look, she wants to come and help."

"Oh, lord." Josephine thought fast. The last thing they needed was Gaia lost underground. "She might want to but it would be more of a hindrance than a help. She's only a baby. Can you keep her for me?" she asked the youth. "We don't want her to go missing as well."

He nodded. "I'll do that. She's a lovely pup. I'll make sure she can't follow you."

Josephine inclined her head to show her gratitude, smiled and gathered the reins. "My thanks. Hold on," she said to Rose. "We won't go too fast, and I need you to be my eyes and ears. You have to tell me which way and when."

"I can do that," Rose said solemnly as she turned a little to look up at Josephine, her expression serious. "I know where to go." She looked ahead again. "That way."

For the first few hundred yards, Josephine kept Ruby to a walk, to let Rose get used to the sway. Then Rose giggled again. "Can she go faster?"

"She can, and she will. To the top."

"Ye…ssss." Rose crowed the word and twisted her head to look back at Josephine. "I like you and I like Ruby as well."

"Ah, sweetheart." Josephine gave in to temptation and kissed the top of young Rose's head. "I like you too and so does Ruby. She's being very well behaved for us." Was this what it was like to have a child? This blind trust and a feeling you would protect someone with your life? That someone trusted you with their well-being.

I could have this if I marry. She'd examine those emotions later. Would the unstinting love of a child be enough?

Josephine clicked her tongue to ask the horse to move faster and they continued in a brisk walk until they reached the top of the bridleway.

"Which way, sweetheart?" She knew where David had taken them the previous day, but hadn't he said the whole area was riddled with caves and potholes? It was going to be almost impossible to know where to look. She prayed that Rose did indeed have an idea where her brother and his friend might be.

Rose looked back and forth and pointed. "That way, and we need to look for the dragon." She was silent for a minute. "I dunno really if there is much of a castle, mind. Didn't look like it to me. Just the dragon."

That dragon again. And now in the other direction to their ride the day before. A hazy memory of a jagged wall or rock filtered into Josephine's brain, but for the life of her, she couldn't remember if it was something she'd seen recently, or something she had been told about. "What does the dragon look like?" she asked Rose as she leaned over and tied a rag to a bush a few yards away from the bridleway, in the direction they were heading. "Would I know it?"

"I dunno, but if you keep showing our way, someone might."

Hopefully, those rags would be enough to show any followers which direction to proceed in.

"Then I will. Now, let's find your dragon. Is it happy or sad?"

"It's just a dragon, all spiky and scary," Rose said in the tone of a child pandering to a slightly unintelligent adult. "It goes down."

Not an awful lot of help. "Then you keep looking for it and tell me where to go." Rose nodded and Josephine urged Ruby on. For several minutes they rode steadily nearer the base of the crag then Rose pointed to the right. "We need to go that way."

"Through the trees?" That was new territory to Josephine. "Are you sure?"

Rose nodded. "Yes, acos I hid in the trees when Sam and Freddie went down the dragon."

"Down the dragon?" Josephine queried. Was this all a figment of Rose's imagination?

"Yes. You'll see, miss. I heard 'em say if they went into the castle they'd get the treasure. Don't forget to tie a rag to say we've gone that way, eh? 'Cos we want someone to help us if…" She sniffed. "Well, whatever. I bet they get a good hiding when we's get 'em home, eh?" She sounded as if that wouldn't be a bad thing. "Boys, eh?"

"More than likely a scolding, no more." Josephine hoped she could live up to the young girl's faith in their ability to find the lads. "You are showing me the way, and you are a good girl, for reminding me of the rags," Josephine praised her. "I'll do one here and one at the edge of the trees. Must we go through them?"

Rose scrunched up her face as she turned to look at Josephine. "Well, I s'pose we could go around 'em," she said in a voice full of doubt. "But it's a long way. The dragon ain't so far."

"Then I'll trust your judgment, sweetness." After all, she couldn't do much else.

The trees grew close together, and Josephine hoped they didn't run out of rags, or get lost themselves. However, Rose unerringly pointed where they needed to turn, and seemed confident they were going in the proper direction.

Once or twice Josephine thought she saw footprints in the earth, but it was dry underfoot. Little daylight filtered through the thick canopy, but Josephine presumed that also meant not a lot of rain did either.

Gradually, the trees thinned. Josephine looked at the few rags she had left and prayed there would be enough to show in which direction to proceed to those who hopefully followed. Her petticoat would have to be sacrificed otherwise, and she was rather fond of it.

"There." Rose pointed and waved her hand around so it was difficult for Josephine to make out where she indicated. "Over there. That's where the dragon goes down."

Josephine squinted until she noticed something unusual. It looked like a long, ragged gouge out of the ground.

"A gorge?" She hadn't known there was one around. Why hadn't David mentioned it the day before? But then, it was in the opposite direction from where they had visited together. This craggy outcrop they were heading toward, with the deep scoop in the ground to one side, must be several miles away from the places she had ridden past the previous day.

"A what?" Rose asked, perplexed. "I dunno what that is."

"A hole in the ground," Josephine explained. "Big and deep?"

Rose nodded. "Yes, I told you, that's where the dragon lives. He's going into his home. But I can't see a castle. Do you think we gone wrong? But I did foller 'em 'ere. I did."

"I'm sure you did, sweetness. Now, I wonder… Do you think the dragon knocked the castle down with his tail?" Josephine asked. "Swish, swish into bits?" Anything to lift the worried expression from her young companion's face.

It worked. Rose giggled. "Do you really think he's a real live dragon?"

"No, not really, and I can't see a castle either, can you?"

Rose shook her head. "But this is where I saw them, miss, I mean, my lady, honest it is. Then they weren't there and I was worried so I ran home. When he came 'ome later he was sort of excited and secr…secret… You know, not sharing."

"I know, and miss will do. If you say my lady, I will look for my mama."

Rose chuckled again. "Is she very gray...gra... shush?"

"She thinks so." That was for certain. "Right, we better go and see if we can find those pesky boys, eh?"

"Afore the dragon breathes fire in them?" Rose asked in a worried voice. She seemed to fail to remember their conversation of a few seconds earlier. "I wouldn't like that, even if they can be right little rascals with the devil in 'em. It is me brother and his mate, after all."

She sounded so adult with that expression, Josephine bit back a grin. The situation was too serious to treat in a frivolous manner.

"I thought we decided the dragon wasn't real?" she said in a no-nonsense voice. "You know, boys and their silliness. Storybook tales."

Rose smiled. "Ah, I forgot. They are silly, aren't they? I mean, they play with worms 'n' things. Me mam says worms live where they are for a reason, not for boys. Well, then they must have mebbe found the treasure, do you think? And not come back?"

Now Josephine was even more worried, but understood she couldn't show it. "Why would they do that? Boys like their supper too much to do that. Hold on, let me dismount, help you down and tie Ruby up safely. Then we'll see what to do next." Dismounting wasn't as easy as she'd hoped—those darned skirts and petticoats—but she managed, and after lifting Rose down and securing Ruby's reins to a convenient tree, she took Rose's hand. "Right, let's see, shall we?"

They reached the edge of the gorge.

"Look, miss, see? I told you there were a dragon." Rose pointed across the gorge. "It goes down."

Josephine looked in the direction Rose pointed and gulped. The gorge was deep, steep-sided, with scree, scrub and a few trees clinging to the rocky edges, and to her mind scary. However, Rose had been correct. To one side, a set of rocky outcrops did indeed look like the scales of a dragon. Josephine could easily see why it would appeal to two adventurous lads. But treasure? "What is the treasure, do you know?"

Rose shook her head. "Nah, me brother said it was some boy called John's but me dad did tell 'em ages ago it was a load of nonsense."

"Fair enough." She wondered who on earth John could be. Maybe one of the older generation might know? "Now, Rose, what should we do next?"

A faint shout for help told her.

"That's me brother, I reckon, miss," Rose said in a worried voice. "Where is he?"

"I don't know, Rose, but it's the ladies to the rescue." If only David were here to help them. Josephine was out of her depth and knew it. All she could do was hope someone would come and find them, and soon.

Chapter Ten

Hot, perspiring, grimy and tired, David wiped sweat out of his eyes and sighed. "Where have we gone wrong? What other caves are there?" A faint and persistent niggle told him they had missed or forgotten something vital.

Will shrugged. "There aren't."

"There has to be," David persevered. "We must have overlooked somewhere."

"Only those with an opening too small for even them young devils to get through, or them so shallow we could see inside without going in," Will said. Worry tinged his voice and his face was ashen with both weariness and concern. "There's no more caves around here. Hell, Davy, we would have found 'em as kids if there were." It was a sign of his anxiety that he had used the youthful nickname without thought. "We went everywhere."

David nodded. He accepted that was correct, but it was so damn frustrating to think they could be wrong.

"We'll have to hope Bert and the others have better news."

"Bert doesn't," that man said as he walked up to them, fatigue evident in his walk and demeanor. "Not a sniff. I'd even go so far as to swear no bugger been in or over those caves since we did."

"Could the rods have been a red herring?" David asked. He couldn't think of any other reason for them drawing a blank. "To make people think they're here and they've headed, say, to the lake or the river?" Or anywhere.

He looked around, as, along with the rest of the men, grimy, scratched, thirsty and tired, he stood outside the last cave they could search easily and drank some of the water they'd taken with them. "Would they think to be so devious?"

Will swallowed and wiped his mouth on his sleeve as he considered the question and eventually shook his head in a reluctant way. "Not enough time, and we'd've expected the river anyways."

Bert nodded. "He's right."

"Then we have to have missed them somehow." David ran his hand through his hair in vexation and wished he had something to hit to vent his sense of defeat "Dammit, though, where?"

"David, look." Bert pointed back toward the bridleway. They'd long passed formalities. "That looks like young Walker coming up the track. Do you think they're back?"

"Only one way to find out." As a man, they began to walk down the track to meet the youth. When they were within hailing distance, the lad, Billy Walker, as Will told David quietly, "Not all there, but willing and able," began to run.

David caught him as he stumbled and coughed. "M'lord, m'lady said to say it's the dragon," Billy gasped. "She said to hurry to tell yer, there's only me able. Lady Josephine and young Rose have gone to see."

"The dragon?" Will asked as David gave Billy some water and urged him to sip. "You sure, Billy?"

Billy nodded, gulped his mouthful of liquid and cleared his throat. "That were her words. The dragon, oh and a castle and treasure."

"Whose words, Billy?" David asked gently. "Take your time and tell us everything."

"Joe Mannion was left in charge of t'stables, and young Rose and Lady Josephine went for an 'oss. Lady Foster said Lady Josephine 'ad 'eard Rose say she were sure lads went to find the dragon by the castle to get the treasure and she'd show the lady. So she, my lady, told 'em to go get an 'oss and she'd send someone to tell you. She sent me, 'cos Joe were better to stop in case more 'osses were needed. I came as fast as I could. I left me 'oss down there acos I'm not good enough a rider to come up 'ere. I thought of 'oss, you see, and tied him backaways."

"You did well," David told him. "I'll remember. But, bloody hell," he added explosively, "Dragon's Den. How the hell could we have forgotten it? Would they have gone there?"

Will hit his forehead. "The buggers, I bet they have. They've been so full of chatting about caves and stuff I forgot that t'gorge would call to 'em. Best we go there, eh?"

David nodded. "We need to send someone back to let the household know." He turned and scanned the men present. Who seemed most tired and therefore more use back at the house?

"Now, Billy, when you are fit, you go back with...let me see." He named half a dozen men. "Take Mr. Dempster with you. He's at the end of the bridleway."

"Ah, I saw 'im. He said to say he'd do as you wanted."

"Good. Now, we'll probably need gates or a barn door, and water and bandages from the big house. Tom, you're in charge."

Tom Bryars, a burly farmer whose land was nearest to where they stood, nodded. "I've got a couple of new gates waiting to be put up in my barn, and I'll get the missus to hunt out some food for everyone."

"Lady Foster will have that in hand, I'd think. Perhaps Lizzie could go there?"

"I'll sort it. Where do you want 'em? Top of gorge?"

David nodded and waited until the party had departed. Then he turned to his friends. "So, Dragon's Den, I can understand, but a castle and John's treasure?"

Bert sighed. "A few years back, the farm around there was bought by a bloke called Cassel. We knew it as Fiddlers, the youngsters as Cassels. But he was Don, not John."

"Could they have heard wrongly?"

"Mebbe, who knows with lads, but he were just an ordinary bloke, not anyone with more than the rest of us."

David nodded. "No doubt when we find them, we'll find the answer."

* * * *

"Now, Rose, I want you to wait here until I shout and tell you what to do. All right?" Josephine wriggled back from the edge of the gorge, where she had spent several minutes stretched out on her front to study the best way to get to the ground below. She dusted her dirty hands on her already mucky skirts, took hold of Rose's hand and looked at the little girl. "It's very important you do exactly as I say, sweetness. I won't know what I need until I get down." She looked at the rock face and wished she'd been more adventurous as a child. However, she was fit and agile and needs must. It was a pity she had a dress on and not pantaloons or breeches like the men, but she couldn't take it off. It would not be seemly, and her chemise would be scant protection against scratches and scrapes, to say nothing of gorse and nettles — or worse.

Since that first cry for help, they had heard nothing more. "I'm going to wrap these last three rags around my waist, under my dress, in case I need them."

"Mebbe's you should wrap 'em round your fingers so they doesn't get too scratched, or would that make it hard to hold on?" Rose asked. She seemed in a much more positive frame of mind now she had something to concentrate on. "Acos you'll ruin your gloves else. And tie the water bottle in one and sling it over your back."

Josephine thought over Rose's words. "I might need the rags to be clean. They'd be best tucked under my dress." She suited her actions to her words. "My gloves will do. But what a good idea about the water. I'll take one and leave one for you. Now, if they shout again, then tell them I'm on my way and ask if they can show me where they are somehow. Maybe wave. And you shout to me as well. Yes?"

As soon as Rose replied in the affirmative, Josephine scanned the rock face to determine her route. Although at first glance it had appeared sheer, she could tell that, in fact, it wasn't so. There were outcrops and cracks with more than enough foliage to give her decent handholds. She could see how tempting it would be for young boys to climb down the scales of the so-called dragon, but for her own descent, she noticed many more less dramatic but probably safer routes to take.

The first few yards were the worst. There the rock face was steep and crumbly. Several small — and not so small — rocks and stones tumbled down the scree with a noise like thunder. Twice one bounced off her shoulder and she was glad of the thickness of her gown. No doubt she would be bruised.

"Miss, you all right?" Rose shouted. "I ain't heard any more."

"Fine," Josephine called back. She risked a quick look around and gulped. There was still a long way to go. "About halfway down." She was breathless and her body ached from the effort of stretching for hand and footholds. Without haste, she moved downward in a careful step-by-step, steady manner. If only one of the boys would call out again, she would be a lot happier. At least she would know she was climbing to the proper area.

A brisk wind teased her skirt and she uttered a word her mama would have washed her mouth out for. It was difficult enough to move without her skirts hindering her progress.

This stretch was tricky. For a couple of yards, the hand and footholds were scarce and at one point she had only the roots of a spindly bush to hold her. She struggled on and breathed a sigh of relief when her feet settled into a deep and wide crevice. She let her body sag for several precious moments then took another look down. "Only a few yards now," she shouted, and hoped both Rose and the boys — wherever they were — could hear her. No one replied. Undaunted, she set off again and a few minutes later was rewarded by her feet touching solid ground.

At that point, the gorge was around a hundred yards wide, she supposed. To one side of her, it narrowed to end in a semicircle, where a trickle of water showed on the mainly bare rocks. Josephine presumed it would be a proper waterfall in the winter, although now there wasn't even enough water to create a pool at the base let alone a stream over the valley floor. Probably just as well. She didn't want to have to cope with a paddle and wet feet as well as taking care she didn't twist her ankle. Nearer to where she had climbed down was the so-called dragon, and at the far end she rather thought the gorge opened out. No doubt if she had known the area she could have walked in via a track or some such thing. However, as far as she could tell, there wasn't one nearby, so presumably it would have taken an age to get to. Plus, she had now achieved two new things that day. Riding astride and climbing down a cliff, neither of which was to be sneezed at.

"I'm down," she called, even though she had no idea if anyone could hear her. "Going toward the dragon." She had to start somewhere. Very carefully, Josephine began to pick her way across the uneven floor of the gorge. It was chillier there. Very little sunlight reached over half of the area, and the shadows were longer, more menacing than those that danced through the trees above. The goosebumps on her arms were of the unpleasant something-isn't-quite-right sort, not those delicious ones David's touch had given her.

David!

She prayed he would somehow turn up like a knight on a white charger and not rescue her exactly, but aid her. However, unless someone had managed to find him, it was likely the next however long was up to her.

She cast her mind back to remember the youngsters' names. "Sam? Freddie? Can you hear me?"

Silence. She took several steps toward a crack in the rock, very near the base, and shouted again.

Was it an echo or did someone really answer? Josephine scanned the area. "Sam? Freddie? Where are you?"

"Down 'ere." The faint shout appeared to come from a few feet in front of her. Almost as if it originated underground.

"Keep calling so I can find you. I just need to shout up to people at the top." She thought it sounded better to say people rather than one little girl. Josephine checked her position, walked back to where she'd scrambled down the gorge sides and cupped her hands. "Rose? Can you hear me?"

"Yes, miss." The reply was faint but there. That was one thing less to worry about.

"I've found them. Tell whoever arrives to come down the way I did and head to the left then look for a hole near the bottom of the cliff." She thought that would be the simplest way to describe where she was. "Can you remember that?"

"Course, miss. You be careful, acos I'm all by m'self up 'ere. S'long walk 'ome."

Bless her.

"I will, and you won't be alone for long. You're a big, brave girl." Josephine took a deep breath. *Right, get on with it, it's all down to me for now.* She made her way slowly across the uneven ground toward the spot where she had heard the lads. "Boys? Time to shout again. Can you give me a clue where you are?"

"Down the hole. At bottom of dragon. But who are you?"

That was as clear as mud. "I'm a friend of Lady Foster's. Are either of you injured?" Josephine walked with care toward the fissure, which she now noticed extended from the cliff face into the ground. The ground was uneven, boggy and rocky in turn. The last thing she needed was to hurt herself. Little use she'd be then.

Behind her, the sun rose over the horizon and gave her more light. She didn't spare a second glance to see if the sunrise was spectacular.

"Did you fall?" It was hard to keep her voice level and not appear as anxious as she was as she called down to the boys. "And are either of you hurt?"

"Not down it, miss," the speaker, presumably young Sam Bonsall, said with what sounded like a sob. "But Freddie slipped and some rocks and stones and muck fell on 'im when we was in 'ere and nows I can't move him. An' he just sorta groans a bit."

That didn't sound good.

"Ah, well, hold on." She reached the edge of the hole, pleased to see the sides did not slope too steeply, even if on first glance there were few hand or footholds. "Can you tell me if you can see this?" Josephine unwrapped one of the rags and dangled it over the edge.

For a few worrying seconds there was silence.

"Ah, yes, miss." Sam's voice echoed up to her.

"Now, how far above your head is it? Can you touch it?" She held her breath.

"Nah, it's mebbes higher than I could ever jump."

Damn. She supposed it was too much to hope it would be that easy.

"Quite far then?"

"Um, a bit, but I reckon if Freddie were able to move and I stood on his shoulders I would. But he can't."

"Never mind. Now, if I come down, I won't land on Freddie and squash him, will I?"

Sam almost chuckled. "Nah, he's back a bit and I'll keep out of the way."

"Good, then let me just make sure that our rescuers know where we are, and then I'm coming in. Put the kettle on."

Sam did chuckle then.

Josephine tied one of her remaining rags around the nearest tree and, after a swift scan of her surrounds, rearranged a few rocks into a rough arrow pointing to the cave-hole. She closed her eyes and offered up a brief but heartfelt prayer, ignored the butterflies in her stomach and the fact that she'd never done anything remotely similar before and stretched out on the ground. Slowly, and with great care, she twisted until her feet, then her legs dangled over the edge of the hole.

* * * *

The small girl with a tear-streaked face who stood next to a horse screamed as she saw the riders approach her and jiggled from one foot to the other in impatience.

"Dad, Dad, it's our Sam. He's down near the dragon, though Miss says there aren't any left no more, but she's gone to rescue 'em and I've got to be a big girl and look after Ruby here and wait for you and tell you…" She sobbed. "Tell you…they ain't dead. It's all acos of Boy John and his castle."

David let out the breath he hadn't realized he held as he slid to the ground and wrapped his horse's reins around a sturdy branch. Ever since Billy had come upon them, an icy fear had gripped him and a huge lump of dread had lodged in his stomach. Worry for the boys, fear for his lady and an urge to put her over his knee for giving him such a fright and placing herself in danger all vied to be the uppermost emotion. Along with the desire to kiss her senseless.

Then carry her off and make love to her until she agreed that they were made for each other.

"Boy John?" he said quietly. "Not just a mistake for 'Don', then?"

Will shrugged. "Who knows except them young rapscallions?"

Who may or may not have been found by Josephine. Who may or may not be injured. That unwanted thought sent a slither of apprehension down his spine.

Do not even think about that. She will be fine. She had to be.

David didn't have time to dissect his thoughts. He knelt on the ground next to Rose.

"You'll get all dirty," Rose said. "Your mum won't half go on."

"Never mind, you're more important," David said. He had other, more pressing things to worry about than his buckskins. The boys, Josephine and how to rescue them for a start.

"I'm so glad my lady thought to bring you," he said in a soft, unthreatening voice. "What can you tell us?"

Rose sniffed as her papa gathered her into his arms and sat with his back to a convenient tree trunk.

"Miss and me heard the boys so she went to see if she could get to them. She said she's gone down near the dragon so you've got to do it as well, and look for a hole near it. And now she's got into the hole and what if the dragon eats 'er?"

"Didn't she say dragons don't live anymore?" David spoke to soothe Rose, even as his throat closed up and his skin went clammy. She'd done what? He'd like to lock her up for a month.

"Ah, she said. I forgot."

"Not anywhere. So it's not a dragon's den. Just a pothole." That potholes often led into caving systems with a myriad of tunnels and rivers, he didn't dare think about.

"Yes, she said that, but the boys are in the hole and so she had to go and help them. I'm gonna be like her when I grow up." Rose sounded very definite. "And you need to go and help her, acos even if we hate to say it, we ain't as strong in body as you men, even if we is in mind," Rose finished in triumph, as she obviously repeated something she'd been told or overheard. "But without us, you'd've been stumped."

"I don't doubt it for a second." David slanted a swift look at Will. "When Bert gets here, ask him to keep an eye open for the rest with the trestle. I've a feeling we will need it. Otherwise I would have wagered my last guinea they'd have reappeared before now. I'll go down, you take Rose home and come back. The others will stop here with me."

"I aint goin' back. Miss said to stop here so I will," Rose said in an obstinate voice David didn't expect from one so young. "I promised."

David glanced helplessly at Will, who shrugged. "She's as strong-willed as your lady, I reckon."

"Miss made me promise not to move."

David doubted Josephine had meant it so literally, but thought it best not to upset Rose. "Then you must stay here, but now do exactly as your pa tells you. Agreed?"

Rose bit her lip. "'Til Miss comes back?"

David nodded. "Until she comes back. Would you do that?"

Rose sighed in a way David would guarantee she'd heard her mother do. "All right then, but hurry up, will you? I'm fair clemmed."

When was a child ever not? David indicated his saddlebags. "There's a pie or two in there. Just save something for the boys." He gathered up everything he thought he might need, including his hip flask, and slung a bag over his back before he glanced at Will and the other men standing around.

"Can one of you come to the top of the slope? Listen out for anything I might shout. I'll check what's what and let you know what the status quo is."

One, Davy Flixton, nodded. "I will. What else do you need?"

David mentally checked the contents of his bag. "Apart from the trestle, nothing except positive thoughts and good luck." He made his way to the edge of the gorge, checked how crumbly the soil was and levered himself over the grass roots and scree. "I'll need plenty of that. I've not been over this edge for nigh on twenty-five years."

Will let out a bark of laughter. "And it were a lot easier in those days, even if it did seem like the side of a mountain."

It might not appear so high these days, but he was a lot heavier and the scree less firm. As if to reaffirm that thought, loose stones accompanied him as he climbed lower. Several hit his head and arms and one bounced off his shoulder so hard he cursed under his breath. If he got down in one piece, it would be a miracle.

Miracles did happen — didn't they?

* * * *

Josephine washed her mouth out with the tiniest amount of water she could manage and passed the container to Sam. She sat back on her knees as she surveyed the two boys in front of her. The amount of light from the hole above and behind her was negligible and ahead all she could discern was a yawning blackness.

Freddie Killer, dark-haired and skinny as a rake, lay at an awkward angle, with his eyes closed. His breathing was shallow and interspersed with a low groan every so often. Josephine could see that his right arm was twisted in an unnatural position and what she was convinced was a sliver of bone poked through his shirt. One of his boots had come off and Sam Bonsall, tow-headed and grubby-faced, had put it near the entrance.

While Josephine surveyed their surroundings — not that there was a lot to see — Sam stuffed his mouth with food and grunted his thanks. When he'd finally swallowed the last mouthful, Josephine decided he might be ready to answer her questions.

"Now tell me all about it," she suggested in an unthreatening voice.

"Me dad'll kill me," Sam said gloomily. "An' if he don't, Will's ma will. See, we knows we aren't supposed to come down the holes or in the caves. Both our dads told us it were dangerous. But we know they did it, so why shouldn't we, eh?" he asked passionately. "And when we heard of that boy John's treasure, well, why not?"

She could understand his reasoning even if she didn't condone it.

"Boy John's treasure?" she queried. "What's that?"

Sam shrugged. "Dunno, we just overheard old man Cassel, him who bought the farm over by, sayin' he were sure Boy John's was in his cave, not just at the castle. Well, stands to reason it's got to be that John's treasure that were in the caves, and it'd be a right fortune. Reckon if we found it, it might be finders keepers or sommat. At least a reward."

Did he mean Blue John? The gem David had talked about? But surely she remembered David saying that was only found around Castleton, which was a fair few miles away. Was that the castle? Had the boys misheard somehow?

"Did you find anything?" she asked Sam, as if it wasn't overimportant. "Or was the cupboard bare? You know, like Old Mother Hubbard."

Sam sniggered and shook his head. "We didn't hardly look afore them bits of muck and stuff started down on us. Then, as we was coming out, Fred slipped on some stones and, well, that were it."

A hail of small stones and earth fell onto her head and Josephine cursed. "Has this happened a lot?" she asked as Sam brushed her shoulder clean for her. "The stones and things?"

"Ah, a bit. More and more, really."

Josephine shivered as the possible consequences of that hit her. If more fell and they were smothered or cut off, the results were unthinkable.

"Sam, we need to move Freddie near the opening," she said, and hoped the fear she experienced didn't manifest in her tone. "After all, he can't shield himself from soil and stones, can he? And if more fall, one might hurt him and— Run to the entrance now," she added urgently as the next shower of stones descended. She leaned over Freddie and bit back an agonized groan as several large rocks bounced off her shoulders.

"Nah." Sam's voice wavered. "Come on, miss, we do it together. What do I need to do?" Sam asked her in a stronger tone. "He's me mate and mates help each other."

"True, and as I now consider you and Freddie my mates, we'd better move him, eh?"

Hopefully, the idea of mates helping mates meant that David was on his way to aid her. Sadly, they were not true mates. But could they be? Josephine turned her mind away from what might be to what was. A pressing need to move.

"Where did he hurt himself, his leg and his arm?" she asked Sam as she carefully ran her fingers over Freddie's head.

"Nah, just his arm, but he curled up like that and I durn't move him."

"Good boy. It was wise not to. Now, though, knowing where he is hurt makes it easier." Without any regard for propriety, Josephine found her last two rags. Sam didn't blink, in fact she wondered if he'd even realized he was getting a bird's-eye view of her petticoats. All his attention was focused on his friend.

"Now let me see if we can tie his arm to his chest and then drag him. How does that sound?" she said once she'd rearranged her skirt. One side had a long, jagged tear in it, where, she assumed, she'd caught it on a rock. Josephine shrugged philosophically. No doubt it would be a lot worse before they returned home.

Another rumble of stones and soil brought that thought to an abrupt end to be replaced by the horrific one of...*if we get out.*

"Sam, it won't be comfortable for Freddie, but I can't see how else we can move him." There wasn't enough room to lift the lad. "We must, though. This roof is collapsing by the minute."

"Hard, but we'll do it." Sam appeared to grow in stature at her assumption — flawed though it was — that they could manage. "And the roof has been at it ever since we got down into the cave. After all, that's what did for ole Fred here."

"Then let's see what we can do." By dint of pushing, shoving and thanking the Lord Freddie didn't really come to, they anchored Freddie's arm somewhat clumsily to his body. Then Josephine fixed Sam with a hard stare. "This will hurt him, so it follows it will hurt you because you are his friend. But" — she coughed as yet more stones fell — "we have to do it. It is not safe here. Do you understand?"

Sam nodded, white-faced under the grime that dusted his skin, but resolute. "I get it, miss. It'll be all' right. I won't cuss and he's too gone to be able to."

Josephine thought she'd probably cuss enough under her breath for the lot of them. "Right then, on three. We will have to drag him one leg each." Heaven knew what other injuries he would sustain, but better than being killed. "So on three...one, two...three."

They heaved.

Chapter Eleven

Whether it was the rising sun, which had a hard time to appear between the ever-growing black clouds, or the ominous stillness in the air that made him twitchy, David wasn't sure. The atmosphere was heavy, sultry in the wrong way even, and tiny black thunderflies began to appear and settle on him.

He climbed cautiously down the rock face as fast as he dared. Hand and footholds were a lot easier to find than in their younger days, but conversely a lot tighter for his now larger hands and feet to get into. At one point, a seemingly sturdy root snapped and he swore as he scrabbled for purchase on a large boulder.

Once he thought he heard a rumble of thunder but, with the noise of his boots scraping and his heart beating, he couldn't be sure. It could easily have been his stomach. Food seemed a distant memory.

David made his slow and steady way ever downward. Once he stopped and wiped his clammy hands on his buckskins in turn. A stone bounded off his head, followed by a shower of smaller pebbles, and he stopped abruptly, several yards from the bottom. When the bombardment stopped, David shook some muck from his head and eyebrows and took a cautious glance upward. Will looked worriedly down from the top of the scree.

"You okay, Davy? That was a helluva fall."

"Am I mistaken in thinking this scree is a lot less stable than when we were lads?" he asked. "I swear we didn't bring half as much down, and even though we were lighter there were three of us."

"I don't rightly know," Will said in an anxious voice. "I've not been around here for years."

"Then fingers crossed I make it down in one piece." David began to move again and didn't add… 'And that we get the boys and my lady up in one piece each.' That would be understood, and worried over without him heightening the disquiet. He scrambled down the last three or four yards and breathed a sigh of relief when he touched the ground.

"When I get them, is it easier to go down the gorge toward the farm and home via Apple Lane?" he called up. It had been so long since he'd been in this exact area, his memory may well be faulty.

"Ah, longer, but probably better for injuries. Shall I send the trestle down that way when it gets here? Might be better for it, else it might get broken."

A further rumble of thunder echoed around the gorge. "How long would it take?" There was silence while he reckoned Will made mental calculations.

"'Bout an hour to you from here and mebbes two back home. There's only a plank over stream unless you go around by Becketts." Using the plank wouldn't work with a body on a trestle. It was dangerous enough with all your limbs unencumbered.

"Hmm." David thought over their options. Via the bridge at Becketts added a good couple of miles to the journey. "That's probably too long. Send the trestle down here on ropes and we'll decide then."

He went over the instructions young Rose had relayed to him. It sounded easy, but instead of getting lighter, the early morning was rapidly appearing like dusk, or beyond. A definite rumble of thunder sounded to the west followed by a second, which he would wager was closer. Time was of the essence if he was to find Josephine and the boys and get them up to the others. He well knew that if it rained to any great extent, the bottom of the gorge could be flooded.

"I'll shout when I know more." He waited to hear Will's reply in the affirmative and began to scour the area.

"Josephine?" He projected his voice until it bounced off the walls of the gorge and reverberated around him over and over again.

"David?" The shout was faint but he would have sworn it came from near the base of the cliff. In the area Rose had reported was the place to head toward. For the first time since he'd discovered Josephine had headed out with Rose, he allowed himself to hope, just a little, that all might turn out reasonably well.

"Keep calling." He'd save his breath and ask all the other questions he needed answers to when he found her and hopefully the boys.

"Near the cliff, and, oh, David, please, come as fast as you can. It's caving in…" Her voice faded and he caught the noise of a sharp cough and splutter.

What? He began to run, heedless of how close he was to an injury. As he skidded over a damp area of long grass, he saw a rag, an arrow of stones and a hole in the base of the cliff that opened up like a monster's mouth. Gaping and intimidating.

David stopped abruptly and levered himself to the ground before he looked down over the edge.

Two worried and grimy faces peered back up at him.

Two? "Hello, fancy meeting you here," he said with an insouciance he didn't feel. "What are you doing in a hole?"

Sam giggled. "Ah..."

"Trying to get out now," Josephine said in a raspy voice. "But it is too far for me to climb, and Sam will not use me for a stepladder to get out."

"I can't, miss, I needs to stay and help you with Freddie, and you agreed." The uneven tones of a youth whose voice had only half broken floated up to David.

"Of course you must," he said gravely. "No true gentleman would leave a lady in potential danger."

"You're right, and Sam is very much a gentleman." Josephine coughed. "Ugh, sorry, that last shower of muck fell into my mouth. Sam and I have dragged Freddie as far as we can. I think it is only his arm that is broken. Or it was before we decided it was best to move to where we might have a better chance of not being entombed. But, David, we need to get him out. The roof is crumbling and I fear this cave is at the end of its lifespan. I don't want it to be the end of ours."

That pronouncement, said in such a prosaic way, made his skin go clammy. "Give me a second." He stood and, now he knew where he was, took scant seconds to reach the base of the scree.

"Will? I need one of you down here now. We need another sturdy rope tied to the top and dropped down. It is imperative that we get the lads and my lady out as soon as we can."

"You found 'em?" The relief in Will's voice was obvious. "Thank the Lord."

David didn't have the heart to tell him how worrying the situation was. "Found but not safe yet. It's a cave below the overhang, and it's not that stable. I imagine it's man-made, not natural. I don't remember it from the odd occasion we came around here. I'll leave a rag outside."

"Got it, and I'll come down."

"Fine." David didn't wait to hear more. He went straight back to where he had to be.

With whom he had no doubt was the most important person in his life.

Three minutes later, he had anchored a rag with a rock, tied one end of a rope firmly around the trunk of a sturdy sapling and the other to his waist, and was ready to descend. "Will I kick anyone as I come down?"

"No, we won't let you. We value our skulls, even if they are thick."

David smiled to himself as he began the descent. At least Josephine could still make a joke.

The scramble down wasn't hard when you had a rope to use, but he could understand how difficult it must have been for Josephine, especially as she would have been encumbered by her skirts and petticoats. He reached the bottom with only a single maneuver of his legs by someone.

When his feet finally touched the ground, he took a deep breath and clapped Sam on the shoulder. "Sam?"

"Ah, that's me."

"And Freddie." Josephine nodded. "To your right."

"And you?"

"I'm here, unharmed apart from two broken fingernails."

"Thank the Lord."

"That I broke my nails? How ungentlemanly, eh, Sam?"

Sam guffawed. "Me mam'd agree with you, I reckon."

"Fingernails can be repaired. A broken skull cannot." Unheeding of Sam, David dragged Josephine to him, plastered her as close to him as he could and kissed her long and hard. She returned the salute with fervor. Her lips softened and parted under his. David teased her tongue and drank in her soul. He didn't even realize he had moved his hands to her bottom and started to caress her through her skirt in tiny but ever-increasing circles. For once in his life, he truly let his senses dictate to him and ignored everything else.

"Cor."

Sam's one word spoken in a voice of awe made him break the contact and laugh, even though he half wished the lad to perdition. It was perhaps as well Sam was there and he had brought David to his senses, so David stopped before he actually got started.

Out of the corner of his eyes, David watched as Josephine took a deep breath, licked her lips — damn her, that sent his desire soaring and his body tightening — and smoothed all the loose strands of her hair from her face. Even dirty and bedraggled, he wanted her.

Mine. Very caveman, but then, they were in a cave after all.

"Very 'cor' indeed," he said to Sam with a wink and a cheerfulness he didn't feel. It was so dark now, he doubted that Sam could see the gesture. Which thankfully meant he would also not be able to see the state of David's body. Aroused and throbbing was a mild description.

"And that, young Sam, is what a gentleman does when he finds the lady he loves is unharmed. Even if he does have the knotty problem of how to get her and two young lads out of a hole in the ground."

Sam sniggered. "Ah, there is that."

David perused the lad's face for a moment. "Can you climb that rope?"

"Yes, but I need to stop with Freddie." Sam's expression was mulish. "Mates don't leave mates."

"They do if it is for both their safety. And the well-being of a lady. You need to be our scout," David said evenly but with enough force to show he meant what he said. "I am relying on you. Your pa is on his way down. You have to get up there so you can show him where to come. I'll sort Freddie out, so when your pa gets here we can lift him and Lady Josephine out. Deal?"

He waited, his pulse overfast as Sam bit his lip. Slowly, the lad nodded to David. "Deal."

David let his breath out in a soft whoosh. *Thank goodness.*

Josephine watched as Sam shimmied up the rope with ease and scrambled over the lip of the hole.

"The agility of youngsters," David said wryly. "It would have taken me three times as long."

"And me four." Josephine gave in to the luxury of leaning on David and absorbing some of his strength.

He looked down at her and kissed the top of her head. Not a sexual want-to-learn-more kiss, but one of reassurance and, she fancied, strong emotion.

"All right?" he asked softly. "Everything will work out."

"I hope so, and I am fine now you are here. I will be even more so when we get Freddie out. I have a nasty premonition this cave is not at all stable." As if to agree with her, thunder rumbled and once more several large stones fell from the roof a few yards farther in. "The boys were convinced John's treasure was here. In Cassel's place." She searched her mind. What had Sam's exact words been? "Sam said, and I hope I remember this correctly, that they overheard Cassel saying he was certain Boy John's treasure was in his cave. Cassel's cave I presume, not John's. I did wonder if he meant Blue John and Castleton and the boys got it wrong. Whichever, here they arrived, here Freddie got hurt and here we are. I saw no sight of any treasure, but then I have been more concerned with the boys' welfare than supposed treasure."

"And here we will soon not be," David said. "Time, I think, is of the essence. Plus, if there were any treasure, I suspect it would have been found by now. And it certainly would not be Blue John. Too far away from the only place it is found. Now it's time for you to go up."

"What? Why? I thought mates stayed together," she said. "Does this mean you don't want me?" She got a mouthful of earth and spluttered before she had a chance to finish her sentence.

In the gloom, David's teeth showed as he grinned. "I do. Very much. But not here, and sadly it cannot be now. However, hold on to that thought for later."

"I didn't mean—" she began indignantly.

He put his finger over her lips. "Don't spoil it and dash my hopes."

Josephine's pulse sped up. Goosebumps dotted her arms and her breasts became heavy. Was it wrong to want to suck that digit? How forward.

"I did," David said in a tone that curled her toes and sent darts of arousal through her body. "Mean it. But first, I want you to go up. It will give me more room to maneuver Freddie. And you can help me guide him."

It sounded plausible, but… "You're not just trying to get me out of the way for my own safety, are you?"

His arms tightened for a second and Josephine felt the shudder that went through him. "Of course I am," he answered, in a tone that made her realize he meant what he said. "Well, partly. But there is more to it than that. I do need the space, you can guide me from up there, and if you are out of here, that is one less person for me to worry about. One less thing to divert my mind from the best way to rescue Freddie."

Put like that, she couldn't do anything but agree. "I was never that good at climbing."

"If you slip, I promise to cushion your fall. Just make sure you miss the delicate parts of my body. After all, when we are wed, I do want to be able to give you enjoyment and father our children."

That was going a bit too far. "I have not said I will marry you." Although, maybe she might consider it a bit more later. After all, didn't his care and concern now show there was more to him than met the eye? Would either of her parents have done even half as much as he had? An almost-forgotten memory of her as a nine-year-old trapped on the upper story of an old barn when the ladder had disintegrated flashed into her mind. Her parents hadn't even realized she was missing, much less come to her aid. Only the fact that she'd managed to open the door through which bales were hauled inside the hayloft and shouted to a passing cowman had rescued her from a goodness-knows-how-long incarceration.

She'd been missing for almost four hours. Her governess had been frantic. She had hunted high and low, then had told Josephine's parents their daughter was nowhere to be found. That Josephine had told Miss Govering she was going to collect leaves for their nature table and would be back within an hour.

Evidently, her father had merely said, "Well, if someone has the time to look, so be it. She'll come home when she is hungry." It was not a comforting thought to think that could be the normal behavior for a parent.

"I need to think more."

"You have a day or so to think," David agreed. "You haven't said you will be my wife. Not yet." He hugged her.

She gasped at his words. There was no way she could deliberate on any of it at that moment.

"But I live in hope, my love. You might not believe me, but I love you." It appeared he'd forgotten Freddie could be all ears and would no doubt report back to everyone what David said. "I never thought I would feel this way about anyone. You are my sun and my moon. Any children would be my stars."

Josephine swayed and clutched his shoulders. *What a time to say that.*

"Now please," he added in a strained voice. "Please, up you go and let me get young Fred ready for when the rest of the help arrives."

Time to show she was a capable woman, even if her hands shook and her mouth was dry.

"I don't suppose there is much point in telling you to avert your eyes, is there?" she said in an attempt to lighten the atmosphere.

"No," David replied cheerfully. "I need a good memory to hold on to whilst I get Freddie and me out. Now go. For the sooner you are up, the sooner I have room to move and then once Will is here, we can do what is necessary."

Josephine gave in to temptation and kissed David's cheek. It was the only part of him she could reach with ease. "Right, so the best way is to use the rope as a handrail and sort of walk up? Like Sam did."

"Just like that. But I will tie the end of the rope around your waist as well." He didn't say why and she chose not to ask.

Within seconds, she was three feet up the slope, and thankful she'd had the forethought to slip her riding gloves in her pocket and had thus been able to now wear them. The soft leather not only protected her hands, it gave her purchase.

"Nice ankles."

Trust him. At least he hadn't said 'nice thighs'.

Josephine bit her lip as she concentrated. Hand by hand, one foot after another, she inched her way upward.

"You are doing well, love. Over halfway now. Shut your eyes." The last three words cracked out like a whip.

A few pebbles tumbled past her. It was nerve-wracking. Why, oh why hadn't she been more of a tomboy as a child? Her papa had remarked disparagingly about her boyish figure and lack of curves often enough.

'If it's not bad enough she's female, she doesn't even have a figure to show for it,' he'd said on more than one occasion. *'No womanly curves. How will that encourage a husband? Bony, all arms and legs.'*

When other girls of her age had begun to burgeon, she had stayed stubbornly boyish. Of course, she had eventually become shapely, but never to any great degree. Josephine had always thought she was happy in her skin, and her lack of obvious curves didn't bother her. But perhaps those scathing pronouncements from her papa had stung more than she'd realized. Was it that which had turned her against the sort of things both sexes of children might get up to in the country? Or was it that she preferred sketching and reading to climbing and fishing anyway?

"Love, Will is above you now and has a hold of the rope. Move again." She nodded, aghast at how she'd forgotten where she was and what she was doing. As the rope tightened, it became easier to climb, and within a few minutes Will helped her over the edge and to her feet.

"There now, miss, I mean, my lady. Our Sam has some water for you and a blanket. You sit down a sec, while I see what Davy wants me to do next."

Josephine nodded, too out of breath to speak, and let Sam guide her to sit down on a blanket.

"I've got a chicken leg as well if you fancy it," the lad said as he handed over a bottle of water. "The men brought more food."

"Thank goodness, eh?"

Sam sighed. "Ah, 'cos it's a long time since yesterday's scran, ain't it?"

"A very long time." Josephine ate a mouthful of the succulent meat before she spoke again. "I don't even know what time it is. I seem to have smashed my watch." The tiny timepiece attached to her jacket had somehow been cracked. Most of the face was missing and only one hand remained. Just as well it held no great sentimental value to her. "It only has the minute hand, which isn't a lot of good." Even that was bent.

Sam squinted at the dark clouded sky. "No sun to tell either."

There was a flash of lightning to their west and he began to count. He got to twenty before they heard the thunder. "A goodly long way away. Me dad says if you count slowly like I did you can tell where lightning's gonna land. Over up the peak, I reckon. So we're safe for now."

"Good." After all the alarms and excursions of the day so far, and the revelations about David — and herself — the last thing she wanted was to be struck by lightning. There was too much to discover about what might be. "Now, as we seem to be the only two around here, what can we do to help your papa and Davy when they bring Freddie up?" She realized she'd used David's nickname, but didn't worry about it. This was not a time for formality, anything but.

"Mebbes we need to find somewhere for shelter?" Sam suggested. "Or make one. 'Cos the others haven't got the trestle back here yet, and if it rains we'll need to keep Freddie dry." He made it sound as though there was nothing wrong in him, and others, standing in the open in a thunderstorm, as long as Freddie was dry.

"True, so what do you suggest?"

Josephine watched how Sam preened as he realized she needed his advice. She wasn't going to make any suggestions unless he became stumped. He needed to be kept busy so he couldn't think about the predicament his friend was still in.

"Never under a tree in a thunderstorm," Sam said sagely. "So lemme think. Mebbes we can find sommat at edge of rock face? 'Cos if it rains it usually comes from behind it. A crevice or a little cave or sommat should keep most of it off." He grinned an urchin grin that for once made him look his age. "One that's not gonna fall in."

Josephine laughed. "Preferably, eh? Very well, let's look. Keep your ears open for your papa and Davy if they shout."

"Well, what now then?" Will hung over the edge of the cave, a dark outline against the lowering and menacing sky. "Can we get him out?"

David didn't bother to give the answer he ought. That there was no 'can' about it, they had to, and soon. Even in the few minutes since Josephine had begun to climb, there had been several more falls and now the cave was half its size. The back, where Sam had intimated Freddie had been injured, was a jumble of rocks, stones and earth. There was hardly enough room for David and Freddie in the space left, and David had to stoop.

"I don't want to wait for the rescue team," he said slowly as he considered his options. "This place is falling in. There's not enough room for me to get him on my back. I think we're going to have to risk me tying him to the rope and then attempting to push him up until you can reach him."

Not the ideal way, but perhaps the only one.

He knelt down and studied Freddie's face. It was so dark it was hard to tell but was there a little more color in the lad's cheeks? He touched one carefully and was rewarded by a faint groan. "Freddie, lad, can you hear me?" Freddie's eyelids moved a little.

"Da?"

"No, it's Davy, your da's friend."

"Where's Sam?" The words were hesitant and low, but David could hear the worry behind them.

"Sam's up top." He used the words most likely to work for Freddie in his dazed state. "We need to get us there as well. You first because of your arm."

"Me arm?"

"Don't move it," David said urgently. "Sam and Miss Josephine tied it to your body so you don't hurt it more." He used 'miss' rather than 'lady' on purpose, guessing it would be less worrying to Freddie. He wouldn't want to think he'd caused any trouble for a lady. "So you'll be a one-armed climber, eh? Well, not really a climber, more a helper. Now, how about we see what we can do to get you out?"

Freddie nodded and moved one leg. His boot scratched the earth at the side of the wall and a crack appeared above the point he'd touched.

"Careful," David warned the youth. "This cave doesn't want to be a cave anymore. We need to get out before it's a pile of earth. If I step over you, do you think you can wriggle to the bottom of the entrance? Very carefully."

"There ain't room for you. I'm up tight."

"Nonsense, of course there is." There wasn't but that was not the point. He had to get Freddie to move. "Once I begin to step over you, you move."

David wondered if he dared brace his arm on the roof. There was no dare, crouched as he was, it was his arm or his back, and surely his arm would be best. "Right, ready to move... Now move."

David arched one leg across Freddie's body as the lad obediently wriggled as best he could and left a few inches behind him. Another squirm and David was able to put one hand next to his leg. For all the world, he imagined he must look like a very ungainly crab.

"That's it, Freddie," he encouraged the lad. "A bit more and I can stop hovering over you like a big, bad bat."

Freddie managed half a laugh. "Mebbe a vampire."

"Grief, I hope not. I prefer ale to blood. Right, so now I'm going to try and lean over you in a better way. Sam's dad is at the top. He'll help pull you up. First, though. If I push and shove, can you stand upright next to the opening?" He hoped so, because otherwise the next few minutes would be horrendous.

Freddie coughed. "Blood...er, blooming mucky down here, eh?"

"True, so...?"

Freddie sniggered. "Well, if I doesn't I'll be hauled arse up, so I betters try."

That was one way of putting it.

Chapter Twelve

Josephine would have preferred to pace. To nibble her nail, or bite her lip, and worry. However, one look at Sam's face told her it might not be a good idea. Not if she wanted even half a chance to keep Sam calm. He bounced with energy, most of which Josephine recognized was nerves and worry over his friend. Plus, she surmised, anxiety over what the outcome of their adventures would be.

"Probably be told we can't go anywhere without a grownup 'til we're twenty," he grumbled to Josephine once his father was out of earshot. "Or made to take Rose with me everywhere, and she's a pest."

"Without Rose, you'd still be down the pothole," Josephine said mildly. "She needs a thank you from you, not a moan."

Sam had the grace to look ashamed. "Ah, well, for a kid and a girl at that, she's not bad, I reckon."

He'd had a cuff around the ear and a hug from his parent, along with a stern admonishment to do as Josephine told him.

"He's been a tower of strength," Josephine said sincerely. "I would have been lost without him."

While Will stayed ready to haul on the rope or not, as David directed, Sam and Josephine scouted around the area. Between them, they decided on a fairly low but deep crevice, which after consultation they concluded would provide the best shelter for two or even three people, as long as they didn't mind being cramped.

"Better cramped than drenched," Josephine said prosaically. "That sky looks very menacing to me, and I swear the thunder is louder and closer."

"Ah, or frizzled by lightning," Sam had said in a straightforward manner. "I durnt fancy that."

He'd told Josephine to stay where they were while he went the few yards to collect the blanket and bag with the food and water in it. By the time he got back, the first few fat raindrops had begun to fall.

"That'll either chase the thunder away or make it worse," he said as he thrust the blanket at Josephine. "Here, keep it out of the wet, eh. I'll just go back and see if me pa needs me."

She didn't even try to stop him. He needed to know he was being useful. "It's not cold, is it?"

"Eh? Nah, why?"

"Because if you took your jacket off and left it here, it would be one more dry thing to use later."

"Ah, we could wrap Fred in it." He shrugged out of the garment and handed it over. "I'll shout to tell you what's what, eh? And if you sees th' others, tell 'em where we are proper."

Josephine mock saluted and grinned. "Yes, Captain."

Sam blushed and stuttered. Josephine took pity on him. "A true man is decisive when he needs to be, but never afraid to ask for advice."

"Then is that t'right thing to do?"

"It really is," she assured him. "You go and see what's happening and I'll arrange our temporary abode. Home," she added at his blank expression.

"Right-o." He ran across the grass with no regards to the rain, the thunder or the slippery surface.

Josephine shook her head at the resilience of children. The minute he had been reassured that David would get Freddie out, he'd perked up and become a lot more like she assumed he would normally be. Not that she'd had a lot of interaction with youths his age, even though her brother, at eight years younger than she, would qualify. George and she rarely met, something that was not to Josephine's personal preference. It was, however, the way things went.

She folded the blanket so it would be both under Freddie if he needed it, and easy enough to wrap around him. She was somewhat hazy as to how they would carry him on a trestle, but no doubt the men would know.

A large crack of thunder overhead made her jump and bite back a scream. Over by the place she assumed David would bring Freddie up, Sam flinched but otherwise didn't move. His father clapped him on the shoulder in a gesture of reassurance. It gave her a pang of envy. Why had she never had that?

Would David be like that with his children? How could she know?

What a time to wonder about such things. But his kisses excited her, his scent teased her and his presence… Oh, his presence made her wonder, what if?

She wriggled uneasily as her body perked up with those stray — and, at that moment in time, unneeded — thoughts. Time enough to ponder, assimilate and arrange her thoughts later.

A shout made the lad look up and he waved to someone Josephine couldn't see. "Ower 'ere. Ower 'ere."

She turned and peered through the rain and ever-increasing mist as best she could. The low cloud made it hard to see much past the place Sam stood. Four men carrying a five-bar gate appeared and stood alongside Will and his son. A brief conversation took place, then Sam hopped and skipped back to her.

"They came down dragon's back with the gate, but me da reckons they'll need to go back the long way. I'm off up back to the house to get a wagon to meet 'em over by Becketts. Bert, that's Freddie's dad, you know, well, he says our Rose has gone back down with Joe Frankel. Oh, and they's brought a blanket so you keep this 'un for now. Will you be all right, miss?"

"Of course I will. I'll wait for Davy."

Sam grinned and, to her surprise and pleasure, gave her a hug. "For a woman, you're a good 'un, miss."

High praise indeed. Josephine smiled as the lad rushed away, obviously pleased to be undertaking something so important. That he might have been sent away in case Freddie's condition was worse than previously thought evidently hadn't crossed his mind.

Meanwhile, she would sit and worry for both of them. Will and two of the men conferred and Will beckoned to her. Josephine scrambled up and made her way across the wet ground toward them.

"Miss, it could get a might damp around here if it doesn't stop raining soon," Will said in a deferential manner. "There's a stream that appears and cuts across the gorge. Davy says you might want to go up top."

"No, thank you. Not unless it is really necessary. Otherwise, I'll stay here," she stated. "I have the blanket and your son's dry jacket."

Will hesitated, obviously torn as to what to do.

"I'll tell David it was all down to me," she said. "I promise to keep out of the way. So what happens next?"

* * * *

David wrapped another rag around Freddie's arm, both to secure it and cushion it, before he tied the rope around the lad's waist. The poor boy's face was ashen, creased with pain, and perspiration dotted his skin. It wasn't going to be easy to get him to the surface, but David could think of no other manner to get him out of the pothole. There was not a feasible alternative.

"Ready?" David asked. "It won't take long once we get going."

Freddie nodded and winced as the movement obviously jarred his arm somehow. "Ready."

"Remember, all you need to do is try not to hit your arm off the sides. Will and I will do all the work," David cautioned Freddie as he crawled behind him. "If you need to swear please use a euph…a pretend word." He didn't think Freddie would comprehend the word 'euphemism'. Especially in the state he was in. "In case my lady is close enough to hear."

"Ah, wimmen don't like us cussing, eh?" Freddie, for all the world, sounded like a man of his father's age, and sage with it.

"Exactly," David agreed gravely. "Now, can you get onto my shoulders like we discussed?"

"I'll give it me best."

It was a tight squeeze, but without too many swear words on either side, Freddie was maneuvered onto David's shoulders and very carefully David stood up. That gave Freddie a good few feet start toward his climb — or assisted rope walk — upward.

"Pull up now," he called and watched as Freddie moved steadily away from the dank, dark cave and into the open air.

Once the youth swung and used his feet to stop himself brushing his injured arm on the side. Stones rattled down and David ducked to avoid a face full of earth.

Then cursed roundly as a large stone fell squarely onto his right foot.

"What's up?" Freddie twisted and looked down, anxiety etched on his features.

David took a deep breath. "A rock that I really didn't want to make contact with. All's well now, carry on."

"If you says so." Freddie resumed his awkward scramble upward.

Pain radiated from David's foot so swiftly it caught him unawares, and knocked the breath out of him in one long hiss. He tried to move his leg and found it impossible. The rock had wedged itself in such a way that he couldn't dislodge the foot with ease. No matter, he would do it once the lad was safe.

Not until Freddie's body disappeared and Will's face filled the aperture instead did David breathe a sigh of relief. "All right?"

"Yes, he's tucked up under a blanket and they've started back via Becketts. Now to get you up, eh?"

David thought rapidly. If it was only him and Will around he could swear and use rage to get free. "In a minute. Who's left?"

"Just me. Oh, and your lady."

"Hell. Couldn't you get her to leave?" He didn't want her to witness his attempts to get out. Silly, male pride or whatever, he preferred her to think him invincible, or as near as.

"Not a chance," Will said. "She's stubborn. Worse than my missus, and that's saying sommat."

David had already guessed that. Normally he'd be pleased she wouldn't suffer fools gladly and had a mind of her own and was not afraid to use it. So unlike the fade-into-the-background young lady he had first met. Now, though, he wished to high heaven she was one of those debs who had been brought up to think a man's word was law and his directives to be followed come what may.

However… No wonder she more than intrigued him.

"Then tell her to put her hands over her ears. We might have a problem. That last push by Freddie gave me a rock on my foot."

"Bloody hell." Will's voice rose to a screech. "So what now?"

"I move my foot. You ask her to come over here. I try to send her back. Then you come back for me. Nothing to it."

"Sounds easy. If anyone can do it, you can." Will didn't sound too concerned. "Once you're out, we can get off back for breakfast." David was about to upset his equilibrium.

"It won't be," David said darkly. "Easy. I'll wager with you on that."

"I'll get her and see." Will didn't appear convinced by David's edict. "She'll abide by what you say, won't she?" He didn't sound too sure. "Don't young ladies of your class listen to their menfolk?"

"Not always, and sadly she's not mine." *Yet.*

"She'll listen," Will said confidently.

"Would your Maggie?"

"You have a point."

He soon found out that Josephine had no intention of being sent away.

"Categorically no. Not a chance, my lord. Think again." Josephine was adamant. "I am not leaving until you are up here and safe. Send Will with Freddie. I will wait for you, and we can go back together. Will might be needed to help get Freddie back. We need no help."

"But…" David searched his mind for how to say it wouldn't be seemly. "Are you not worried about the thunder and the proprieties?" he said at last.

"What?" Josephine appeared amazed he should even feel the need to mention them. "David, please do not be silly. It's daytime, for heaven's sake, and we are merely out for a ride. With your godmama's blessing."

He thought it best not to say that made little difference to the tabbies whose one aim in life was to spread gossip, whether they — and those they maligned — were in the capital or not. Gossip somehow became known all over the country. Shared via the air, maybe? It often seemed so.

"Besides," Josephine continued, "Will needs to go, you need to get out and I need to wait for you. That is the total sum of it."

David shrugged and glanced toward Will. There was no point in arguing anymore. He wriggled his foot, ignored the sharp and instant pain that slight movement brought and thought he'd be able to release it from its confines with relative ease and a lot of agony. "As she says. Go and reassure Bert all will be well. We won't be long."

"You don't need a hand up?"

David shook his head. "Come on, Will, I might be getting on in years but I can still manage a climb like this, especially with a rope." He didn't mention his foot, now on fire and doing its best to split the leather of his riding boot. "Just get the lads home, reassure their mothers they are alive and tell Lady Foster to have hot water ready for us. Say we're making this damned place secure or something." He waited until Will nodded. "Anyway, if we go back over the plank, not by Becketts, we may well beat you home."

"Don't forget you need the 'osses. You'll have to come back for 'em."

"Damn." He'd forgotten they were at the top of the gorge. "I'll get them, and we'll see you back at the estate."

Will, obviously still reluctant, nodded. "I best get off then."

Josephine watched Will walk away with reluctance in every step. He must have sensed something was wrong as well as she. She knelt and peered down the opening to the pothole. "What now?"

"Now you close your ears to my cussing and wait until I get out."

I knew it. "And the cussing is why?"

"My foot was hit by a rock when I was pushing Freddie out. I have a feeling it is now the size of a football."

"Then get out before it won't let you. What can I do to help?"

"Stand far enough back that you do not hear me swear."

"Very well, shout if I am needed." She had no intention of doing anything other than moving out of his range of vision. A few cuss words wouldn't harm her, and if he did call for aid of any description, she intended to hear him.

And give him succour? Where did that idea come from? In fact, when did this nervous energy and worry for him arise? It was all very confusing. In a few short weeks he had turned her thoughts and intentions on their head, and now... *Now I need to see what happens next.* She was under no illusions that he wouldn't come back to her and push for marriage. But even though she accepted that something about him called to her, she had no idea what.

First things first. He seemed to be taking an awful long time to reach the surface. *Stand back indeed.* Josephine inched forward and peered over the edge of the hole.

David was halfway up the side of the pothole and swearing softly under his breath. He looked up as she took away some of the light that showed and grimaced. "Sorry if you heard that. My damned foot is proving to be almost as much of a liability as Freddie's arm."

"Is it broken?" she asked worriedly. If it was, how on earth would she manage to get him to the relative warmth of the cave?

Drag him like a heathen. Or an animal? Well, if I have to.

"No, thankfully, I think I've just wrenched it. However, as I can't put weight on it, my ascent is not as easy as I'd hoped. No matter, I'm on my way. Watch your head."

She took that as a subtle directive to move back and did as he requested.

Five or so very long minutes later, David's head appeared over the rim of the hole, followed by his torso. He grunted with effort as he managed to wriggle out and flop onto the ground like a stranded fish.

The thunder, which Josephine had thought had left the area, echoed around the crag once more, and yet again raindrops descended, ever faster.

"You can't stop here," she said forcefully. "You will get soaked if you do. As I have no intention of leaving you alone, therefore so will I. It is miserable enough without being soaked to the skin. Plus, if I am not mistaken, there is a storm brewing." She didn't mean over where they were together, without a chaperone, or with regards to the boys' behavior. "Can you crawl toward the crag? There's a sort of cave there where we will be dry."

"You go."

"Do not be daft," she said in a forceful, brook-no-nonsense tone. "If you don't try to crawl, I'll get hold of your hair and drag you that way."

He smiled and grunted. "Forceful lady."

"You better believe it. So, hair or crawl, the choice is yours."

"Some choice," he grumbled but his expression belied his annoyance. "Crawl, of course. Please note I have never crawled to a woman before. Enjoy it whilst you can."

"I'll enjoy it a lot more when we are dry and out of this storm. Come on."

"Despot. Where to?"

Josephine pointed to where she'd left her jacket and the blanket. "About thirty or forty yards back. Under the crag. It's not a big overhang but it will be better than being struck by lightning."

"Then please go first, love. You get there and give me the incentive to follow."

She opened her mouth to argue and he forestalled her. "No point in us both getting soaked. Unless, of course, you want to disrobe in front of me?"

Drat the man. Even out there, at the mercy of the elements, that idea made her tingle.

"If—" *Lord, I almost said when.* "—if I did, it wouldn't be in a cave in a storm, believe me."

He got up onto his knees and swayed. His expression kept her where she was. Help was evidently not wanted.

"True. I suppose somewhere a little more comfortable would be better. However, as the best we seem to have is a cave of sorts, I'll make an assignation to meet you there as soon as possible." He winked. It was obviously an effort. "It may well be me disrobing for you."

"Hmm." The pictures that conjured up. "Well, get a move on." Dare she appear a little risqué? Why not. "Or all I'll see is goose pimples and you'll catch your death. Neither is appealing."

"There's an incentive," he called as she moved away. "My lady waiting for me to undress in front of her."

"In your dreams."

"Oh yes, now go."

Crawling and sliding on the slippery surface, with the soil turning to mud and the storm increasing and getting closer, was not the best way to improve his temper.

At least she'd stopped arguing and retreated to where she could be dry. David gritted his teeth and moved slowly toward the part of the crag Josephine had indicated. He remembered that cave, although it could hardly warrant being called by that name. It was better than being where he was — or down the ex-cave where the boys had been. He hadn't mentioned the fact that just as he'd reached safety, the rest of the cave had disappeared under a heavy fall of rock and soil. Luckily, the noise had been drowned out by a large thunderclap and Josephine hadn't noticed.

David crawled on. He didn't look up to check how far he'd gone. It would be what would be. Somewhere to his left, there was a shower of sparks, a crack and a hiss. Slowly an old elm split in two and sank gracefully to the ground. A flash of flame glowed and disappeared in the steady rain. It showed him how close the storm was, and he did his best to increase his pace. He didn't fancy being burned to a crisp.

"Come on, stir your stumps or there will be no brandy left." Josephine sounded whimsical. "You are almost here."

David let out an inarticulate sound and crawled the last few yards and under the overhang. Into blessed dryness. He rolled over onto his back and did his best to catch his breath as his chest heaved and he fought for air.

"You said brandy?" he asked hopefully once he decided he could speak in a semi-normal voice.

"I lied. I have water, bread and cheese, oh, and half a pastry. Sadly, no brandy."

"Ah well, it's probably for the best. Then I can't be accused of being under the influence." David looked down at his bedraggled appearance. He hadn't realized just how wet he was. Every contour of his body was outlined in faithful detail. He glanced at Josephine and noted just where she looked, looked away and risked another quick glance. She caught his gaze, and in the dim light he fancied she blushed.

"Never be afraid to look at me, love. Though, unless you are ready to study a lot more of me, maybe avert your eyes." He moved his injured foot without thinking and bit his lip on the sudden pain that caused. "Damn. No need."

"Pardon?" She sounded bewildered. "No need to what?"

"I was going to get out of my buckskins and try to dry them," he explained. "But I best not take my boot off, for I will never get it back on. I can't get them over my footwear, so therefore that outcome is not achievable." In spite of himself, he shivered. "Ah well."

"Take your jacket off and wrap this blanket around you." Josephine held out an old but warm blanket. She waited until he started to struggle out of his wet thorn-proof jacket and sighed. "Men."

"Men what?"

"Never ask for help. You cannot do it by yourself, can you?"

He raised one eyebrow. She was, of course, correct. His jacket was ideal for what he'd had to do earlier but a bugger to get off in the confines of their temporary accommodation.

"Here, let me give you a hand." Josephine grabbed hold of a sleeve and pulled. Eventually, between her tugging and him wriggling, they managed to get it off. Josephine shook it out and splattered them both with water. "Idiot that I am. I'll spread it out over that lump of rock." She suited her actions to her words. "That should help a little."

David looked at his shirt. "This is only damp. Best I keep it on." He untucked it and wafted the hem around. Damp or wet, either was unpleasant.

"If you want pneumonia, well, yes. Otherwise do not be daft." Exasperation colored her voice. "Just take it off."

"But I'll be half-naked." He felt obliged to point that out.

She sighed. "The most innocent half," she said impatiently. "I promise not to let my urges overtake me. Well, I would if I had any."

David nodded and pulled his shirt over his head before he wrapped the blanket around himself. He made certain she didn't have a chance to see his scars. There was no point in bringing them into the conversation at that point. "What about you?"

"I'll be fine." She shivered. "I just got a little chilled waiting for you."

"You will get even more chilled if you do not keep warm." Even in the dim light of the cave, he noticed the fine shivers that rippled over her skin that wasn't covered. "We're stuck here for a while so come here." David shuffled until he sat with his back to a part of the wall that was reasonably smooth and spread his legs and arms wide. "Come on, I won't tell if you don't. Bring the food, and the water."

Her teeth showed white as she grinned. "What about the brandy?"

"You said we had none."

"Ah well." Josephine crawled over the floor of the cave, dropped a large sack by his uninjured foot and carefully moved about until she sat in the circle of his arms and legs. Not touching. "I lied. I wanted to save it for when it was needed. Like now, to warm you up."

As his body was on fire from her scent and her close proximity, being warm was not a problem. "You'll do that, by being where you are."

Josephine stiffened and tried to move forward.

"This is ridiculous." David pulled her back. "I promise not to give in to my urges. I do have them, but I'm perfectly capable of controlling them when need be. Now let's get comfortable, eat something, drink something, and then... Why, then we can discuss our future, perhaps? What do you say?" He held his breath.

The silence seemed to last for ages.

Chapter Thirteen

What exactly did he mean? Tight as a bowstring and scared to move a muscle, Josephine did her best to relax. It wasn't easy. Every fiber of her body appeared, to her scrambled brain, to be immersed in him. The only thing she could sense was David.

Outside, the storm was noisy, almost overhead, but she was hardly aware of it. Rain sheeted down and made a waterfall outside the cave's entrance. Lightning showed the streams of water in flickering colors. At any other time she would have been entranced. Now she barely gave it a second look. If she moved just a tiny bit, her bottom would rest against his...his... *Oh lord, woman, say it.* His staff, his manhood, his body. Dare she? Just to discover what it felt like. Would it be fair when she still hadn't made her mind up about their future?

"Here. We'll need to share the flask." David handed it to her. "No goblets or brandy balloons here."

"Ohh dear, I must have forgotten to pack them. What a failure." She took a healthy swallow and let the fiery liquid warm her from inside out. "That's better." She passed the flask to him, bent forward and found the pastry that was left. "I've no idea what's in this." She broke it in half, passed one portion back and sniffed the piece she still held. "Meat of some description."

"Meat of any description will do when you're hungry." For a few moments there was silence then David sighed. "That's better. So what shall we do now to pass the time?"

"What do you mean?" she asked in a voice full of suspicion.

"I mean it innocently," he said quickly. "Not as an invitation or innuendo."

"But what if I wanted to take it as such?" She reddened and coughed. "That just slipped out. Ignore it.

"I can't. And if you do mean it, my resolve will be tested. I swore to you and myself I would take no liberties. So we will ignore any opportunities for dalliance and talk about oh, I don't know, the weather."

"It is storming. Next topic."

"Damn it, woman, I have no idea, you choose. But for the love of God, not about wanting what we shouldn't. Perhaps share with me any more thoughts on marrying?" His body thrummed with nervous arousal at the thought of her as his wife. He had to believe that would be her final answer — nothing else would do.

"Lots, none conclusive. Maybe I best tell you about my childhood. That was to be my intention tonight, so I'll just bring it forward a little. It might turn you away from me. Heaven knows it is enough to show how unsuited I am to be a wife."

He noted she didn't add 'and mother'. *Interesting*.

"Tell away. Come on, get comfortable and we will be open and honest." He touched her shoulder. "If you hold yourself like that for too long you'll get rigwelted. Like a sheep, stuck on its back with its legs flailing in the air and unable to move. Be in that position forever more."

Josephine giggled. "Such a lovely word for a horrible thing." She edged back to lean against him and slowly her body relaxed.

His body chose to react in the opposite way. His staff stiffened and even his nipples became hard nubs. Lord above, and that was with her fully clothed. Goodness knew what would happen if they ever did get naked.

David counted to ten in his mind. And ten again. "You were going to tell me about your childhood," he prompted. "I bet you were a pretty little girl. What is it they say? Cute and bright as a button. Did you have ringlets and were you unable to pronounce the letter 's' properly?"

"Ringlets, sadly, yes. A speech defect, no. I had very little else to recommend me, though. You spoke of how your father was toward you. At least he gave you some attention, the wrong sort though it surely was."

A tremor ran through her. David wrapped his arms tight around her and rested his chin on her head. "You don't need to tell me if you would prefer not to. I can't see why it would have any bearing on our future."

"Ah, that's where you are wrong," she said sombrely. "It has every bearing on our future."

That sounded ominous. "Then perhaps you should share it with me. Then I can offer my opinion." He nuzzled her head and dropped a gentle kiss where his chin had rested, before he resumed that position. "I promise to be honest."

"I'm sure you will." She spoke in a soft undertone he had to strain to hear. "But it is hard to open up and show my parents for what they are."

"I know, love." He waited for the ache in his scars. Again, it didn't happen. Relief flooded him. Perhaps he had truly accepted what he was about to say, and no longer paid lip-service to it. "I promise you that after the first revelation, things get easier. And with each disclosure, it tears away a little of the bitterness. I now accept it was not my fault I was treated the way I was. Those failings were my parents'. Specifically, my father's. My mama was not a strong enough character to disobey him. I wanted to blame her as well, but I couldn't. She was weak and knew it. But, for her sake, it was perhaps as well she was. To defy my father comes with grave consequences."

"The scars?" Josephine asked softly. She tightened her hands over his in a silent gesture of sympathy. "I could not help but see them, however I promised myself I would not pry."

"The scars," he confirmed. "Both those outside and those within. What I do know is I can learn from it, and make sure I am nothing like my father."

"Then I have hope as well. Tell me…" She stopped talking. The only sounds around them were the patter and splash of rain outside as it bounced off rocks and into the sodden earth, a distant rumble of thunder and their own breathing.

If the rain didn't ease soon, they'd have trouble getting out of the gorge. Oh, they were safe where they were but it wasn't the sort of place you'd want to be stuck in for long. At least the side where they were was on a slight incline, or they would be in danger of a ducking. David well understood how dangerous flash floods were in the area. He remembered many a time hunting for stranded animals, and on one horrific occasion, a shepherd who had gone to rescue his flock. They had arrived too late to rescue the man.

"Tell you what?" he prompted. Anything to stop worrying about things he had no control over.

"If, hypothetically, I agreed to marry you, what would you expect of me? I know we touched on it, but, believe me, this matters. It's important."

"Before you tell me about your childhood?" he asked.

"Before then," she confirmed. "What do you expect from a wife? All of it that you know and intend should happen."

Now he was puzzled. Surely he had explained everything previously? However, he was willing to reiterate his desires. "To be the other half of me. My wife, my lover, the mother of my children. My helper, my rock, my completion." The words burst out from him without conscious thought. They came from the heart. "To run my households, of course." *What else?* "To grow old with me."

"Hmm." She turned until she knelt facing him. This close in the gloom, her green eyes shone with a mysterious glow. "Let me describe to you a hypothetical scenario.

"You are married and, at this moment in time, ensconced in your county home with your wife and child. A girl, say. No heir as yet."

"An heir doesn't matter," David interjected. "There is little entailed these days and my own money would go to my wife and child or children. The title is irrelevant because it holds no happy memories for me. I would give it up if it means we can be together. I would imagine there's an odd second cousin or someone tucked away who is next in line. If not, the title dies when I do. Whether I have sons or daughters or we are not blessed is irrelevant."

"But you said you'd like to keep it."

He nodded. "Not at the expense of happiness for us."

She gulped. "Ah…very well. However, that aside, I wondered what you would expect if your daughter injured herself. Say, oh, I don't know, broke her leg. She, of course, would want attention. But you had to return to town. What would you expect your wife to do?"

"There is only one answer to that, surely."

"Which is?" she asked huskily.

"If I could possibly not go to town, I wouldn't. If I had to, say for an important vote in the House, then I would go and be back as fast as I could."

"And your wife?"

"Would stop with our daughter, of course. What else?"

"Even if you had a ball or something to go to in London?" she persisted. "Or you just wanted her with you?"

"My needs are a poor second to the needs of a child. Especially *our* child. Nanny or governess aside, this is one time where a child takes precedence over everything possible. I would have responsibilities, and one of the most important ones, if not *the* most important one, would be my family. My child or children. Along with my wife, that would be my priority. My workers, my estates. They come next. My papa might not have shown me how to behave but by God he showed me how not to."

"My parents were not like you say you will be," she said so quietly he had to strain to hear. "I broke my arm. They left me with my governess. I had chicken pox. They didn't even come home to see how I was. My papa wanted a son. He said girls were worthless. They just cost money. I overheard him tell my mama that I wouldn't even be a good catch, even with the money he could give me for a dowry if he felt so inclined. *'No man would want to lie with a skinny under-endowed woman.'* Then I heard him tell my mama she should make a push to find some poor sap to marry me, and I'd be off their hands with someone else to be forced to look after me. For, as he said, *'this tomfool idea of mine to move to my own house might put me out of their orbit, but, unfortunately, not ultimately out of their care'*."

If her papa had been anywhere in the vicinity, David would have happily shown him the error of his ways. "Your father is an imbecile, and doesn't deserve any consideration at all. You, to me, are perfect. Everything I want in my wife. Every last thing." What else could he say?

"To know you would expect our children to come first is music to my ears," Josephine said. "Not all the time but you know… Not when…"

"They are fit and healthy and we want each other. No, not then. That would be our time, and we would enjoy it on a normal occasion without any interruptions." David ran his hand over her bosom. "These are a perfect handful that I ache to try."

Josephine swallowed. "Then will you kiss me, please?"

He wondered what was in her mind. "Anything to oblige, my lady." He drew her close and set his lips to hers.

Passion flared as though it had been ignited by a flaming branch. David moved his mouth over hers. Her lips softened and carefully, gently, he let his tongue slip between them He wanted — needed — to show her how much more he could give her than an ordinary kiss. How a kiss was only the beginning. Josephine moaned deep in her throat as her tongue meshed with his, a guttural unearthly sound that vibrated through him and touched his soul.

The blanket slipped down as she swayed until her breasts, those neat round orbs he ached to touch, rested firmly on his bare chest. Even through her clothes, the heat of her body scorched him.

David tore his mouth away as he moved one hand to knead her breast over her blouse. "Lord above, I want you. Want all of you. But we cannot."

"Why?" Her hands moved to the placket of his buckskins and he removed them before she managed to undo it. She was drunk on passion and he doubted she really understood what she asked.

"Why? You are an innocent. If I take you, we marry. I promised I would do nothing to force your hand."

"Not even if I beg?"

"Not unless we are betrothed, no." How difficult it was to say that.

"Damn it. You were a rake. "

He rested his forehead on hers and moved his hand to give her other breast the same loving treatment as he had delivered to the first. Josephine pushed into his palm and sighed. "That creates so many delicious emotions inside me."

"*Was* a rake is the operative expression. Stop it, Josephine. I'm trying to be noble here and it is bloody difficult."

"Couldn't you revert for a few minutes?" she asked plaintively. "Just long enough to show me what I need to know."

"Hell, love, I can think of nothing nicer than burying myself in you and loving you as you deserve to be loved. But not here, not now. And believe me, when I take you, if I take you, it will be for more than a few minutes. I intend to set several hours aside for our first loving. If it happens," he added hastily. Too much was at stake to act as if it were a foregone conclusion.

"Hours?" She blinked as if she were coming out of a trance. "It takes hours?"

"Hours," he confirmed. "If we wish to savor every minute and make long, slow, lingering and exquisite love. And in a bed. Much better for your first time."

"First time. But…" She paused and took a deep breath. "You mean we do it more than once? But I thought… Oh, never mind what I thought, it sounds incorrect. Glory, what have I done, what do you think of me? How forward." She put her hands to her cheeks and closed her eyes. "I can never look you in the face again."

David moved her hands and kissed each eyelid until she opened her eyes. "That's better. You have done nothing except for giving me hope. All I can ask is you mull over what I said and believe me. I can't do any more, because let's face it, only time and the occasion will prove me to be honest in what I vow. Now trite, but true, I do believe the rain is easing and we need to get out of here."

Or you do, it's not going to be as easy for me.

Josephine sighed. "I suppose so, but it is so cozy."

David burst out laughing. "This? Cozy? You are easily pleased, I'll have to remember that."

She punched his arm lightly. "You know what I mean. Away from all the people who try to influence me."

"You mean your parents. I'm so sorry I spoke to your father. However, I felt I better do things properly. For once. Will it matter?"

"Who knows? No, it won't. I will do as I think fit and he might not like it, but will accept it is so."

"That was the impression he gave me," David said. "Something about a mind of your own."

"Exactly. So how do we get out? Bearing in mind I doubt you can walk and I do not think I can carry you."

This was it. "You'll have to go and get Will or Bert to come and help me."

"No, no and categorically no. You are not stopping here by yourself. What if no one can get back? What if the cave floods, what if…?"

He put his hand over her mouth. "Shh, stop that, I promise you the cave will not flood. The land here is too high. However, I'd hate you to be stuck here overnight. It might be safe and dry but it definitely wouldn't be comfortable. What if you please do as I say and put my mind at rest? I'll need help. Male help. Have a look outside and relay to me what you see."

"Rain, I would imagine. And not much else."

"Humor me, please, love." He was apprehensive about what she would report. If the storm didn't appear to be passing, she'd have no option but to stay, and that would put them in an awkward position. She would be well and truly compromised.

Josephine wrinkled her nose but nodded in the manner of pandering to a particularly annoying companion. "Ah, very well." She wiggled away from him and once more he was treated to the view of her perfect bottom. If she chose not to marry him, he didn't know what he would do.

"Good grief, David, apart from a few yards close to us, the place is underwater. The sky is brightening, I can't hear thunder, the rain is less heavy than it was and there are several brand-new waterfalls. Are we really safe in here?"

"We are, but honestly I need you to try and get back to the house. That way I cannot be accused of compromising you."

She sat back on her knees. "Hmm. I'd not let it bother me."

"Perhaps not, but your papa could see it as the ideal way to make you marry me. I'd be the one vilified."

"Ah, I hadn't thought of that. Very well, what shall I do?"

"Supposing your horse is still where you left it and hasn't bolted, your best way is to go up this side of what Rose and the boys called the dragon. It's reasonably stable, albeit a bit longer. Then, well, then ride to the stables, and get someone to say you had a groom with you. Lord, whatever you do will not be easy. Luckily it is not yet noon."

"It isn't?"

He shook his head. "My timepiece is still going. It wants but twenty minutes to ten."

"Then I stand a good chance of getting back without my parents knowing what I've been doing. If I can get up to the horse."

David looked beyond her and grinned. "The cavalry is here."

"Ha. He means me, Lyddie, Will and Bert," James said as he ducked his head and crawled in next to them. "You do choose your times for an adventure, David.

Couldn't you have waited until the storm stopped, and done yourself an injury then? Is it broken?"

"I think so." David groaned. "Big mouth."

"Broken? You informed me it was just a wrench," Josephine said accusingly. "You lied."

He shrugged. "Guilty. But I lied in a good cause. I promised you that you would not be forced to marry me. I want your decision to be as easy as possible for you."

Josephine wished she could just say, 'Drat it, yes, I will marry you.' She was so almost there but... She needed to sit and think very carefully about every little thing. Preferably when she was not under pressure. To marry was the opposite of all she had ever intended. A decision that would change everything. She smiled at David and hoped he could see how much she appreciated him and all he was doing for her. "So, what is the plan?"

David held his hands in the air. "Don't ask me, love. I'm as much at his mercy as you are, probably more. I have no doubt he will remind me of it forever more."

"Of course, how else will I ever be one up on you?" James chuckled and sobered rapidly. "Now to get back to the point. The most feasible story we could concoct on the way over, Josephine, is that you and Lyddie decided to ride out once the storm abated, to get some fresh air. It had, you both agreed, been very stuffy. You very properly took Will and Bert with you because everyone else was busy. Lady Foster gave her permission, as your parents had not at that point showed their faces."

Josephine shrugged. "If the sky fell in, they would think, 'Ah, well, it has nothing to do with us', and ignore it."

"Their loss," David commented, and she flashed him a swift grin.

"My hero."

"Oh yes."

"Meanwhile," James continued, "once you two have stopped all the billing and cooing and return to the here and now, I shall continue."

"I do not bill and coo," David said. "I speak the truth."

"You make us sound ridiculous," Josephine said as she noticed David struggle to hold back his appreciation of James' humor. "Only pigeons and doves do that, and if you are insinuating I am either one, well, ask David about my fist."

James looked horrified and she sniggered.

"I got you worried."

"Wretch," David said. "Poor James *was* worried for a moment."

"I was," James agreed. "And I will steer clear of you when you are aggrieved about anything. But we digress, and we must get our stories straight. Therefore, David and I are off somewhere else. I have no idea where, but no doubt one of us will think of something before we get home."

"Castleton, to discover if anyone knows any more about Cassel's hare-brained ideas," David suggested. "That gives us plenty of time to get me out of here. Plus, it is easy enough to report no one had a clue what Cassel meant. If anyone is bothered enough to inquire."

"Ah yes," James said with satisfaction. "Perfect. So, Josephine, if you accompany Lyddie and the men, I will get back as soon as possible with Peg Leg here."

"And then we will see what happens next," David added with a wink. "To any or all of us. So, love…"

"It's up to me and Lydia to play dumb?" Josephine said. She ignored his endearment. Time enough to think of the connotations it suggested later. "I'm not quite sure I can manage dumb."

"Well, not quite dumb, but not knowing or caring what we are up to."

"Oh, that will be easy. We can roll our eyes and mutter about pea-brained men and their little foibles."

David gave a crack of laughter. "Precisely."

"And curse idiots who hurt their foot and get stuck in a cave in a storm?"

"No doubt. But do it in a positive manner, I beg you."

"I'm not sure that is possible. However, please take care and do not get yourself killed. I would be most annoyed not to be able to say my piece because you were so careless as to lose your life."

David had to laugh. "Yes, my dear."

She grinned. "It is no laughing matter, and I know a pander-to-the-little-woman voice when I hear one. Right, moan over. What do I do?" She kissed David, unheeding of the way James watched with interest. "I mean it. Both of you take care." She moved so her mouth was next to his ear. The next sentence was for him only. "I promise to talk to you tonight with my decision."

"Then it behooves me to get back to hear it. Off you go." He patted her bottom and she scowled even though she didn't attempt to move his hand, which he left on her derrière for several seconds. She supposed

253

she'd better complain for form's sake. "And do not make free with my body."

"Yet."

Would she ever get the last word? "Maybe never."

Did he really mutter, 'God, it better not be never'?

Josephine followed James out into the drizzle and yelped as water almost immediately sloshed over her feet. "James, tell me honestly. Is he really safe?"

James inclined his head. "As long as we get a move on. Will says there's more rain to come. The cave, so I have been told, won't flood, but it could be difficult to get him out. Especially if he can't put any weight on his foot."

It was as she feared. "He can't. He crawled there."

James hit his head with the palm of his hand. "Therefore, as Will said, we need to move swiftly."

"Then shouldn't Will have stopped here with you to help you?" That seemed the simplest thing to do.

"Not when you are dealing with David, who is directing things as he knows they should be done. Me, I go for straightforward. He covers all angles. Which is why Will's going to take you and Lyddie back and he and Bert will show themselves. Just in case anyone queries your story. Then they will come back here. If we can all pull together, our story will be taken, if not as gospel, as acceptable." He indicated the rock face. "If you go up as he wants, I promise I will do everything in my power to make sure he suffers no more injuries."

"Thank you. More than you will ever know, I needed to hear that." Josephine took a deep breath. "I'm ready."

"It's a rope again, I'm afraid, but Lydia thought these breeches might be a help. I was to tell you she often wears them under her skirts and rides astride. Her suggestion was you wear them without your skirts to make the climb easier. She has a clean riding habit with her for your ride home. I promise to avert my eyes. I prefer my face arranged the way it is, and I have reason to know how thrawn David's temper can be when all does not go as he thinks it should."

She could well believe it. An aristocrat to the core, with those imperative demands and intentions to care for and cherish those who mattered. A sweet sensation of being wanted filled her. It was a novelty, and she wished she had time to savor it. "After all I've been through, a rope without a shower of mud raining down on me will be child's play." Or at least she hoped it would be. "With no skirts to hinder me, it will be even better." She took the proffered trousers, waited until James turned his back and pulled them on. Her petticoats she gathered up and knotted around her waist. The simple solution would have to do. At least she'd worn a skirt the day before and not a dress. That had made the change so much easier.

The sensation of no gown to cover her, of being exposed, wasn't unpleasant, but it was definitely unusual. However, she could see how much easier it would be to clamber up the cliff with no skirts flapping around her legs.

"You can turn around now. What do I do with this?" She waved her soiled and ripped skirt.

"I'll take it back with me and David. I'll tell him you left it for him to take care of — before I explain what you are wearing and going to dress in. Shake him up a bit."

"You are incorrigible. Do you always behave like this?"

"To him and him to me? Always," James reassured her. "We bait each other but would fight to the death to aid the other if need be, and know anything we do would never be harmful. When we were growing up, I suspect we kept each other sane. And I stopped him really cutting up the traces. His father was enough to drive anyone to excess. He is a thoroughly unpleasant specimen."

Just as she'd thought.

"Let's do it." Before she changed her mind and insisted she stay with David — propriety be damned.

Chapter Fourteen

Five minutes later, Josephine was on her way upward, and less than a minute after that could appreciate how scrambling up the scree and the side of the gorge was so much easier without skirts. No wonder men were such daredevils and took things like rock climbing and potholing in their stride. To say nothing of archery or swordplay. What a pity ladies' pantaloons could not be regular wear for any strenuous activity. The fact said ladies were not intended to undertake such things was not lost on her. The grand dames would swoon at the thought of what she was at that moment attempting, let alone her wearing such clothes as she did.

James had foreborne from mentioning how she appeared in her unconventional attire, but she had caught the glimmer of admiration in his eyes before he'd masked it.

"On penance of your intended calling me out, I will do my best not to look at you as I guide you," he'd said with a smirk.

"My what?" Bother him. She refused to get drawn on that subject. "You're ahead of yourself there. I have not said I will marry him."

"But you will," James said confidently. "The pair of you mesh, match and complement each other."

That was good to hear, but two could play at that game. "As do you and Lydia," she said sweetly. "When do we congratulate you both?"

"At this rate, never. Now climb."

She climbed.

Her gloves were soon sodden. She'd had the forethought to put them into her pocket earlier, so they hadn't become soaked through, but now she wondered why she'd bothered.

Halfway up her climb, the rain, which a few moments before had been a fine drizzle, came down in earnest. Water dripped from her eyelashes and nose. Her hair escaped its untidy knot and added to her misery as it stuck to her face. Josephine blew at it without much success. All she could do was carry on and hope there was a hot bath at the end of it all.

No doubt any cross-examination would ask why on earth she and Lydia had chosen to go for a ride in such weather. Their only response would be to insist they hadn't thought it would get worse so fast.

Other than that... Her thoughts skittered to David alone in that tiny crevice of a cave, and with no idea what was going on. How would he and James succeed in getting out and back to Lady Foster's? Would their story be accepted or would it throw up more questions than they could answer? What if he wasn't able to move? What if...?

Enough. Lord, she was becoming morbid, and it was neither the time nor the place. Josephine managed to move up another three or four feet before she leaned on a smooth part of the rock face to catch her breath. Right then she couldn't care less what people said about anything. Her attire, her attitude, her future. Nothing mattered except David being rescued.

"Josephine?" Lydia called down from the top of the gorge. "Is anything wrong?"

"No, I just needed to catch my breath. Last push coming up." She took a deep breath and fumbled for her next handhold. Either she was becoming used to climbing or the incline was less steep, because it seemed a very short time later when her wrists were grasped and Will and Bert hauled her over the side.

Josephine collapsed into the grass, unheeding of how wet it was. She was little better. Even her chemise was damp.

"We've got her," Bert called, presumably to James. "We'll be setting off soon."

"When you drink this and we pop behind a bush for you to get changed," Lydia said with a grin. "You do look like a drowned rat."

"I feel like one as well." Josephine grasped the flask and, uncaring of how unladylike it was, took a hearty swallow of the fiery contents. The brandy warmed her insides as it slid down her throat and she almost sighed with satisfaction. "That's better."

She used the tiny square of toweling Lydia passed to her to dry her face and mop up some of the wetness in her hair. "Thank you. What happens next?"

"We get you out of those sodden clothes and into the dry ones I purloined from your room. They've been wrapped in oilskin so should be fine. I've reconnoitred and, if you can squeeze between those two bushes, there's a small clearing amongst all the trees which is hardly wet at all. That will be the best place to change. Of course, you'll need to get damp all over again, because we will have the eyes of everyone at the manor on us. Lots of tutting because we have been silly enough to ride out and be caught in the reoccurring storm. But at least you won't be in the same clothes as earlier."

That made sense. Josephine followed Lydia across the bumpy ground and slid between the indicated bushes. Lydia handed her a parcel. "Do you need any help?"

"Probably. I'm all fingers and thumbs." Although the brandy had warmed her insides, her fingers were icy and she fumbled with buttons until Lydia brushed her hands away.

"Think of me as your ladies' maid, albeit an inexperienced one." Lydia worked swiftly, and within a few moments had divested Josephine of her blouse and jacket and slipped a deep red woolen riding dress over her friend's shoulders. "I thought this would be the easiest thing for you to put on, and I have the jacket to go with it as well. Now all you need to do is get out of the breeches, which I will say look so much better on you than me, and do something with your hair. There's a brush and some pins here. Keep the breeches. You have the figure for them. I look like a lumpy sack of potatoes without the proper underpinnings."

Josephine laughed. "That's the first time someone has said anything positive about my figure." She ignored the compliments David had given her. Men said things to please, to help them get their own way. *He is not that shallow, is he? Of course not. He is a true gentleman.* She answered her own question. "Almost, anyway."

Lydia raised her eyebrows. "What?"

"It's true. For me, I accept we are all shapes and sizes and how good that is. The world would be very boring if we were all the same. To my parents, though, I am everything a woman should not be. As I can't, and never could, do anything to please them, I stopped trying long ago and did what I wanted instead." She considered how to continue. Those newly found feelings for David were too personal to share yet. Plus, in the cold light of day, he might regret what he'd said. She knew she wouldn't. "In a few weeks, I move out of their house and into my own. I cannot wait. No more ton, and I imagine no more parents. Which, as I rarely see them anyway, will be no hardship." She shrugged and smiled at Lydia.

"Jo…sephine, how awful."

Josephine patted Lydia's hand. "Do not look so aghast. I learned at a very young age that, as a female, I was of no account to them." It was a relief that every time she said that out loud, a little of the hurt she'd carried all those years left her. "As time goes on, it matters less and less."

"If I may be so bold, your parents are ill-informed and pathetic," Lydia said passionately. "It is their loss. Why, when I left they'd asked for breakfast in their suite. I believe they were informed about the alarms of the early hours but told the maid it was nothing to do with them. Selfish, they have not even asked if all was well." She put her hand over her mouth as she realized her faux pas. "I'm sorry. They may be your parents, but still. I'm sorry to be so blunt, but they do not deserve a daughter like you."

"Oh, it does me good to hear that. I've often wondered why I deserve to be saddled with them. As they say, we cannot choose our family, more is often the pity."

"There's just one thing." Lydia paused and tilted her head to one side. "Would you say we are now friends?" she asked.

"Undoubtedly." There was no doubt in Josephine's mind.

"Good. So, as a friend, I must ask. I thought you were going to marry David. Is that not what this whole house party is all about?"

Now the reason for their invitation made sense. "Not as far as I'm concerned. I came under duress and this visit is the last thing I will *ever* be forced to do. My swansong in the ton."

Lydia laughed. "Does David know all that?"

"He does now."

"And what did he say? He is a very determined man. When his mind is set on something, he rarely deviates from it."

It was Josephine's turn to laugh. "That he'd try to change my mind."

"Dare I ask if he has?"

Josephine rolled the wet breeches into a ball and took the hairbrush Lydia handed her. She doubted she'd be able to do much more than pull her hair into a bun and pray no one looked at it too closely. "Not yet. He's working on it, and I...well, let's say I'm enjoying it all. But marriage is a big step. As far as he or anyone else knows, my next move is to my own house," she lied shamelessly. "Men cannot have it all their own way as they seem to assume is their due."

"Don't I know it," Lydia said gloomily. "What next?"

"We ride."

* * * *

"Look, James, just go," David said wearily, several hours later. "There is no way I can walk, you can't carry me in this weather, and there is no point in us both being stuck here. Apart from anything else, there wouldn't be enough food and you are like a bear with a sore head when you're hungry."

"I am not leaving you alone," James said stubbornly. "We'll get you out somehow."

David gestured to the flooded gorge bottom. No grass could be seen except on top of the small outcrops of rock or hillocks. "How? Be sensible, Jamie. If nothing else, make sure Will and Bert know where I still am. Once the rain stops, the three of you can get me out and onto a horse, even if you have to carry me on a bloody gate. Hell, once it's dried out a bit, they will get a horse down here, and I'll ride back without recourse to a gate or piggyback."

"And how long will that be?" James folded his arms. "You could be here for days."

That was the rub. "Honestly? I have no idea." David squinted up at the sky. "But I doubt days. And in any case, if that seemed likely you could replenish my food supply." He laughed at James' first mulish, then horrified expression. "Seriously, if it seemed it would be an age, I'd agree to being dragged out somehow." He squinted to peer outside, where dark clouds scudded overhead. David thought there might be a break in them to the east. Not enough to make a gnat a garter, as his godmama was wont to say, but it was a positive sign.

"This appears very localized. Hopefully, it will pass before much longer, and I swear, once it does stop, the ground will drain quickly. One of the bonuses of all those caves and potholes. Listen, Jamie," David said earnestly. "I'm safe and dry in here. We'd need a hell of a lot more sustained rain to flood this cave. Plus, half the county would be underwater. That is not a scenario that is likely to happen. Nevertheless, you will have to go and tell Lady F. what is going on and stop her worrying. She'll cover for us if need be, but you have to speak to her and make sure she hasn't got the wrong end of the stick. Will and Bert aren't likely to sensationalize, but all they really know is that their boys are safe, and I've hurt my foot. The longer it is before either of us shows up, the more she will imagine the worst." David waited as James considered his words. Everything he had spoken was true, but he understood James' dilemma. They had always watched each other's backs. Always.

"And tell my lady I am thinking of her," he added.

"Is she your lady?" James asked in a quizzical manner.

"I have no idea, but once I get out of here, I hope I discover she is. So will you go?"

James sighed. "I suppose I have no option. What do I tell anyone who asks why I am back and you aren't?"

David went over various scenarios in his mind. "I think the best answer is that I went on to see someone, name not supplied to you, who had information but wouldn't speak to anyone but me. And, ah, rather than you hang around in his terrible weather, I suggested you go back to reassure everyone. You could add that I said if necessary I'd stop around Castleton until the storm passed over. How's that?"

"Flimsy, but not easy to dispute. Very well. What else?"

"Nothing. I sit and wait and contemplate my future.

"Better than your past."

"Maybe so."

* * * *

"Where are they?" Josephine muttered for the goodness knew how many times. Her return had been simple and undramatic. Once she, Lydia and Will had arrived at the stables, the girls had walked into the house via the back door, and Will had departed to get fresh horses.

They'd met no one except a maid and a footman as they'd run Lady Foster to ground in her private sitting room.

Gaia had howled and leaped from the chair she'd occupied and hurled herself at Josephine. She'd picked up the dog and stroked her as Gaia had made little whuffles and squeals of excitement.

"So someone is glad to see me."

Lady Foster had looked up as they entered and rolled her eyes.

"Cried incessantly. Now what do you two look like? Two drowned rats. What have you come to report? And do you want food? I can get Chef to find you something to keep you going until luncheon."

Josephine had glanced at the clock, amazed it was not yet lunchtime. So much had happened in the past few hours. "Please," she and Lydia had said at the same time.

"Hungry work this gadding and saving lives." Lady Foster had rung the bell and relayed her instructions to the footman who appeared. "You eat in here while we talk," she'd said as soon as the man bowed and left the room. "So begin."

It had been a matter of minutes to relay all that had occurred, interrupted only by the footman with a loaded tray. Afterward, as soon as she possibly could, Josephine had made her excuses and, Gaia following her, looked out of the window. With one eye on the weather, she'd gone to collect her cloak then made her way upstairs to disrobe and towel herself vigorously before donning a morning gown and sitting in the armchair. Gaia had plonked herself at Josephine's feet, chewed on a hank of knotted rope and appeared as if she had no intention of ever moving.

If only she could do the same. Josephine re-anchored a hairpin and winced. Her scalp was sensitive. Had she knocked her head and not realized?

Probably. I was too busy concentrating on other things to notice the odd bump. She pushed the sleeves of her gown up and registered a few discolorations on her skin, which she was sure would become spectacular bruises before long. If only she'd had time for a long bath. However, mindful of the part she had to play, she'd decided it was out of the question. She rolled the sleeves down again and made a mental note to ask Lady F. for some salve. Josephine was certain her housekeeper would have some sort of liniment with a special ingredient sure to take away aches and pains. Most ladies of that ilk did.

For now, though, she intended to sit and think things over.

The door burst open and crashed back on its hinges with a loud thump that shook the china ornaments on the dresser.

Josephine glanced up as her mama burst into her sitting room and came to a halt just inside the door.

"Where have you been?" her mama demanded. Her color was high and she looked decidedly out of sorts. "And for goodness' sake, what is that animal doing here?"

"Keeping me company. Why?" Josephine saw no reason to embellish her query. She stood up, found a dry pair of gloves and put them next to her cloak. Gaia growled and Josephine hid her grin as she picked the puppy up before the animal decided it was her duty to protect Josephine from her mama.

"Why? You infuriating girl. Your papa and I need to know if you are betrothed! We must do all that is needed."

"No."

"No?" Her mama screeched the word and started to shake Josephine. "Why not? It was all but done. How could you *not* have succeeded?"

Gaia barked and showed excellent teeth before she growled and wriggled to be put down. That was the last straw as far as Josephine was concerned. A red haze filled her vision and she struggled to hold onto her temper and the pup. "Do not"—Josephine shrugged her mother's hands off her shoulders—"ever touch me like that again." Her voice was icy. "For the past twenty-four years of my life, I have been nothing but an encumbrance to you and my papa. Worthless, and not to be given a second thought, except how to absolve yourselves of any responsibility for me. Just because you see marriage to his lordship as an acceptable manner for that to happen does not mean I will fall in with your plans. My life has always been mine to control. You neither choose to remember about me nor care, unless it is for your own ends. Enough is enough. I absolve you of all responsibility for me. Oh, and it is getting harder and harder for me to hold on to the dog."

Gaia growled. From such a small pup, the noise was loud and full of menace. The animal added a bark, wriggled and bared her teeth.

With a wary eye on Gaia, Lady Bowie took several steps back. Once out of bite range, she stopped and glowered at Josephine. "What do I tell your papa, you ungrateful girl?"

"Exactly what I said. No more. I will go straight to Northumberland. There. See how easy that was? You can wash your hands of me. Forget once more you have a daughter. Go and do whatever you want, wherever you want." She sighed. Gaia yowled mournfully. Josephine forced herself not to smile at that. The puppy seemed attuned to Josephine's moods. "You know, I would have enjoyed your love, Mama, and had plenty to give back. Ah, well, now it's too late." 'Not my loss', her tone implied.

"In that case, there is no more to be said. Your papa and I will leave today. You no doubt will do as you wish. I will arrange for your belongings to be sent to Northumberland."

Just like that. Josephine nodded. "Why not? Then I can decide what I wish to keep and what can go to the needy." Not something her parents thought a lot about.

"Wasteful."

"Not at all, exactly the opposite."

Her mother sniffed. "I bid you good day." She gathered her skirts out of the way.

As if I will sully them, Josephine decided, amused. She waited until the door closed in a controlled manner behind her parent. Nothing so uncouth as slamming it, even if she was riled. After all, the outcome was what her parents desired, even if it had not been achieved in a respectable way.

Josephine wrapped her cloak around herself, found the leash for Gaia that David had discovered somewhere. The long leather thong had, he'd said, been used on one of Lady F.'s dogs who was too unruly to be allowed to run free. It was ideal to control a young pup who had yet to learn how to behave amongst other animals. Once the leash was secure, Josephine made her way out of the house with Gaia. She met no one, although a few snatches of conversation came from behind closed doors, and once someone sang a cheerful ditty about some cherries and a blackbird in a pleasant contralto.

She walked purposefully toward the tiny summerhouse situated on a knoll that overlooked the way by which the men would hopefully return, and dropped her cloak onto one end of the chaise positioned in front of the window. By then the rain had eased, and although the sky was dark and menacing, she hoped the storm was over.

How would David get back? He might have tried to behave as if his foot were hardly injured, but she knew better. He had been in considerable pain, and had done his best not to show it.

And when he did get back, how would she answer the inevitable question?

It was time to examine her feelings. Savor those delicious tingles his attention and touch gave her. Try to analyze what they meant, and how much more of them she wanted to experience, and why. And, most importantly, what did she want from the rest of her life, David or to be alone?

David and children or alone?

Chapter Fifteen

The rain might have slowed to a drizzle but it hadn't stopped. David propped himself against the knobbly back of the overhang and squinted out and upward. Was he deceiving himself when he decided the sky was a little brighter than before? He picked up the bottle of brandy James had left and eyed it thoughtfully. It might be good to ward off chills but getting bosky wasn't the best aid to getting out safely. He checked his watch — still working — and realized that James hadn't been gone an hour. Swift calculations showed him it was going to be a considerable time until help arrived. James had to get back to his horse, ride to the house and let Lady F. know what was going on without alarming her. Then gather up the men and equipment needed to get David out of the gorge. It was a devil to get someone injured out of.

David was glad it wasn't him doing all the organizing. Not that his godmama would panic, far from it, but it would need coordination and decisive action, and he'd bet his last guinea someone would try to be 'helpful' and delay things.

David chuckled to himself. He could imagine it. *'Barn door or a trestle?'*

'What about a gate?'

'Do we put him in a wagon, or drag him on the gate, door or trestle?'

'Can he walk at all?'

He rather thought a couple of sturdy farmworkers to carry him to a horse or gig would be best. Hopefully, James and Lady F. would sort out the swiftest method and make sure it happened as soon as possible.

Meanwhile, what was the best thing he could do?

Wait or get on with it?

The slow advance of a menacing black thundercloud to the west decided it for him. If that broke, who knew how long he'd be stuck?

Get on with it.

David pondered his options. He couldn't stand on the foot with a broken ankle but if he could somehow get to the dragon, surely he could haul himself up?

He managed to get to his feet—just. He even stood swaying and cussing for a while before he gingerly moved his injured foot and pressed on it. Just a little.

Little was too much. Pain shot into him like a bullet, or a red-hot poker. He swore long and low as the pain radiated out and reminded him just what a broken ankle meant. Sweat dotted his clammy skin and he swallowed hard to stop nausea overwhelming him. It was bad enough feeling sick, he was damn sure he wasn't going to vomit. Even a slash with a knife when two ruffians had set upon him hadn't hurt to the degree of agony he was now in. If this was a mere broken ankle, heaven help anyone with another broken limb.

Long minutes passed before he decided he wasn't going to pass out, throw up or collapse in a heap.

What next, he wondered?

If only there was a branch or something he could use as a crutch, he could limp or hop. However, in that part of the valley, it was mainly coarse grass and the odd gorse bush. The nearest tree was halfway up the cliff and its scrawny branches wouldn't hold the weight of a child let alone a fully grown man. He mulled over the various options that occurred to him.

Crawl? That was a possibility, except after all the rain, the ground was boggy. Combined with the uneven terrain and the large rocks that littered the area, it wasn't a journey he looked forward to. Even if he did manage to get to the scree with only one useable foot, how could he heave himself upward? It wasn't a couple of feet, and if he fell, it would be a long and bumpy, not to say dangerous, drop.

A loud clap of thunder made him jump. Fat raindrops began to fall and dampen the rocks. He'd been so deep in thought he hadn't noticed that distant cloud get closer. That was all he needed. More rain, and less chance of getting out in a hurry.

David slid down the rock face until he was sitting on the ground again. He had to face it, he was stuck until help arrived. He refused to think what might happen if, for whatever reason, it didn't. He wrapped his coat around himself and closed his eyes. There was no point in doing the 'what ifs' or the 'what if nots'. What would be would be. He wasn't going to drown, he had the brandy, there was plenty of water around, so he wouldn't die of thirst, and if his stomach rumbled so what? He'd managed without eating for several hours before, he could do it again. Meanwhile, he could catch up on the sleep he'd missed the previous night. Didn't they say the noise of raindrops was soporific?

* * * *

The sound of voices woke him. David opened his eyes and yawned as the voices became clearer and more recognizable. He brushed his hair out of his face and wished he had a comb, a damp cloth and a chance to look half presentable. Which in the circumstances was stupid. Who could look presentable in the situation he was in?

An urgent need was pressing. Thankfully, it was James who got to him first. He stared at David's disheveled appearance and raised one eyebrow. "You look worse than I thought you might."

David smiled wryly. "I tried to see if I could meet you halfway." He shrugged. "Not a cat in hell's chance of even one-twentieth of the way. I got to my feet and that was it. Now, though, I need to get to my feet again and relieve myself before I have an accident. Help me up, will you, please?"

James nodded and hauled David vertical. "I'll help you hop outside, and then we'll get you out of here before it's too dark to see." He maneuvered David to a convenient gorse bush and stood behind him as a prop.

Several seconds later, David gave a sigh of relief. "To be basic," he said, "I needed that."

"Too much brandy?"

David shook his head. "I forgot about that. I fell asleep. What time is it?" Balanced as he was, he didn't trust his stability enough to search for his fob watch.

James consulted his own timepiece. "Just shy of five. We need to get moving. Sorry it took so long, but after damage limitation for the boys, the playacting to convince those who mattered that you were in Castleton, not that anyone paid a lot of attention, and sorting out who and what to bring and make it look innocent, time went by. Lady F. insisted we ate and brought you something to eat." On cue, David's stomach rumbled.

"I think this is where, as Will would say, I'm fair clemmed. What do you have?"

"A turnover — beef and onion — chicken leg, couple of apples, no idea why she put those in, and some ale." He handed an oilskin bag over to David, who opened it and began to rummage inside.

"Oh, and a threat that if you don't do as you're told, you'll be put to bed without any supper."

David laughed. "She always uses that threat. It's never worked before."

James rolled his eyes. "She said you'd say that. But, in all honesty," James continued soberly, "she's worried. The boys, of course, after they realized people were glad to get them home in one piece, broken arm and some scrapes and scratches apart, were full of how you had to stay in the hole for a while and couldn't walk. They got scolded and then the focus was on you and what to do."

David nodded, his mouth too full of pastry to reply without covering James with crumbs. He swallowed, emptied his mouth and coughed as a crumb got stuck. "Went down the wrong way," he croaked and drank some water. "That's better. So, what *did* you decide to do?"

"Feed you first. It seemed we were correct in that decision." James indicated the few remains of food in the bag. "Then, one Caleb Thomas and Ru...Reuben I think it is, something or other, the two strongest men around according to Will, will carry you out of here. There's a gig with blankets and cushions waiting at a barn near Oak Copse. I think I have that right. I came down the dragon—the others have had to come a longer way. The scree is very loose after the rain."

"Caleb Thomas is the innkeeper. Runs a tidy house, as my godmama says. No one would dare try to go against his wishes. Reuben Gates is the local farrier. Wins the village fete wrestling every year and is the backstop of the tug-o'-war team. A gentle giant. I can understand them not coming down the dragon." Both men were big, burly and weighty. "I couldn't wish for better men to help me."

"Just as well, they're on their way now." Will joined them, closely followed by Bert. "We can't go up at the end acos the waterfall's back after all the rain. We've had a quick scout around and think the track across the Backbarrow side'd be best. Even longer than the end, but less likely to get drowned."

"That bad?" David frowned as Bert nodded. The waterfall and pool only appeared after heavy rain and, once the weather improved, usually drained into the limestone as fast as they had come. Only in really bad weather did they linger. It seemed this was one of those times. Backbarrow Farm was on the 'wrong' side of the gorge from Lady F.'s house and, if they had to go up that way, they'd be hard-pressed to get back before dark.

"Three foot and filling, I'd say."

That settled it. "Then let's go."

"Hold on a sec." Bert put his hand on David's shoulder to stop him trying to get up. "We need Caleb and Reuben first. They're almost here. Then we can set off."

David sighed. "I feel so bloody helpless," he said explosively. "A right idiot."

"Was those young rascals who were the idiots, not you," Will said. "If it weren't for you, they'd be dead and buried now. That cave's gone as if it were never there."

"I know, and I'm sorry I'm such a bad invalid." David smiled ruefully. "Lord knows what's going on back at the house."

James grinned. "Oh, the usual. Evidently, the chef is cooking all your favorite foods. Josephine's parents have washed their hands of her—to her delight, I believe—and the boys have been bathed and told early bed. The sawbones has set Freddie's broken bone and is ready and waiting to do yours. Everyday life, if you listen to Lady F."

David nodded. "Well, as she had me on her hands a lot when I was a lad, I guess, in some ways, she's not far wrong." He had the uneasy thought that history was repeating itself. At least now he didn't have his father to chastise him in the way the man preferred—with his fists or whip. To his delight, his scars no longer itched when he remembered those days. *Thank goodness for Josephine.* She seemed to have somehow cured him of that reaction.

The skyline disappeared as a scraping noise, a shout and a guffaw indicated Caleb and Reuben's arrival.

"Now then, m'lord, let's be sorting you." Caleb's gruff, deep voice echoed around the overhang. "Get you back in a trice now, me and Reuben will." He pulled David to his feet as if he weighed no more than a child. "Right then. You hold on to Will for a sec until me and Reub get us arms right."

David did as he was told, amused to see how Caleb — usually quiet, apart from his booming voice — took charge, and the others meekly followed his instructions..

"Now you let us sort it all. Don't try and help acos I'll be betting you'll make it worse, not better, begging your pardon, m'lord. No offense meant."

David laughed. "None taken. You tell me and, if it's in my power, I'll do it." He watched as Caleb and Reuben linked arms as if they'd done it every day, and moved behind him as Will still held him upright.

"Now if Will moves to one side and yes, that's it. Let us do the work."

David had the strange sensation of being swung off his feet and onto the crossed arms of Caleb and Reuben. He put a hand onto each shoulder to steady himself. "I've helped with something like this a few times," he remarked. "But never been the recipient."

"First time for everything," James said as the procession of men began its way across the uneven ground. "My first time for wading in a bog. My boots will never be the same again. My valet will squawk and hand in his notice, and my reputation be sullied as badly as my boots."

Pools of water were everywhere. Tussocks of grass appeared like tiny islands, boulders like cliff faces. The noise of squelching feet was loud in the still air, along with the odd muttered curse as someone went knee-deep into mucky water. David laughed. "You're having a great time, admit it."

"Well, not great, but it's a lot better than being chased by eager debs."

David nodded as his thoughts turned to Josephine. What on earth would she think? He grabbed on to Caleb's shoulder as, with a grunt, that man lurched over a wet, rocky area and almost lost his balance.

"Bugger it, that were close." Caleb righted himself and the procession began to make its way steadily up a winding sheep track. "This 'un's the tricky bit. Just hang on and let us do work."

David couldn't have done anything else.

He tightened his grip as Reuben grunted and began to walk, crab-like, up the steep sides of the valley. Not as vertical here as the dragon, but still difficult enough to have his carriers sweating before long. Behind them, the rest of the man followed in grim silence. David almost held his breath, conscious that any move from him could unbalance the other two.

Once his foot glanced off a rock and he bit his lip to hold back a yelp. Several stones rumbled down the slope as they were dislodged by one man or another.

It wasn't a pleasant half-hour.

He'd bet every one of them was grateful to climb over the lip of the gorge and see the gig and several horses tethered close by.

"That's the worst," James gasped as Caleb and Reuben lowered David carefully onto the back of the gig. "Just to jolt you home now." As he was one of the best carriage drivers David knew, any jolt would be unpremeditated and unavoidable.

"Jolt on." David turned to the rest of the men. "Thank you all. Now, let's get home, get dried and get fed, eh?"

* * * *

The sun was setting behind the house and the grayness of the day changed to inky black with only the stars and a sickle moon to relieve its darkness. A few clouds scudded across, the remnants of the earlier storm. Josephine hardly noticed them. David and the others were still not back. She'd been restless all afternoon, as she'd done her best to keep out of her parents' way as they'd packed up, ready to leave, and tried not to show how worried she was about everything else. Every time one of her parents spied her, the scowls and dark looks she was given were enough to make anyone annoyed, and Josephine was no different. Each time she was asked tersely if she had come to her senses.

Each time she replied that her senses were as they always were. Eventually, with a muttered "Ungrateful child," her papa had reiterated her mama's earlier words, and said that he washed his hands of her and that her goods and belongings would be forwarded. He'd added, "And I no longer have a daughter."

To which Josephine had retorted, unrepentant, "It seems I never had a papa," and left him gobbling like a turkey as she took refuge in the kitchen, where the chef gave her a pastry and told her not to mind selfish men and their unpleasant ways.

Gaia hadn't left her side, and after almost tripping over them for the umpteenth time, Lady F. shooed her out of the house saying she'd have dinner brought down to her if her parents hadn't gone by then. It seemed they were determined to depart, even if only to the nearest suitable — in her mama's eyes — inn.

Now the die was cast, it couldn't come too soon.

As Josephine sat in the summerhouse, her chin in her cupped hands, she contemplated how, over the past few days, her ideas on life, love and marriage had changed. How her parents would crow if they knew. Which was why she had been determined not to say anything to them. Unrepentant and unbowed, she intended to see how things went. See if David was still of a like mind, and determined on marriage. If so she could well become the person she had, it seemed, never realized she wanted to be.

A wife.

Strange but exhilarating.

Why him she didn't have a clue. Why after all this time she had decided on something she had thought she abhorred she also had no idea. But it was exciting, to say the least.

If…

If they did both want the same things. If… Such a little word with a big meaning.

"I do trust him," she said out loud. "He is what he says he is." She sighed. "Oh, David, where are you?"

"Here. Limping, on crutches, but here."

She looked up and gasped. Immaculate clothes, perfectly brushed hair, two crutches and with an expression of apprehension on his face, David stood in the doorway.

"Oh God, I thought you were dead." Josephine sobbed and ran across the summerhouse. Deep in thought, she hadn't known he was there until he'd spoken. "How did you find me?"

"My omnipotent godmama. Who says to tell you the coast is clear, your parents have left, and you are welcome to stay as long as you would like. I suspect you have a story to tell me there. Later." There was an almighty clatter as David dropped the walking sticks he held and missed Gaia by inches. "Daft dog. No, I cannot bend down to pet you."

Gaia *woofed* and went back to sit on Josephine's cloak that somehow the pup had managed to pull to the floor.

"Much later," Josephine agreed as she drank in the sight of him. Exhausted, with hollow cheeks and a bruised and battered look, he was, she accepted, all she ever needed or wanted for a partner. A warm, happy and relieved sense of utter contentment rolled through her.

Mine. Mine forever.

"I'm just so grateful you are alive and almost in one piece," she said and gulped back a sob. "I thought you might get killed. Drowned or fall down that damned cliff."

"Not that easy to kill a rake, you know. We lead charmed lives."

"What about ex-rakes?"

"Even harder, for we have something we want to live for. Or I hope so." He was silent for a moment. Then he took the three steps to stand in front of her and gather her close. "My love, do not cry. I'm here." He brushed her hair back from her face. She had dark shadows under her eyes, her expression was troubled, and he had never loved anyone more than her.

David inhaled deeply and buried his face in her hair as she rested her head on his jacket. Her scent, as ever, surrounded him and filled his senses. The rightness, the feeling of coming home and of being where he not only wanted but *needed* to be encompassed him.

Please let her be mine, and me hers.

"I thought I'd lost the chance to tell you I want to be your wife," she said, her voice muffled by his cravat. "I do, you know. I want to be yours."

The words were music to his ears, but he had to be certain.

"Are you positive, love? Do you promise me you've thought long and hard, and no one has tried to influence you?"

Josephine looked up at him with a tear-streaked face. "Except for you? No one. Whilst you were in the gorge and I was here, worrying, I had plenty of time to think about you, me, us, our lives and our future." She took a deep breath and her bosom swelled and tantalized him. His hands itched to undo the buttons of her pretty day dress, slowly slip the ribbons of her chemise loose, lower the top and feast.

Maybe soon.

"I decided I've been letting my past affect my future. I am not my mama and you are certainly not my papa. We are people with minds of our own."

She was silent for a moment, and as David waited for her to continue, he gave in to temptation and stroked her back in gentle circles, then let his digits drift lower to cup the gorgeous roundness of her bottom. She wriggled slightly and he stilled the movement.

"No, don't stop. I like it. It makes me feel cherished and wanted." Josephine sighed. "I saw you with the boys, I heard you stick up for me, I recognized your compassion. Do I love you? I honestly do not know. I've never really been loved, so how would I recognize it? Can you love someone in such a short time? I have no idea, but the idea of us parting, of me never being close to you again and watching you marry someone else, fills me with dread and sorrow. Is it enough?"

David kissed her forehead then her mouth. Her hands slipped around his waist and tightened.

"Could it be?" she asked anxiously.

"It is for me, love. I have all the same symptoms. I cannot imagine life without you. I want us to grow old together. If we are blessed, then to have children." He smiled. "We know how not to bring them up, so to give them all the love and attention they deserve will be easy. The hard bit will be not to spoil them."

Josephine put her hands under his jacket and stroked his back over his shirt. Just where the scars of his childhood criss-crossed his skin. The scars that no longer bothered him.

"As you said, the one thing we can both take from our childhoods is what should not be done," she said slowly. "It can help us now to discover what is right and what is wrong. To guide us along the complicated path of life."

"Exactly. No one knows what the future will bring. All we can do is strive to do the best we can. Do we do it together?" He waited, conscious that his heartbeat had sped up, and that the rest of his life hung in the next few moments. "I can't get down on one knee unless you want to witness me as a pathetic heap of misery when I try to stand."

"I'll take it as read, then, shall I?" she said softly. "And just listen with all my heart."

"Then, Josephine Bowie, will you marry me, be my wife and perhaps, God willing, the mother of our children? I can't promise you all will be easy — in fact, I'd say it is more than likely to be the opposite. My father will have a fit when he eventually finds out who bought all his land. He will do his best to show me in a bad light."

"Let him try. I won't let him speak about my husband, my hero, my beloved, in any foul-mouthed way. Ah…" She looked up at him, her face alive with laughter.

"Ah?"

"It seems my mind knew what I hesitated to say. You are all of those things, or I hope soon will be. So, to answer your question, I would be honored to be your wife and the mother of our children. You've given me something I never thought I would have. Love."

Epilogue

"Chicken pox," the doctor said cheerfully. "Not too bad. I'll leave some lotion and wish you luck."

Not too bad? Josephine looked at the two spotty children in her arms and groaned under her breath. Both were flushed, breathing heavily and grizzling. Thoroughly unhappy. At least they had their parents to comfort them. Not like it had been for her. That thought no longer had the power to hurt her. The thought of what her children now had to endure did.

Gaia took one look at her, sniffed the twins and hid under the sofa.

"Thank you." Josephine decided she would be polite to the doctor, even if it killed her. Wishing her luck was not very helpful.

Why now? They were due to depart for town the following day on one of their infrequent but necessary visits.

"There's a lot of it about." The doctor answered her unspoken question as he repacked his bag. "No doubt one of the staff carried it here. Not quite an epidemic, but enough cases to keep me busy. I'll call back in a day or so to see how they are getting on, and won't be surprised to see several more victims."

"I'll see you out." David opened the nursery door and ushered the man from the room. He was back within a few minutes.

"Where do we have all our commitments listed?" he asked as he took one toddler from Josephine. "There, sweetness, Papa will promise not to ask Mama to sing to you. If I sit down and you and I get comfortable, Mama can pass your sister to me as well, and she can go and get the delicious syrup Cook has made for you both." He sat on a large comfortable sofa, rolled his eyes at Josephine and mimed vomiting. Gaia scrambled out from her hiding hole and wriggled onto the settee.

Josephine bit her lip as she passed David Twin Two, and somehow kept a straight face. Three years wed and he could still make her giggle with unexpected statements and silly facial expressions. "I'll go and do that now. And wine for Papa?"

"And Mama, and maybe some tempting nibbles for us all. I have news. Big news."

"News? Good or bad?"

David did a very dramatic raise of his eyebrows. The twins giggled.

One of the twins patted his cheek. "Silly papa."

"Me?" David said in a loud exaggerated manner. "Never, 'tis your mama who must wait and curb her impatience."

Josephine shook her head in amusement. "No nibbles until you tell me."

He sighed, very theatrically. "A low blow."

"Of course. You taught me well." She blew him a kiss. "But you wouldn't have me any other way."

"Of course not. I love you as you are."

"And I you." Josephine enjoyed the way their girls giggled and echoed, "Love you." "But you can't leave me in suspense, not after such a dramatic statement. Big news. Is it good, bad or indifferent?"

"I imagine that would depend on from where you view it."

He paused and she shook her fist in a mock threatening manner.

"David Suddards. Enough. Tell me." She sobered. "Seriously, is it bad news?"

"No, not really. Well, not for us at any rate. It seems my papa has discovered who now owns all the un-entailed lands. It appears that information came out at the last country dance. The one we missed because we went to godmama's for her birthday. Apparently, in the middle of the evening, Lady Duggan over at Fowdlers, she who is a crony of my mama's, asked if he'd met up with me now we were neighbors and wasn't it a good idea to make sure the estate was all together, or some such thing. She'd heard from someone, no idea who, that the land had been sold. And I suspect my mama must have confided in her about the estrangement at some point. Lady Duggan, I suspect, has never been overfond of my father, so there was a little malicious glee involved. Evidently, he gobbled a bit, this is third- or fourth-hand I believe, so accuracy is not guaranteed, said he hadn't seen me lately—very true thank goodness—and marched off."

"Ha, I love it. Anything else?"

"According to Jacobs, our new man of business, he accosted him the next day. My father accosted Jacobs, not the other way round, and tried to say that I had acquired the land through stealth and foul means. That it was unethical and he intended to sort things out. What things were not specified."

Josephine glowered. "The cad. He can't cause trouble, can he?"

David laughed. "No, he cannot. Jacobs gave him chapter and verse. By the time he'd finished, I believe Father was red in the face and not in a good temper. Because, of course, he'd thought he could bully Jacobs and that is not possible. Plus, there were no underhand dealings so the only person who came out of it in a bad light would be Father. And, to cap it all, it is now all round the district that I had to buy my own lands to ensure the estate prospered. He's not a happy man."

"Good." Josephine thumped the table and one of the twins jumped and let out a startled squeal. "Sorry, my pet. But that man."

"Is no one to worry about. We both have rotten parents and these two" — David looked at the twins — "these are their loss."

Josephine smiled. "True."

"Now that's over, nibbles, please. Hungry, aren't we, girls?"

Josephine shook her head in mock sorrow. "Why am I not surprised, even though you have only just had breakfast?"

David looked from one spot-covered daughter to the other. "We need to keep our strength up, don't we?"

Amelia nodded. "Custard."

"Yes, custard," her twin, Louisa, echoed. "Cook makes such good custard."

"And custard," Josephine agreed. "As fast as I can."

"Bring the appointments diary back with you," he called as she reached the door.

She stopped and turned around to stare at him. "Why?"

"So I can ask Jacobs to write and cancel anything we've committed to. The girls will need a lot of attention over the coming days. They would hate town in this state and so would we. Here, at least we can both keep them occupied during their waking hours." He winked. "And occupy each other whilst they sleep and others keep watch for us."

Josephine rolled her eyes and smirked before she walked back to him, to kiss the only part of him easily reached. His ear.

"I don't know if I've told you lately, but I love you," she said quietly, sincerely. "Not just for this, but for everything."

"Spots and all?" he asked quizzically.

"Yes, why?" she replied, somewhat puzzled by the wry expression on his face. "Spots and all, I love you, and our girls."

"Good. Because I itch. I think our daughters have passed their chicken pox to me."

Want to see more from this author? Here's a taster for you to enjoy!

The Duke's Temptation
Raven McAllan

Excerpt

Whenever had a knife twirled so fast it became a vicious, glittering blur of metal?

Never.

Gibb Alford, the Duke of Menteith, had expected to be bored. Or on guard against any female who had somehow wangled her way into the spectacular. Or, although he devoutly hoped it wouldn't be so, both. Not that any woman should be there, but he was by now much too cynical to expect what should be so to actually be thus.

What he also hadn't envisaged was this unfamiliar tug of arousal directed toward the main act of the night. Who was a female, although he presumed an invited one. One who stirred his senses in a manner he'd almost forgotten.

Gibb didn't do arousal. Not now. Or, he amended, he hadn't. He stood on the terrace, amidst his peers but alone, a glass of the finest French brandy in his hand. In silence he watched the Chinese firecrackers and flaring sconces set around the lawn vie with the moon and stars for brightness, and willed his body to behave. Not for the first time he wondered what he was doing there. Why wasn't he at home on his beloved Scottish estate? At times being a conscientious peer was annoying to say the least.

Someone bumped into him and apologized as Gibb scowled. He didn't want his concentration spoiled, or his brandy spilled by an idiot like Algernon Follet.

As Follet swayed, Gibb held his goblet out of the way. Good brandy was not to be wasted. Gibb watched his fellow spectator stumble away, miss the fishpond by inches and lurch round a statue, before he ignored the man and instead turned his attention back to what was happening on the lawn. Only to tug at his suddenly too tight cravat because of what he once again saw in front of him.

In the middle of the perfect, manicured, luscious grass, a wooden platform had been erected in front of a large, plain white, thick canvas screen. Before it, the curvaceous raven-haired beauty who had attracted him minutes earlier stood with her arms outstretched, her crimson lips wide and an invitation to every man in the vicinity to stop, stare and give her their undivided attention. Dressed in something made of two-tone material, the like of which he'd never seen before, with hidden slits up each side, she presented a picture of contradictions. Gibb was sure she made each and every one of the audience imagine what the gown might or might not conceal.

The illusion of material not really there was very clever, Gibb mused. The flesh-colored silk that swung loose from her shoulders matched her skin, so he couldn't see where skin finished and material began. The bodice fit snug around her generous breasts in such a way he had to wonder just how it stayed in place. Her lustrous hair swung loose over her shoulders in a riot of curls and sparkling jewels hung from her ears and around one ankle, just above one of a pair of sandals that from a distance appeared flimsy and delicate. In her left hand she held a wicked-looking knife—a stiletto, he noticed—now still and unmoving. Even so, it shone in the twinkling lights that surrounded her.

The last firecracker sizzled and died, and with just the flickering torches to light her, the woman bowed to the assembled men. "I need," she said with a husky, seductive French accent, "a man."

The howls and catcalls would have overwhelmed anyone without a strong determination. She waited, arms folded and with an amused look on her face, until there was once more silence. Then she raised one eyebrow. Even at the distance he was, Gibb realized the woman was toying with them. Teasing them about something they thought would happen and she knew would not.

To his annoyance, his body tightened even more. He did not want this reaction to an unknown woman. Hell, he didn't want it with regards to anyone known to him either. Gibb Alford wanted no one to disturb his well-ordered life. The life where his mind never let him shy away from the sole thing that tore into him. His wife was dead and he was to blame. He was never going to be put in a similar position again.

Never.

The lady fixed her gaze on one of the men near to the front and beckoned to him in what some might call a seductive manner. Gibb chose to interpret it in a different way. Her body language showed nothing of seduction, except for that curled finger. Was it a come-hither gesture? He thought not. However, it worked. Young Lord Denby Crowe bowed in an extravagant manner and swaggered toward her.

God, Gibb mused, he felt old and jaded. Why could they not see the act for what it was? Entertainment, not innuendo. Why was he here? Because it was better than sitting alone in an empty house and wondering why it had all gone wrong. Here were no scheming mamas or desperate debs who saw him as a challenge or a poor wounded widower who needed a new wife. To his horror, not long before, a brazen and giggling chit had even accosted him outside the card room at one of the few soirees he'd felt compelled to attend and suggested he looked at her daughter.

No, no and no.

With an inward shudder of distaste at the memory, Gibb returned his attention to the vista in front of him and the very different woman in their midst.

"Take off your coat, my lord," the woman said with a slow and throaty drawl to her... Her what? Victim? "Pass it to one of your colleagues so it does not get in the way."

Crowe did so, smirked at his friends and stood with one leg bent in a suggestive manner before he put his hands to his cravat.

She shook her head. "Oh no, m'sieur, I would not do that. That is a good guard in case my aim is wrong."

Lord Crowe stiffened and half turned. "Aim?" he croaked. "What aim?"

"Scared?" she taunted Crowe.

Am I the only one to see the derision in her eyes? Gibb wondered. To realize she held them, if not in contempt, damn near it.

"Are you worried that perhaps women do not have as good an eye as men?" the woman asked with a lilt of humor in her voice. "Or indeed that we are better?"

Denby flushed. "Not a bit," he said tersely. "You're a mere woman."

"You think that means I will not hit where I intend?" She quirked one eyebrow and mocked him. "Oh dear. I suspect only time will tell." The knife in her hand soared into the air, whirling almost lazily as it did so. It appeared as if she would cut her palm as she caught it.

Gibb gulped as she put her hand out and caught the stiletto without even looking. The insolence, the certainty she had nothing to worry about hit him like a cannon shot. A woman in command of her senses. Not someone to rely on a man, or demand attention. However, she had secured his. All of it. He couldn't remember the last time anything had done that, let alone a woman.

Not even his wife.

From behind Gibb someone shouted out, "Women can't aim and hit to save themselves with anything. Aim for his bollocks and hit his brain."

She laughed and gave a gamine grin that to his surprise went straight to Gibb's groin.

"As I am the exception to your absurd rule, that is exactly what would happen, for we all know where a man's brain is located." The amusement that followed was good-natured and she curtsied. "Let us begin. Sir, I hope you can assure me you will stay as I direct?"

Denby scowled and pointed his finger toward her. "What are you, anyway?"

Gibb had wondered when Denby was going to get around to asking that.

"Ah, that is a question many have asked," she said in that husky throaty voice Gibb had noticed earlier, then laughed. "Wait and you'll find out," she advised him as she once more twirled the knife in her hands. Even from where he stood, Gibb could accept and admire her mastery of the weapon.

So it seemed could Denby Crowe, who was getting paler by the second. Gibb had an amused idea that the man might vomit or run. He hoped he didn't as the spectacle unfolding on the lawn looked as if it was definitely going to be the highlight of the evening, if not his whole sojourn in the capital.

"My name is La Belle Evangeline," the woman said in a slow and husky undertone. "Stand with your back to the screen, and then be careful you make no abrupt movement."

All of a sudden Gibb understood what she was all about. Her stiletto was not for security or effect, it was part of her act. A knife-thrower. He'd seen one, once many years before, although then it had been a man holding the knife. Now it seemed there was a woman about to do the tricks and at one of his fellow members of the ton, not at a partner.

It could be interesting.

It was.

Gibb had no idea if it was the way she caressed the knife like a lover, or how she was in control of what happened that sent his body into an unexpected and uncomfortable state of arousal. Whichever, he wasn't amused by his visceral reaction. He didn't need it, didn't want it and as sure as hell had no intention of acting on it. Danger for danger's sake should not be and would not be in his present, or his future. If it were up to him, he would never be privy to emotions that arose from such a thing.

Or from anything else.

With that resolution firmly in his mind he willed his body into rest — he was not entirely successful — leaned back on a marble pillar and prepared to be entertained.

Denby Crowe stared wide-eyed and stood as rigid as the statuary dotted around the grounds. Gibb watched, entranced as La Belle Evangeline, with a grin he decided was best described as wicked, leaned toward the man.

"Do not worry," she purred in a voice that curled around Gibb like hot chocolate. "I rarely miss." She paused and contemplated the knife she held. Picked up another and spun it between her fingers. The blades seemed ten times longer than before and forty times as dangerous as they shone and glinted in the flickering lights. "And if I do it will be a very sudden death." She waited for the beat of three as the crowd erupted into nervous laughter. "Not, alas, the little death, but one of greatness and finality. So I suggest, my lord, you do not deviate from my desires."

Within seconds, knives were thrown toward Crowe from every direction. When the sultry knife-thrower told him to spread his legs and not to flinch, Gibb wouldn't have been surprised to see him run. She was more than most men could control, and most would not attempt to.

He could. He wouldn't.

To Denby's credit he didn't move — although it was more likely a result of sheer terror than bravery — and Gibb joined in with the applause as the last knife stuck, quivering, into the screen behind Crowe, a mere three or so inches from his bollocks.

Evangeline kissed her volunteer's cheek and held his hand so they could bow together.

The audience cheered once more, resumed their chatter and began to wander back indoors, no doubt to replenish their glasses. Gibb had no intention of drinking anything else. He considered his duty done and therefore as soon as he could find his host he'd make his farewells and head home.

He watched with interest as, once Evangeline and Crowe disengaged, she slapped the man's hand away from her breast. Whatever she hissed at him, and he was certain hissed was the correct word, Crowe wasn't fazed and once more tried to touch her. The knife she held up appeared as if by magic and, amused, Gibb saw Crowe hold his hands in the air and walk away with a brisk step. It seemed La Belle Evangeline knew how to look after herself. Strange, Gibb mused, that his own erection didn't diminish at the thought of her with a readily available knife. Was he unhinged or was it just the novel experience of desiring someone without wanting to? Complicated thoughts for so late at night. Whatever, it was all immaterial. He refused to let his uncomfortable arousal take charge. He would not be at the mercy of his vagarious body.

Gibb turned back toward the house and hunted for his host. Enough was enough. Time now to go home and ponder why his body had chosen to react to La Belle Evangeline and no one else since —

Stop it now. It is over and you do as you wish. And he did not wish for emotions to hold sway. Never again would he allow that, whatever they were. It led to anguish, tortured thoughts of 'what if' and 'if only' and people hurt. He hadn't been able — or cared enough — to curb his wife's wild side, and she'd died because of it. Because of him.

Never again would he put himself in the position of being responsible for someone else's happiness and wellbeing.

Home of Erotic Romance

Sign up for our newsletter and find out about all our romance book releases, eBook sales and promotions, sneak peeks and FREE romance books!

About the Author

A multi-published author of erotic romance, Raven lives in Scotland, along with her husband and their two cats—their children having flown the nest—surrounded by beautiful scenery, which inspires a lot of the settings in her books.

She is used to sharing her life with the occasional deer, red squirrel, and lost tourist, to say nothing of the scourge of Scotland—the midge. As once she is writing she is oblivious to everything else, her lovely long-suffering husband is learning to love the dust bunnies, work the Aga, and be on stand-by with a glass of wine.

Raven loves to hear from readers. You can find her contact information, website details and author profile page at https://www.totallybound.com